DEATH UNDE

DEATH UNDER PAR

Dennis Casley

Constable · London

First published in Great Britain 1997
by Constable & Company Ltd
3 The Lanchesters, 162 Fulham Palace Road
London W6 9ER
Copyright 1997 by Dennis Casley
The right of Dennis Casley to be
identified as the author of this work
has been asserted by him in accordance
with the Copyright, Designs and Patents Act 1988
ISBN 0 09 477160 X
Set in Linotron Palatino 10 pt by
CentraCet Limited, Cambridge
Printed and bound in Great Britain by
Hartnolls Limited, Bodmin, Cornwall

A CIP catalogue record for this book
is available from the British Library

1

R.D. Price-Allen had seen men die, indeed, had contrived on occasion to stage death in strange as well as horrible circumstances, but he had not envisaged that his own death would come in such a bizarre manner. He clung to the slippery rock and watched the crocodile watching him. It was only the fact that he was pressed against the rock and motionless which kept the crocodile from nosing in. If he were to attempt to swim for the shore he knew that his clumsy splashing strokes would not achieve more than a few yards before those great jaws would close around him. On the other hand, his present tactic of keeping as still as possible would only serve for a short time before the patient predator, eyeing him from its semi-submerged position, would investigate this possible meal. Price-Allen twitched involuntarily as he felt something touch his legs below the Nile's water level. No, a false alarm. A passing piece of flotsam or an inhabitant of the river less deadly than the one who had, yes, definitely had, moved closer in reaction to the movement of the prey.

The hired assassin who had pushed him out of the dug-out canoe would in due course return to camp and explain that the *mzungu* had fallen in because the boat tilted due to a surfacing hippo, or some such story. Then a party of his fellow guests would come looking for him, but starting further upriver where his staged accident had occurred. There was no reason why the boatman should hurry back, indeed, the reverse was the case. No doubt he would have the wit to appear breathless as he arrived with the dreadful news, but a short sprint over the last few yards would achieve that. No, help was an hour or two away and Price-Allen knew with absolute certainty that his mortal span was measured in minutes at most. He had introduced death too often to others not to recognise its approach.

So, in all probability, Kiwonka and Aramgu would win because they had disposed of him with such an insultingly simple tactic. Take advantage of his presence at the President's tented camp below the great Falls in Uganda, where the Nile commenced its long journey, bring him a message via a boatman that a Kampala associate of his had urgent news and awaited him in the village on the other side, and push him into the darkening waters as the predators, now the heat of the day was past, looked for their supper. As the great river gathered him into its current it was a fluke that he had been swept against this rock to which he clung, not so far in physical distance from the shore, but a distance which in his present plight might as well be infinite.

The eyes he could still just see in the rapidly intensifying gloom suddenly disappeared. The croc had submerged and that terrible snout would now be boring towards him. Price-Allen heard death arrive bellowing with triumph. But no, his mind, which had started to lose coherence as the terror gripped, fought to re-establish contact with the external environment. The bellowing was real, not a fantasy. Price-Allen looked across to the shore. There standing in the shallows was a large bull elephant, a huge old tusker trumpeting its claim to this area in which it chose to take its evening drink. Price-Allen fought for reason to reassert itself. He had felt no terrible pressure as teeth closed around his legs. Surely the attack would have come by now. It was as if the elephant had spotted the crocodile about to strike and had warned it off. Had it worked? Had the crocodile, temporarily at least, conceded to the greater animal's claim? Price-Allen had never been slow to make a decision once having weighed the options, and now it took him but a moment to launch himself fully into the water and splash desperately towards his saviour.

The crocodile had, indeed, retreated from the elephant's challenge and Price-Allen neared the shore unmolested. At this point the frying pan to fire analogy became relevant. The area around the elephant's claimed domain was devoid of crocodiles because the elephant was intolerant of sharing its space, which was now invaded by a splashing object of dubious origin. The elephant interrupted its intake of water and, flapping its ears, turned to examine the intruder. Price-Allen gained his feet in the muddy shallows and looked up at the huge bulk of the animal looming over him. The trunk now rose menacingly as the elephant bellowed another warning. A huge foot rose and fell as if the animal was stamping in petulance: mud and water spurted towards Price-Allen as the foot sank with a wet, sucking, squelching sound into the ooze. Into Price-Allen's mind came the memory of an old Kikuyu servant telling him as a child that an elephant would give way to nothing within its experience, but it was susceptible to being taken aback by a novel occurrence. He raised his hand and smacking it repeatedly to his lips let out an ululation like a demented pygmy Tarzan. The elephant seemed to rock back at the impact of the discordant sound; the ears flapped, but indecisively, the foot rose and fell, but this time as if pawing the mud rather than asserting a stronghold, slowly the head turned away, the great body following it, and the confrontation was broken off. Slowly Price-Allen moved inland but at an angle to the elephant so that the distance between them slowly grew whilst enabling the elephant to observe and digest the unthreatening attitude of this peculiar trespasser. Once into the cover of the bushes Price-Allen moved faster, although great speed was impossible, for the twilight now was such that it was with difficulty he avoided the roots and tendrils which could yet trip him, causing a broken ankle and turning triumph into disaster. The elephant waited until it was sure the disturbance was over before turning back to the water.

Price-Allen was aware that he was on the wrong side of the Nile in terms of the camp from which he had come, so, having gained the relative security of an outcrop of rocks near where he had entered the water, he reconciled himself to waiting for the search party to arrive. The boat from which he had been pushed would no doubt be grounded on the other side. Price-Allen awaited his encounter with the boatman with relish, but he didn't allow himself idle, indulgent thoughts: the attempt on his life meant things were moving to a head. The Omuto enquiry was drawing the noose ever tighter around Kiwonka's neck. Aramgu, back in Kenya while his boss kept out of harm's way in London, was organising fast and presumably knew that time was short. The trouble was that the President refused to take seriously Price-Allen's warnings that trouble was brewing: he had the false confidence of one who had surrounded himself with relatives and sycophants and given generous unofficial income-producing opportunities to his generals. He assumed loyalty could not be eroded or corrupted. Well, maybe he would listen now, particularly if the boatman's links with Aramgu could be established. But, with or without the Big Man's blessing, Price-Allen knew it was time to make his move. Aramgu the Black Knight had sallied down the board in an attempt to take the White Queen, but now lay exposed to the counter-thrust. Price-Allen liked chess, but he liked the world of African politics better – you could win in chess, but in life you could win and also achieve that wonderful sensation that came with the infliction of great pain. Killing Aramgu would not be enough – it must be done with style and in such a way that Aramgu would know who was responsible before he died. There were, however, one or two other details to take care of first, in addition to the boatman. Were all his pawns in place? He believed so, including one whose positioning had been a subtle work in its own right. He had secured the vital witness he needed for the Omuto enquiry and as a bonus the shipment of that witness had brought about the return of a valuable pawn: Odhiambo was back in Nairobi ready, albeit unwillingly, to be put into play.

The elephant, trundling back towards the trees, turned its head once more as a second strange sound reached its ears. Satisfied it was unthreatening, the elephant continued its journey – human laughter was not a sound it could identify.

2

Chief Inspector James Odhiambo left the buildings housing the Nairobi High Court later than he had intended. He glanced at his watch as he descended the stone steps flanked by pillars which formed the entrance to the old colonial-style building. It was seven o'clock in the evening. The day's proceedings of the enquiry into the death some twenty years ago of a rising Kenyan politician had adjourned four hours earlier. Odhiambo had used the hours to catch up with outstanding paperwork and complete the duty rotas for the remainder of the week. In truth, however, he could have wrapped up his work much earlier; much of the time he had been mooching about, his mind refusing to concentrate. He had no incentive to go home; there would be no one to greet him. Face it, he said to himself, life is unsatisfactory and boring. Grief compounding sorrow leading to despair. Had he read that somewhere or had he just made it up? He rolled it around his mind again – if it was his own he liked it. For some peculiar reason he felt better. Perhaps he would go and have a beer in the Safaris Hotel. See which of the girls tried to chat him up before her colleagues warned her that he was off limits. Probably no one would, he supposed they all knew who he was by now. He had been stuck in this part of town since the enquiry started six weeks earlier. When Chief Superintendent Masonga told him he had been put in charge of security at the court for the duration of the enquiry he had welcomed it. He would be able to keep an eye and an ear on the proceedings, look after his father-in-law, and watch the major players perform in the unfolding drama. With his increasingly suspicious mind he believed there was more to his assignment than a random selection, but so be it.

But that was then. Six weeks on, Sam Bito's dramatic evidence had faded from the headlines. Omuto had become in death a legend of hope snuffed out, the man who might have led Kenya to greatness in succession to the revered Kenyatta struck down on the eve of independence by an assassin's bullet. Now here was this middle-aged academic saying in his quiet but unflinching voice that Kiwonka – today's putative leader in exile – was the man who was responsible for the assassination. For two weeks even the international press and television gave the enquiry considerable prominence. Price-Allen, and what Odhiambo had heard people in Washington describe as his spin doctors, managed to get across a positive image: Kenya, mature enough to face old scandals, clearing out the skeletons from the past, moving on to a brighter future. Meanwhile, Kiwonka lay low in Europe waiting for the initial barrage to end. Now the enquiry had entered a dreary phase of witnesses trying to implicate other lesser figures of today who happened to be out of favour. Odhiambo was sure that a large part of the evidence now was but thinly based on fact – it seemed as if it had been decided that the enquiry was to serve a wider purpose of settling a raft of old scores. And in so doing it was in danger of losing sight of the original issue.

Meanwhile, rumours were circulating. Odhiambo picked them up through his official contacts, but he had also caught the whispers around the tables in the Safaris Hotel. He had even gone to his old favourite bar well off the city centre – the bar run by a fellow Luo who heard a lot and was careful of what and to whom he spoke. But Odhiambo was too well known now and too notorious. His exploits abroad had been reported, his relationship to Bito was well known and no one in his old haunt spoke – indeed, he felt the isolation of being removed from the trust of his own kind. Is that what he now was, a sort of half-breed, half *bwana mkubwa*, half son of Luo soil, trusted by neither his new circle nor his old? The rumours continued: Aramgu, the aggressive bully-boy, exiled to Algeria after the Eagle's Nest affair, was Kiwonka's front man and was back in town; a prominent commander of one army brigade had been slighted by the President and had sold himself to Kiwonka; someone close to the President himself was plotting his downfall. And so it went.

Odhiambo had welcomed the decision, clearly Price-Allen's, though conveyed through an officer of the court, that his in-laws, Sam Bito and his wife, were permitted to return to their Washington home with an understanding that they would not speak to the American press on the matter – an undertaking gladly given. His wife Cari had gone with them. Her firm Metroarcs had once again shown flexibility in assigning her back to Nairobi so that she could accompany her husband, but wanted her back to attend a conference in New York. That, plus the need to see her parents safely back into the life from which they had been rudely wrenched, enabled Cari to salve her conscience and leave her husband to his own devices.

Odhiambo had covered the few hundred yards to the Saltlick, the public bar of the Safaris Hotel. Because Nairobi sat almost astride the Equator, twilight was short and darkness had already blotted out the lingering remnants of the inflamed underbellies of the clouds. The lights of the tourist hotels were bright as they sparkled from a multitude of floors, promising a luxury that most of those in their shadows would never sample. Again, Odhiambo felt the terrible loneliness of one who was not only away from home, but exiled from his past, a stranger in his own land. He entered the bar; at this hour some of the after-work drinkers had already departed and there were spaces at the long bar and at the small tables. His mood, having lifted on the steps of the courthouse, now became sombre again, so he sought the solitude of an empty table. He ordered his beer from one of the girls who greeted him with a smile that was intended to be no more than just a greeting for she recognised this large, dark, handsome man. It wasn't just that he was a police officer – she knew of many such who were more than approachable – it was something about him that set him apart. She had heard of his wealthy, beautiful wife and his association with those of whom it was dangerous to speak, but it was more even than that. Her mother was a fortune teller in rural Machakos and she had inherited something of her psychic powers. Around this attractive man was the smell of death.

Odhiambo took a deep draught of the cool lager. One thing at least was better here than he had found in England or America and that was the beer. He wondered if Cari and her parents had arrived safely. He hoped Cari would not suffer a reaction returning to the area where she had witnessed such bloody deeds. Although Price-Allen had delivered on his promise to look after Cari's father, Odhiambo still blamed him for much of what he, Cari and her parents had endured in those days. He had not been able to secure a personal meeting in order to vent his pent-up anger until a summons to the presence arrived last week – a summons which had then been postponed. Odhiambo's enquiries from a contact in State Security revealed that Price-Allen had been ordered to join the President who was enjoying a tented safari in Uganda as a guest of his Ugandan counterpart – the man who had ousted the dreaded Idi Amin. Odhiambo took another swallow from his glass and shook his head: if only half the rumours were true, both the Big Man and Price-Allen would be well advised to stay home. What was the old Masai saying? 'While you hunt the lion, the hyenas steal your cattle.'

'Och, are me old eyes betraying me, or is it a braw sight I'm seeing? James, as I live and die.'

Odhiambo looked up, but the voice could belong to only one man – Robert McGuiry, the master of Eagle's Nest. This time his spirits rose to stay.

'My God, Robert!' Odhiambo rose. There McGuiry was, a little more grizzled, slightly more rounded of shoulder, but the lean figure still looked fit enough. Moderately tall though he was, McGuiry found himself looking up at the flashing teeth. 'You're a sight for sore eyes. Sit down, have a drink!'

'I've heard strange tales of your doings, mon.' McGuiry sank heavily into the proffered chair. 'But from far-off places, mind. Dinna expect to see ye here in Nairobi.'

'Nor I you.' Odhiambo obtained the attention of the hovering girl. 'What'll it be? A whisky, I think.'

'Ay, a dram to celebrate auld acquaintances would be fitting, right enough.'

The two men eyed each other as the whisky and replacement beer were put in front of them. For a minute or so neither spoke, but it was the silence of old companionship not the embarrassed silence of an unwelcome reunion. Odhiambo was the one to break it.

'It's been a while, Robert, and it seems longer. Ever since I met you my life seems to have gone crazy.'

'And you've become too grand for the likes of me. That Cornish business got you a braw lot of attention here. I should've told ye. Go up to Scotland if ye need a change of air. Not to the heathens in the west. And then your tangling with our American cousins. More to that I dare say than got in the papers here.'

'What about you? Still hosting all the tourists at Eagle's Nest?'

'Ay. Getting too old, mind ye. Thinking of calling it a day. Fuller than ever, mind. That business made it more famous. "Where did she fall?", "Are these the same elephants as killed her?" Get sick of daft questions. Yanks are the worst. Yanks and women from wherever.'

'You're an old chauvinist, Robert. What brings you to Nairobi?'

'Had to see some of these government laddies that control your life these days. Resident's permit, gun licence and such. Try and deal with them together best one can. Saves more trips.'

'Are you staying here? In the hotel, I mean.'

'Och, no. Tourist and tart trap this. No, auld friend of mine, lives out at Karen, lent me his place. He's down at the coast.'

The two men chatted amiably on as their glasses were replenished at McGuiry's request. Odhiambo found himself telling this old settler things he had told none of his professional colleagues. It had been like this when they first met. A comfortable rapport and mutual trust had been established that first night. Strange, really: the white game ranger, running the game-viewing lodge in the trees of the Aberdares, and the black policeman. They wouldn't have expected there to be much in common, but there was. Odhiambo had often mulled it over and decided they did have a lot in common: two men who loved Kenya but found themselves almost like displaced persons as the country changed so quickly in the first years of independence.

12

'So you're a grass widower at the moment.' McGuiry leaned forward in his chair, placing his empty glass on the table with a steady hand. 'No bonnie lass to go home to. Tell ye what we'll do, James. You come back with me. I told the houseman to leave me supper out – cold it'll be, but plenty for two. And we'll have a dram or two like we did the last time we were together.'

'Oh, I don't know, Robert. No need for you to – '

'No bother. You owe me one, James. The last time you ran out on me when I was sleeping. Come on, mon. We may not see each other again. Stay with me and I'll run you back in the morrow. Early as you like.'

Odhiambo looked at the face across the table. Why not? It was obvious McGuiry wanted his company. It was almost a plea he was making. Was there more to it than an excuse to get drunk with a friend? He looked into McGuiry's eyes, the skin around them lined and browned by many years of exposure to the Equatorial sun, remembering the twinkle. He couldn't see it now, rather, in the intensity with which they gazed back into his own, he detected concern.

'OK. You're on, Robert. As long as you've got a cold beer. I've never had a taste for your Scottish firewater.'

'Dinna blaspheme now, James. You're a queer one: many of you Kenyan laddies acquired the taste right enough. So let's get away on home and see what victuals we've got on offer.'

Odhiambo sat beside his host as he drove his ancient Land Rover along the road past the entrance to the Nairobi Game Park towards the suburb of Karen, site of the home of Karen Blixen whose story *Out of Africa* was now showing on the wide screen of Nairobi's poshest cinema and giving rise to complaints by politicians because the black actors were cast as either ignorant villagers or servants. Site too of the notorious murder of the future Lady Delamere's lover. Her husband's murder trial probably took place in the building he was now guarding, thought Odhiambo. Or had it been rebuilt since the thirties? Odhiambo knew that these thoughts of the colonial past were not inappropriate – Karen was still home to many of the old white families. If one wanted to find vestiges of the old lifestyle as enjoyed by the whites in colonial days, Karen was probably the best place to look. There was one most noticeable change: the expansive lawns and flowerbeds and the airy, high-ceilinged houses were hidden now behind tall hedges with steel fencing inside the

13

hedges and gates – strong, padlocked and bearing the ubiquitous sign *'Mbwa Kali'*, literally Angry Dog. Crime had come to the colonial suburbs, presenting more of a threat to the residents' lifestyle than the pre-independence troubles had ever done.

McGuiry drove sitting upright, body almost pressed to the driving wheel, staring intently into the, admittedly poor, pool of light cast by the headlamps. A typical posture for someone used to driving on tracks full of pot-holes, rocks and occasional passing animals. He muttered occasional epithets at drivers of *matatus*, various makes of van and minibus, loaded with passengers, going towards the city centre and appearing to favour the centre of the road.

'Ach, these laddies, nothing stops them, does it? Unroadworthy, overloaded and driven by lunatics.'

Odhiambo smiled. 'One police inspector tried to stop them a few years back. City life nearly came to a stop and there was a huge outcry, including from businesses. *Matatus* are the main means of public transport – an example of a thriving indigenous industry. Don't knock it, Robert.'

A grunt demonstrated lack of sympathy for the travel needs of Nairobi workers. 'I'd sooner track a wounded buffalo at night than drive these roads. I remember when the worst hazard on this road was the odd gazelle that had wandered off yon park. I tell ye, James, this modern life's no good for man nor beastie.'

Yes, Odhiambo thought, you're probably right. Kenya was changing for good or ill and the McGuirys were as threatened by it as the rhinos. Not to speak of the Odhiambos. Kenya was no place for a simple Luo boy trying to do his job without fear or favour. Cari had seen it coming before him; rather, she had recognised the likely consequences sooner. She had wanted him to leave, settle in America where she had been brought up and where she had a high-paying job. He couldn't do it. He felt guilty enough enjoying a lifestyle here funded by her salary which was many times an inspector's pittance. But he had to admit that, returning after nearly a year's absence, he noticed the stresses and strains more than he used to. He was too close now to the political intrigues, too familiar with deadly figures such as Price-Allen, and given jobs with political implications like the Omuto enquiry.

Odhiambo was jolted out of his glum reverie as McGuiry suddenly braked and swung the Land Rover sharply to the left.

14

'Damn turning! Always creeps up on ye. Hold on, James, we be there just about.'

The Land Rover slowed and turned again, nose up against a closed gate which looked less fortress-like than many Odhiambo had seen. The lights and a hoot on the horn produced a figure in what seemed to be an old army greatcoat that came down to his ankles. Latches were undone and the gate swung open, the nightwatchman giving a clumsy salute as they drove through.

There were lights on in the house and the door was unlocked. Odhiambo presumed a servant was still about and indeed one appeared while McGuiry was settling his guest in front of a fireplace laid with logs on top of kindling. Further up into the Highlands, over a mile above sea level, a fire was much to be desired in the cold of night – here in Nairobi at half that altitude a log fire was a colonial indulgence. The servant was preceded into the room by two large Ridgeback dogs who greeted McGuiry with familiarity but turned their rather evil-looking eyes on Odhiambo with suspicion, allowing the ridge of hair from which they drew their name to bristle. The owner of the property presumably placed his faith in a loyal staff and large dogs rather than high fences and solid steel gates.

The dogs' suspicions were allayed by reassurances from the servant who then proceeded to light the fire, whilst assuring McGuiry that supper was laid on the kitchen table and should he lay another place. Odhiambo was amused that he addressed the dogs in English but conversed in Swahili with McGuiry who, confirming Odhiambo's position as a guest, asked for a guest bed to be prepared. With a curious look at Odhiambo and a polite greeting the servant withdrew, followed by the dogs.

'We'll help ourselves to a plate anon and eat it in front of the fire, James. But first a dram. Och, you'll be wanting a beer – I'll see what's in the fridge. Settle yourself down, mon.'

The next hour passed pleasantly as they ate their fill of chicken, ham, beans and potato salad. Odhiambo found himself waiting, however, for McGuiry gave increasing signs as time passed of a man who was wanting to get something off his chest.

'No boy at home waiting with your supper?' McGuiry chewed away at a leg bone as he spoke. After a drink or two the old vocabulary tended to emerge. 'Should you have rung?'

'No. It's his day off.'

'When does your wife return?'

'In about a week. She's escorting her parents back to their home in Washington and then has to go to some meeting in New York. I expect you read about the Bitos – my in-laws. Back in his youth he was in Nakuru when Omuto was gunned down. He knew Kiwonka, the man behind it.'

'I remember those days.' McGuiry sipped from the heavy, deeply cut glass that seemed to glow as the liquid reflected the now brightly burning logs. 'Seems like another world. Your father-in-law was like a voice from the past. I wonder if he would have turned out any better than the rest of them. Omuto, I mean. The young idealists lost their ideals in favour of land, Benzes and their cut of everything once they got the chance.'

Odhiambo shifted uncomfortably in his chair. He agreed with the older man's complaint, but he didn't feel it was right to listen to such criticisms – after all, he was still a government officer.

'Kenya's not done too badly since independence, Robert. You've not done too badly, come to that. No one has stopped you carrying on your involvement with the game – in a different way, perhaps, but I don't see you running back to Scotland.'

'Och, I'm sorry, James. I shouldn't embarrass you like this. You're right – here I am and here I'll be until they bury me in the Aberdares. That's why I grieve for what might have been. I belong. Or hoped I did.'

'You're in speech-making form tonight, Robert. I remember you as a man of few words.'

McGuiry put his glass carefully on to the small table beside his chair. He had drunk three generous portions since they settled by the fire, on top of whatever he had had earlier, but Odhiambo noticed his hand was rock steady. He leaned forward, his face alternately lit and shadowed by the flickering flames.

'I'm a silly old man, James. Blathering on' cos I can't get to the point. So here goes. Tell me to mind me own business if y'like, but would I be correct in saying ye've got mixed up with a certain Price-Allen? When you were last here?'

Odhiambo looked more intently at the lined face. McGuiry was getting to the point, it seemed. His instincts back in the Safaris Hotel were right – McGuiry had more on his mind than drinking with an old friend. He spoke guardedly.

'I know him, yes. He has a sort of semi-official role in certain matters. You know him, too?'

'Did, James, did. God rot him. No, don't stop me. Let me get it off me chest. Got an old friend who's still in the safari busi-ness. He was in charge of a big party in Uganda this last week or two. Luxury do. Draped tents, champagne, the works. Presid-ent of Uganda on safari around Murchison Falls. Our leader, honoured guest. Our mutual acquaintance on parade also, it seems.'

'I heard something about this. So what, Robert? Glad to hear Uganda still has game left to go and look at. Amin's men had machine-gunned the lot was the way I heard it.'

'Some of the beasties hung on, same as some of us. My *rifiki* is back in town. Had a few drams together in Langata. Told me a strange story.'

McGuiry suddenly sat back in his chair as if having second thoughts. He reached for his glass, his fingers tapping anxiously on its side. Odhiambo waited a few seconds before his natural impatience got the better of him.

'Come on, Robert. You've either said too much or too little. What happened on the safari?'

'Maybe I shouldn'a started, James. Not my *shauri*. Wouldn'a want to risk our friendship.'

'For Chrissake! You are, what did you call it, blathering now. Get on with it, man.'

McGuiry leaned forward again. 'Price-Allen nearly drowned in the Nile. Mysterious circumstances. He and a boatman alone. Boatman says he fell in. Search party goes to look for body. Lot of crocs there, too, of course. Price-Allen waiting for them on the other bank.'

Odhiambo smiled. The thought of Price-Allen fighting the cur-rent and assorted predators was an attractive one.

'Couldn't happen to a nicer fellow, many would say.'

'Ay. Would give even a croc stomach-ache, would yon Price-Allen. The beastie avoided him, I'd say. No, the point is my *rifiki* notices Price-Allen, couple of security chappies and the boatman missing next morning. Price-Allen and the heavies return with-out the other laddie. Later he overhears two of the people around the President talking. Tents have thin walls. One says, "The *mzungu* says it was Aramgu. He wants to deal with him himself. Says we're toothless old women." And the other says, "He may be right – perhaps they're going to try something be-fore the enquiry's over. We'd better tell the Big Man." And the first man curses Price-Allen, says something about pity he didn't end up as the crocodile's *chakula*. "Always looking for plots. Let him and Aramgu fight it out." '

McGuiry had an attentive audience now.

'Aramgu! He is back here then? I heard as much.'

'Ay. I thought ye'd remember our friend the Administrator. You had some problems with him during those days.'

'Price-Allen suspected him of plotting then. That's why he was exiled, sort of.'

'Well, he's back, laddie. I can tell ye that. Saw him in Nyeri afore I left.'

Odhiambo shrugged.

'So he's back and he bears a grudge against Price-Allen. That man your friend overheard may be right. Let them get on with it.'

'Ah, but Aramgu has no nice memories of you, neither. And there's one thing more, James. Some of the foot-soldiers my friend uses – you know, locals for the menial jobs around the camp – they told him later the boatman's body had been seen in the Nile. And said the word in the village was the *mzungu* had tortured him before throwing him to the crocs.'

Price-Allen up to his usual tricks, thought Odhiambo. Nothing would surprise him about that deadly white man. The unofficial master-mind and executioner of State Security. He pulled his mind back to McGuiry.

'Why tell me this, Robert? I'm only a *toto* as far as two old bulls like Price-Allen and Aramgu are concerned.'

'There's all sorts of rumours running around, James. Some people are betting on trouble a plenty.'

Odhiambo waved his hand angrily as if sweeping rumours aside.

'You've been in the bush too long, Robert. There's always rumours in Nairobi. But what's it to do with me? Or you?'

There was a strained silence, punctuated by the musical note caused by the tapping of McGuiry's fingernail on the cut-glass. Then the words came with a rush.

'When I saw ye, in the bar, I said to this fellow, "I must go and say hello. That's Chief Inspector Odhiambo. Wonder if he'll remember me?" And he said, "Be careful, McGuiry. That's a Price-Allen man you're looking at." So I thought I owed ye a warning, unless you're right in the middle already. In which case put it down to the ramblings of an old man.'

So that's how one gets contaminated, thought Odhiambo bitterly. Mud sticks. That's what they whisper now, is it? 'He's a Price-Allen man.' McGuiry's face seemed to blur as Odhiambo felt a wave of nausea rise from his stomach to his brain. He turned to face the fire: irrational though it might be, he felt anger towards McGuiry. He could sense his companion watching him anxiously. Before he could resolve his mix of emotions there was an interruption as, with a scant knock, the servant entered in a rush.

'*Bwana*! *Samahani*. Scusi. But something very bad. You must come.'

McGuiry and Odhiambo both rose at the distress evident in the man's voice. Odhiambo waited for McGuiry to take on the interrogation, but he found it necessary to hold himself in check. At last McGuiry spoke.

'What is it, man? What has happened?'

'I go to walk for dogs. On place for golf. The dog he find something. You come quick, *tafadhali*.'

'I . . . What are . . .'

McGuiry was trying to gather his thoughts, but Odhiambo could refrain no longer.

'Let's go and see, Robert.' He turned to the frightened servant. 'Right. Show us.'

'*Asante, bwana*. You come, you see.'

The two men followed the scurrying figure through the kitchen and out of a back door. Their guide was clutching a torch and, waving this somewhat erratically in front of him, he led the way across a lawn to what seemed to be a slight gap in a broad hedge that loomed in front of them at a height above Odhiambo's eye level. Gingerly, McGuiry and Odhiambo eased their way through the gap to see the torch bobbing along in line with the hedge to their left. Odhiambo's eyes were adjusting to the darkness lit fitfully by a pale moon. They were on closely cut grassland with a line of trees just visible, running parallel to the hedge. As they hastened after the receding torch, Odhiambo remembered the servant's words, 'place for golf': they must be on the golf course at Karen. He saw a moving shape pass through the beam of the torch and heard the bark. The dogs had presumably been left behind when their walker went for help. The torch came to an unsteady stop as Odhiambo and McGuiry caught up with it. The beam swept around before settling on a mound beside which could be discerned the second dog. Odhiambo walked towards it. It was gazing at the bank of the mound, with an anxious whine seeping from its muzzle. Odhiambo bent forward, following the direction in which the dog was looking. The mound seemed partially grassed with an area of bare and disturbed soil. Odhiambo felt the hair on the back of his neck rise in sympathy with those on the Ridgeback as his eyes focused and adjusted to the dim light. Yes, he was not mistaken – out of the mound protruded a white hand.

3

The bar and lounge of the Royal Ngong Golf Club could be described as small compared to the expansive interior space of the newly rebuilt, nearby Karen Club; the panelled room and corner bar had even been termed poky by some, but for the limited membership the old-fashioned, slightly musty cosiness somehow contributed to their sense of being exclusive. The Royal Ngong had survived the transition from a colonial club modelled on the old establishment London clubs to a club whose membership was now over one-third black. It had achieved this by carefully identifying those who aspired to emulate the colonial clubman, often the sons of the newly powerful who, educated in the more prestigious public schools of England, had acquired the tastes and mannerisms of their former colonial masters. They were not particularly numerous but there were enough to maintain the strength of the RONS, as members of the Royal Ngong were jocularly known. Golf to the RONS was not so much a matter of expertise in holing out around the tree-lined and manicured course but, rather, an open-air and healthy aid to the social and business bonding which was their main motivation. To hold a low handicap was not a disadvantage in itself, but the expertise it denoted should be displayed by a RON as a casual talent rather than one acquired and maintained by long hours of practice. In fact, the increase in black members had raised the standard of play because they were more naturally talented in acquiring a smooth rhythmic swing than their white fellow members, many of whom were less than well co-ordinated.

Francis Hill-Templeton, the long-time Secretary of the club, as he looked around the few members still present in mid-evening, could congratulate himself on the balance between black and white faces that met his eye. He would, if he had consciously thought about it, congratulate himself also on what his eye did not see – the Royal Ngong had no Asian members. He leaned his languid frame against the dark mahogany wood of the bar and watched for a moment the only group still seated around a table in the lounge. Stefano Iocacci and his wife Gianna, both dark and handsome – they could be brother and sister rather than husband and wife. Manager of a motor company in Nairobi he might be, but it was a posh motor company. Moreover, he represented old Italian money and manners which eased his acceptance as a RON. Michael Silent, slightly built, impassive, saturnine, living up to his name with the ever-present half-smile that was so close to a smirk. The woman next to him was Pauline Florislow, daughter of an old Nairobi family, divorced and a businesswoman in her own right. She seemed to have joined the Dennison-Silent circle, Hill-Templeton thought, which surprised him slightly. She had sex appeal although one could scarcely call her beautiful, but he had assumed she was too intelligent to fit easily into that effete and depraved group. The remaining person at the table, directly facing Hill-Templeton, was Anne Dennison. He grimaced slightly at the sight of her, a few drinks and her blonde, brassy vulgarity came to the fore. How a man like Dennison had come to marry her, Hill-Templeton could not understand. 'Let's face it,' he had said on more than one occasion, 'the woman's a tart.'

The missing person in the group was Jim Dennison. Hill-Templeton turned his attention back to his companion.

'Where's your Vice tonight, John? He usually plays on a Tuesday, doesn't he?'

John Matavu, the Captain of the Royal Ngong, looked across towards the group recently scanned by the Secretary.

'Yes. I don't know, Francis. Haven't seen him for a couple of days, in fact. Must ask Anne if he's under the weather.'

'How is he bedding down as Vice-Captain? Pulling his weight, is he?'

'You weren't enthusiastic about him, were you, Francis? He'll be OK. Besides, you and I can cope. We don't need someone horning in. Keep the decision-making process simple.'

21

Hill-Templeton grunted, indicating that he was unconvinced.

'But he's next in line now, John. After you we get Jim. I'm not too happy that he's the right man.'

Matavu gestured at the hovering barman, indicating his and his companion's glasses.

'Don't worry too much about that now. A lot can happen between now and the end of the year.'

Hill-Templeton's mind quickly ran the last sentence through its slow replay facility. Interesting. Did Matavu not intend to follow the tradition and stand down after one year of captaincy? Or did he know something about Dennison's future? He was head of the bank that dealt with Dennison's business accounts. Yes, very interesting.

His musings were interrupted by the appearance of the club's nightwatchman, whispering urgently to the barman who had intercepted him as he emerged from the direction of the kitchen and the back door.

'Hello. Has the nightwatch spotted something?'

He and Matavu watched as the barman turned and hurried towards them. Matavu asked the question.

'Something going on, Sam?'

'Yes, *bwana*. The guard he say police are on course. On number eighteen, I think. He says they are digging.'

'Digging! What the hell is he talking about?' Hill-Templeton was bemused. 'The police digging on the eighteenth?'

Matavu was disinclined to speculate. 'Come on, Francis. Best go and have a look. See what's going on.'

They hurried from the bar watched by the three remaining drinkers at the bar and the group at the table which had recently attracted Hill-Templeton's attention. As they disappeared Anne Dennison spoke, slurring her words ever so slightly.

'Wonder what's bitten those two? Looked as if they'd been told their flies were undone.'

She laughed her throaty, nicotine-stained laugh, drawing the slightest of winces from Gianna Iocacci. Michael Silent's half-smirk widened.

'I somehow get the feeling it could be something that will take them longer to fix than a zip. Who knows, my dear Anne, it may yet touch us all.'

'Well, Robert, at least we got help a lot sooner than the last time we found a body together. They've got the spades from your shed. The body should be clear in a minute.'

The two men watched for a few moments as the torchlights bobbed and the clank of spade striking stone reached them.

'My God, James, I can't believe it. It's . . . it's like . . . I don't know . . . It's like going back to the start of an old film. I mean, we can't find ourselves in the middle of another murder, can we?'

'Let's not jump to conclusions.' Odhiambo did not sound very convincing. 'Although whoever it is didn't bury himself in there. Well, whatever's happened here may not involve us. It was your cook who found him, or rather the dog.'

'Dinna deceive yourself, laddie. You're jinxed, mon.'

'It won't be my case.' But the man's right, thought Odhiambo. How could this happen to him again? Perhaps he was under some juju. Aramgu's witch doctor perhaps. Ever since he'd crossed Aramgu before they both left Kenya his path had led him to a welter of bodies. 'Just a coincidence we were here. Why couldn't some bloody golfer have found it?'

'Ay, that's strange, that. Looks like he's buried in the tee. Ye ken. That's where they start the hole from. They climb up on top and tee their wee ball up. Should have seen something if that hand was there before dark.'

'Might have been the dog that scratched the earth away and exposed it.' Odhiambo saw a torch waving in their direction. 'Why don't you go in and have a dram, Robert? I'll go and see what they've got.'

He moved away; the Scotsman, ignoring the suggestion, followed discreetly behind. A uniformed officer joined Odhiambo.

'We can see the body now. We did what you said, sir. Dug from top. Opened it up. Body is still where it was.'

'Good. Let's have a look.'

Torches were focused on to the body of a man, clad in patterned, casual shirt and slacks. The feet were bare. Didn't look as if he was in the middle of a round, thought Odhiambo. He bent over the body and touched the arm. Cold and with every indication of rigor mortis. He reached out, took one of the torches from the hand of a policeman and shone it on the corpse's face. Middle-aged white man. Skin looked as if it was long accustomed to the Equatorial sun. The eyes were bulging and bloodshot. The mouth was open, giving the impression that the corpse was about to scream. He bent close once more. Yes, there was the cut in the skin around the front of the neck. Something thin had bitten into the flesh. Whoever it was had been strangled. He moved the torch down to shine on the bare feet. Soil was sticking to one in particular. Odhiambo looked closer; there appeared to be dried blood around the toes. He, whoever it was, had cut himself walking in bare feet – white men wore shoes.

A sound behind him like a combination of a cough and a snort disturbed his concentration. Odhiambo straightened and turned. McGuiry was a few steps away and seemed to have intercepted two new arrivals. Odhiambo's eyes found the senior of the policemen present.

'Go and radio for reinforcements. Tell them it's a murder enquiry.' He moved towards McGuiry and the newcomers. 'What have we here, Robert?'

Before McGuiry could respond, a tall white man answered for himself.

'Hill-Templeton – Secretary of the Royal Ngong. This, I assume you know, is our property. Part of the golf course, actually. What is going on? Are you a police officer?'

'And you, sir?' Odhiambo addressed the second of the two men. An African, not as tall as the white man but big-shouldered and broad-chested.

'Matavu. Captain here. And you?'

'Odhiambo. Chief Inspector Odhiambo. A body has been found here in suspicious circumstances. I happened to be on a social visit with this gentleman here in the property beyond the hedge. The crime officer will be here shortly.'

'What do you mean, suspicious circumstances?' This was Hill-Templeton. 'You mean someone's been attacked? A nightwatchman or what?'

'Hold on, Francis.' Matavu's voice carried authority. 'From the little I saw, Inspector, would I be correct in saying it's a *mzungu*?'

'We must wait for the designated officer before proceeding further. But come with me. You know your members, I dare say. And local residents.' He ushered the men closer to the mound and directed his torch on to the dead man's face. 'Do you know him?'

A gasp from Matavu and an expletive from Hill-Templeton gave the answer. Matavu leaned forward.

'How did he die? I'm sorry. Yes. I know him. A Mr Jim Dennison. He is the Vice-Captain of the club.'

'Christ, John! You said a lot could happen before he became Captain. Just a few minutes ago. My God! Anne is in the clubhouse. What do we do?'

'Don't get hysterical, Francis. One thing at a time. This officer will tell us when we can leave to inform his wife.'

Odhiambo's instinctive antennae were twitching. An interesting exchange. He pulled himself together: not my case, just keep everything in order until someone comes to take over. He looked at McGuiry; even in the gloom he could sense the wise old eyes reading his mind. McGuiry slowly shook his head: Odhiambo took it as a gesture of pity. He sighed.

'Robert, take one of the constables here and go with this gentleman – the Secretary – to the clubhouse. Everyone there should wait until someone gets there. OK?'

'Leave it to me, James. We'll see what we can do. See ye anon.'

After some additional protest from Hill-Templeton, Matavu persuaded him to join McGuiry and head towards the lights that Odhiambo could see a few hundred yards away. A constable followed, keeping a few paces behind the *mzungus* and the African who he could tell was a man to be polite to.

Odhiambo watched them disappear into the darkness and turned back to the site of the body. He still had the torch in his hand and he ran the beam over the top surface of the mound, or tee as McGuiry referred to it.

'You didn't dig it all up, did you?' He addressed the corporal who seemed to be in charge. 'Over there in the far corner. You didn't dig that up?'

'Nossir. Only dig around body. From top. Turf is loose. Just put there.'

'Yes, so I see.'

Odhiambo walked around the mound. It was all new: he could see that now. The earth was fresh and the turf on top was in pieces loosely laid. It looked as if whoever was building it had left it unfinished – intending to return, probably. So, most likely, the body had been deposited in the opened earth and turf placed over it.

'How many houses lie behind this hedge?'

'Not knowing, sir. Houses here are for big people. Mainly *mzungus*. Five or six maybe on this side.'

Did one of them belong to the dead man, wondered Odhiambo? Vice-Captain of the golf club – meant he must be a regular player. What could be more convenient than a nice house beside the course? In the distance he heard a siren: reinforcements were arriving. He hoped somebody competent would be in charge.

4

'Why? Why me?' Odhiambo leaned over his superior's desk, anger in his voice and on his face. 'Who says I should take this on?'

Chief Superintendent Masonga crushed out his cigarette in the already full ashtray and turned his chair through ninety degrees as if to avoid direct eye contact. He looked out at the morning sunlight reflecting off the corrugated roof of the building across the yard of the Nairobi central police station. Uniformed figures crossed the yard in various directions. It was a scene he had seen thousands of times, but suddenly it irritated him. There seemed a general lack of purpose to the movement. He felt old and ineffectual. He turned back to look at the real source of his depressed spirits.

'You were complaining to me only last week that your assignment could be done by a *toto*. "Have I been sidelined?" That's what you said. OK, now you are back in the front line. So what's the *shauri*?'

'Superintendent, we both know I wouldn't suddenly be given this case out there in Karen unless there was a reason. I don't like not knowing what's going on.'

'That's your trouble, Odhiambo. Always looking for something. Always thinking someone's pushing you around. You're not needed any more at the court so you're given a prime case and still you complain.'

'The reason I know I'm being pushed about is because I'm an expert. I've been manipulated before, remember? You remember the last case – the white woman? And how I came to be back here a month or two ago trying to find my father-in-law? And you wonder why I'm suspicious? This case has a smell to it. I'm being set up again.'

Masonga pushed his chair back and rose from it to face his subordinate. He still had to look up for he was considerably the shorter as well as the stouter of the two. He reached for his pack of cigarettes as he spoke.

'Listen, Odhiambo, and then go and do your job. We have a prominent white man murdered in strange circumstances. Man with important friends. Needs to be handled by someone with savvy. Someone with experience.' Masonga suddenly grinned, the show of white teeth momentarily lighting up his careworn countenance. 'Someone who isn't put off by interviewing big men and who knows how to handle the *mzungus*. Who better than the famous Inspector Odhiambo, international detective? So you are suitable and you are available.'

'You don't expect me – '

'Chief Inspector, you have your orders.' Masonga's voice was suddenly stern. He bent his head to light his cigarette and then looked back at Odhiambo. 'I am not here to argue with you. You have been assigned. *Shauri quisha!*'

Odhiambo realised that bluster would get him no further.

'What about making arrangements at the court?'

'It's being done, Odhiambo. You forget that and think about the *mzungu* on the golf course.'

It was Odhiambo's turn to break off the eye contact. He paced across the limited space in Masonga's office. Not over-large to begin with, the room was further restricted by piles of files and papers lying on the floor. Odhiambo was sure some had lain undisturbed since the previous year. He swung on his heel and returned to the desk.

'OK. Now, Superintendent, you play fair with me. The dead man, Dennison, he's a big man at the Ngong Club. Vice-Captain. And he's found buried on the course. But he was almost certainly killed in one of the houses near where we found the body. So why this foolishness of burying him under the tee? Now, the little I've been told so far is that Dennison was a director with Mbayazi Estates. You know, that's a company with a lot of former Masai land in the Rift. Wheatland. And coffee farms near Nyeri.' Odhiambo paused as Masonga shifted uneasily from foot to foot, dragging heavily on his cigarette. 'And you know, Mr Masonga, that the chairman of Mbayazi Estates is our old friend Bwana Aramgu, formal Regional Administrator, currently, or so I thought, our Ambassador to Algeria, but last seen back in Kenya.'

Masonga sat down heavily into his chair. He drew deeply once more on his cigarette and then pointed it at his subordinate.

'Odhiambo, for the love of your ancestors, why do you have to go looking for trouble? Why bring up Aramgu? I would have thought you'd had enough of crossing his path. You've got a dead *mzungu* in a *mzungus'* playground! You know what they're like. Golf, beer and sex with your partner's wife. Go and sniff around in their fancy clubhouse. That's where you'll find what's behind all this.'

Odhiambo snorted. He bent his upper torso over Masonga's desk, resting his weight on his formidable arms.

'Why do I get the feeling that you don't believe what you're saying? OK, I'll grill the fancy *mzungus* for you and if one of them did it I'll get him. But, Super, if I smell shit I'll open up the cesspit – you know that. So if you know more than you're telling, pull me off now.'

Masonga sighed as he stubbed out his cigarette.

'I had a quiet time while you were away, Odhiambo. My people did what they were told and they didn't come in here accusing me of being a liar and a stooge of State House. We've had this *shauri* before. I'm trying to do my job and get you to do yours. I can't tell what these people are up to. Go and ask your *rifikis* – you know some of those people more than me. But watch yourself, Odhiambo – these are bad times.'

'I know bastards like Price-Allen 'cos he's been pulling me around like some damn doll. OK, let me go and find out who buried that guy on that damn golf course.' Odhiambo turned to leave, but swung back as he remembered his conversation of the previous evening prior to the events that had then intervened. 'Bad times you said, Super. What I hear, you're right. Look, this Omuto enquiry, it's just about tied Kiwonka down on the ant-hill. Either he does something now or he's a dead man. I told you Aramgu is back. Aramgu is Kiwonka's man, we both know that. And now I hear someone tried to kill Price-Allen but failed. We know what that will make him do. A dead *mzungu* may be the least of our troubles any day now.'

Masonga rose once more and moved around his desk to face his subordinate. His first words were spoken fiercely.

'That's enough seditious gossip, Odhiambo. Leave politics to those whose job it is. We are simple men.' Then his voice dropped to a whisper as he stretched his face upwards towards

Odhiambo's ear. 'Don't open your mouth like a woman. Hyenas chew the bones of those who said less.'

Odhiambo gazed at the face now close to his. He could see the sweat around the temples and the jowls. Although the atmosphere in Masonga's office was sticky with the heat and humidity of the impending rains, Odhiambo could smell a component of that sweat and it was fear. If Masonga believed he could not speak freely in his own office things had worsened more than Odhiambo had realised. He nodded.

'Yeah. OK. I'll get out to Karen.'

'Good. I'll get you a car allocated.'

'And a driver who knows which side of the road he's on, otherwise I'd sooner walk.'

'Always moaning, Odhiambo. Get out.' Then as Odhiambo opened the door Masonga remembered one further piece of advice. 'Before you go on safari to Karen, go and see Ntende, the vice man. You know him? He can fill you in on our friends at the Royal Ngong.'

'Ntende, yes, I know him. Thanks.'

As he walked over to the section where Inspector Ntende would be found, if he was in, Odhiambo mulled over his position. On the face of it, to be given an interesting murder to get to grips with rather than supervising security at the court was a big gain, but his instincts told him that the balance could not so easily be drawn. It was not Superintendent Masonga who had allocated him to the golf-course murder – he was sure of that: orders had come from above, which opened the question of why State House and State Security should be interested in this case. Somewhere at the back of it Odhiambo could sense the presence of Price-Allen. It was time for him to have the long-awaited meeting with this man whose shadow seemed always to be over him like a puppet-master looming over the stage on which his puppets danced. But what could be of interest to State Security in the murder of a golfer, a member of an élitist golf club, a survivor from a colonial era? Odhiambo remained to be convinced that the solution would be found inside the portals of the Royal Ngong Golf Club. A few minutes with his colleague Inspector Ntende, who was indeed in his section's office, went some way to removing his doubts.

'So you've got yourself another dead *mzungu*, Odhiambo. Getting to be a habit, *bwana*.'

'I'm the fall guy, Ntende, same as before, but I don't get given any choice.'

'But you found him. You find him, you deal with him. Seems OK to me.'

'Someone's put the curse on me, Ntende. Someone's killed the chicken and buried the entrails in my *shamba*. That's what I'm up against.'

'Or you move in dangerous circles, *bwana*. If you walk with the night dogs beware the leopard.'

'Yeah, that's very helpful, that is. Typical useless Kikuyu proverb, no doubt.'

Ntende grinned. 'Stay cool, man. Now you want to know something about your new corpse, right? Dennison, right?'

'Anything you know about him and his *rifikis* would help.'

'As it happens I can give you a little *chakula*. The Royal Ngong is like something from the bad old days, except some favoured locals are included now. The new racism is shared by old and new members – there's no Asian members. They're all in the Royal Nairobi. Matavu is the *bwana mkubwa* there and he's got good business and tribal connections. Now, your dead man is also big man there. He is, was, typical front man in one or two businesses for our politicians.'

'Including Mbayazi Estates, I was told.'

Ntende raised his hand as if warding off a blow. 'Don't start bringing that into it, Odhiambo. Some things are taboo, *bwana*, even for a wild man like you. Yes, if you must know, he was. But all I'm doing is telling you what sort of man he was. The left-behinds of colonial days. Can't bear to give up the easy life of sun, servants and safaris, but good for little except using their names to disguise who really owns what. What makes them my *shauri* is that with not much to do they get bored, and hitting a ball about doesn't fill the dark hours. So they have parties, drink a little, sniff a little and swap their women around. There's a few we've looked at who base themselves at the Ngong and the Dennisons are included.'

'I've said this to you before, Ntende. If you have all this dirt on these people, why don't I ever hear of them being arrested?'

'And my answer's the same. Some of these people are more useful as they are, you savvy?' Ntende tapped his nose. 'Through their connections they hear a lot, see a lot and, sometimes, with a little persuasion, can be made to say a lot.'

30

'And was Dennison one of your informers?'

Ntende shifted in his chair and his eyes slid away from contact with those of Odhiambo. There was a silence which seemed to widen the distance between the two men. Finally, Ntende looked back at his visitor.

'Not one of mine, no. I can't vouch for everyone, only my section.'

'You're giving me bad meat, Ntende. Look, the man's dead. He's no good to you now. Come clean with me.'

'It's the truth. We don't have any connection with Dennison.' Again, the pause as Ntende decided on his next words. 'But there's a woman who is in the same social circle. No husband. Businesswoman. You'll be seeing her, of course. She's been helpful once or twice.'

'Helpful about what? Come on, Ntende! I've got plenty to do even if you haven't. Just tell me what you know.'

Ntende smiled as if enjoying his colleague's impatience.

'OK. There's a group that includes the Dennisons. The sort of group I was talking about. Two or three couples in addition to them including a pair of Italians we got interested in. Iocacci. Runs the garage on Mabendu Street. Luxury European cars. He's a user. I'd like to know who he's buying off. That's the sort of thing my contact may turn out to be helpful with.'

'And her name?'

'Florislow. Woman about thirty-five. Attractive if you like that sort of white woman. But thin and a bit hard for me.'

'Who else is in this group of yours?'

'Not mine, *bwana*. No such fortune for us policemen. There's a man called Silent, one or two others. I don't know precisely.'

'What about the Secretary guy? One of those double names. Thinks he's still a colonial ruler.'

'I know who you mean. Hill-Templeton. No, I don't think so. He's too fond of bossing everyone about to get mixed up in Dennison's circle. Can't be sure, mind. He could be involved, but not to my knowledge. Matavu the Captain may be another, but not as far as I know.'

Further probing revealed that he had got as much out of Ntende as he appeared to know, so Odhiambo took his leave. Emerging from the rear of the police station he located the car and driver allocated to him. The driver, Odhiambo noted, was middle-aged and drove steadily and competently. His Superintendent was looking after him, Odhiambo thought: long might it continue.

5

John Matavu sat in the deserted lounge of the Royal Ngong Golf Club and considered his position. Whichever way he reviewed the facts the direction in which they were pointing was worrying. That Jim Dennison had been murdered was bad enough, but his crude burial on the course was an aggravating factor which Matavu considered to be an almost personal affront to himself. The notion that Dennison had been murdered by an angry golfer was obviously absurd, so planting the body on the course seemed to have been an intentional ploy to drag the club into the police spotlight, which was not something that he welcomed, either as the club's Captain or as a private individual.

He had been to see Anne Dennison earlier to pay his condolences and find out what help he could offer. It had been a brief but not easy meeting. Ushered into her breakfast room by her houseman he found her in a dressing-gown sitting at the table with a large jug of coffee and a glass of tomato juice in front of her. She looked terrible, but, to his experienced eye, it seemed more the dishevelled hair and bloodshot eyes of a hangover than the pale face and tear-stained eyes of a new widow. Whatever the reason, she looked her age – which was, he guessed, well into the forties rather than the brave attempt at thirty which she espoused in her appearances at the club.

Matavu muttered his rehearsed words, which seemed even more ineffectual than he had anticipated. The woman looked at him blankly in an extended silence, then at last she seemed to focus.

'It's you. I wondered for a minute who the hell it was. Thanks for coming. You're going to need a new Vice. Christ, what a mess.'

Whatever response he had been expecting it was not this and he floundered.

'Ah . . . I suppose . . . I mean . . . um . . . yes . . . But don't worry about the club. I mean we want . . . I mean . . .'

Anne Dennison laughed; laughter with no humour in it, which turned into a coughing attack. She snatched the glass and drank to overcome her seizure.

'I'm not worried about the bloody club. Just making conversation. Isn't that what ladies are supposed to do? Here . . .' She broke off as if remembering other lessons of etiquette. 'Would you like some coffee? It's one of the few things Amir can do properly. Percolate the bloody coffee. Don't ask for scrambled eggs, he's likely to put the lot in, shell and all.'

Matavu declined the offer: he was already planning an early escape. It seemed likely that Anne Dennison had sought solace from the bottle during what, he presumed, had been a sleepless night. He shuffled from one foot to the other before attempting a return to his reason for the visit.

'I'm sorry to disturb you. You must be distressed. But I thought I should see if there's anything I or the club . . .'

'They said they'd send someone to see me and take me to the mo . . . to wherever they've put Jim. You got good connections with the police, John?'

Matavu shook his head and looked briefly at the door.

'No. Not exactly. Not in the way you mean. I mean . . .'

Again the laugh which turned into a splutter.

'Don't worry, I don't want you to fix owt.' The accent, which she normally took the trouble to suppress, was more prominent than Matavu had previously experienced. 'I was wondering what the form is. What's going to happen next?'

'I'm no expert, I'm afraid. Especially for cases of mur . . . Er . . . have you got . . . I mean, do you have a regular solicitor? You need professional advice.' He sat down in the chair to which his hostess had been gesturing. 'Have you got any friends coming here? A lady, I mean. You need company.'

'Never mind my friends. What there are of them. It's a husband I'm short of.' The voice cracked a little and once more she had recourse to her glass. Matavu wondered if it was just tomato juice in the glass or if she was on her first Bloody Mary of the day. 'I'll tell you what you can do for me, Mr Captain; you can explain how Jim got himself killed. It's not the sort of thing that's supposed to happen at the Royal Bloody Ngong. Aren't you supposed to have nightwatchmen on the damn course?'

Matavu felt a surge of irritation. Did the woman think he had men on every hole? He got up.

33

'I don't think it was a gang. I mean, I don't think he was attacked on the course. The police will – '

Anne Dennison expressed an extreme view of what the police could do. Matavu half turned to go; this was becoming more embarrassing by the minute. She watched him as he edged towards the door, her eyes fully focused now, and, as he turned his head to meet her gaze, he felt their impact as if a message had been conveyed. He waited, shifting uneasily on the balls of his feet.

'Michael phoned earlier. He's coming around. I'll see what he says. But I tell you this, John Matavu, I may not seem like a normal bloody widow to you, but I'm not letting the bastards get away with it. Jim was OK. He was a good man and I'll avenge him. I tell you that.'

With those words and, on his part, a last set of muttered offers of help being available, Matavu managed his escape. As he drove the few miles to the club he considered the implications of Michael Silent acting as the widow Dennison's adviser. There was irony in that, but also a measure of insurance. He should be able to control her. What was worrying, however, was that Silent was a devious as well as malicious character. Matavu was not confident that, if it suited his purpose, Silent would not try to drag him further into this mess. He had appointed Dennison as his Vice-Captain as a favour – given his position in Mbayazi Estates it was thought useful to get closer to him. In that sense he had been used, and now he had a nasty suspicion that he might be used again, but this time in an unwitting and dangerous role.

Now he sat and considered what best to do. He was conscious of the steward sidling up, presumably to see if his coffee cup needed replenishing, but no, the steward leaned towards him and spoke in a voice that was unusually hushed – Dennison's death seemed to have affected everybody.

'*Bwana*, there's a policeman to see you. He wanted Bwana Templeton, but he no be there. So he ask for you.'

Behind the head bent towards him, Matavu could see an approaching figure. It had been dark last night, but he recognised the large frame and the head of a Luo.

Matavu rose and moved to meet the approaching policeman. He started to put out his hand, but withdrew it as his visitor by words and tone indicated the official nature of the encounter.

'Chief Inspector Odhiambo. We met last night. I believe you are John Matavu.'

34

'Yes. That's right – we met out on the course. But it was someone else who came to the club afterwards and asked us questions.'

Odhiambo grunted. He wasn't about to admit that he had left once an inspector had arrived, hoping to keep himself out of the case.

'Well, today I need to ask more questions. Maybe the same ones again. Do you know where the Secretary is?' Odhiambo consulted his notebook. 'Mr Hill-Templeton. I met him last night too. He seemed to think I was a trespasser.'

'He's outside, I think, seeing the professional. I'll get someone to fetch him.'

'No hurry. Perhaps we can talk first? Here?'

Odhiambo looked around. They had the lounge to themselves. The old wood panels, the old-fashioned armchairs, and the existence in the room of only one window situated on the wall furthest from the door gave the room a sense of intimacy, but also gloom. It was how Odhiambo imagined an old colonial clubroom would have been. This, indeed, was what it was; it had probably not been changed since well before Kenya's independence.

Matavu observed Odhiambo's scan of his surroundings.

'Yes. It's private enough. We could go into Hill-Templeton's office if you prefer.'

'You knew the dead man, Mr Dennison?'

'Yes. Yes, of course I did. I told you last night. He was my Vice-Captain here at the Ngong.'

Odhiambo gave the briefest of nods in acknowledgement that he was going over already trodden ground.

'And you're the Captain? Since when?'

'Since last June. Eight months or so.'

'You chose Mr Dennison to be Vice-Captain?'

'Yes. It's the Captain's prerogative. Has to be confirmed by the members at the AGM, but that's usually a formality.'

'So you were a close friend of Mr Dennison?'

'Not that close, no. I've known him for several years. Played golf with him. But he wasn't a personal friend.'

'So why choose him?'

The question seemed to disconcert Matavu. Odhiambo detected surprise, yes, but there was more than surprise: the relaxed confident air seemed to be suddenly deflated. There was a long pause which Matavu covered by signalling for the steward hovering near the bar.

'Do you want a drink? *Kahawa, chai* or something stronger?'

Odhiambo shook his head, but kept his stare on Matavu's face, forcing him to re-establish eye contact.

'You must know why you chose him?'

'Dennison? You don't choose your closest friend for the job necessarily. There's a sort of protocol. List of those thought to be eligible. That kind of thing.'

'And Dennison was top of the list? I don't suppose it's written down anywhere, is it?'

'Of course not. But what has this got to do with anything? You're not suggesting he was killed because he was my Vice- Captain?'

'You're the manager of the Kenya Industrial Development Bank?'

'Yes.'

'Was Dennison a customer of your bank?'

'We don't hold personal accounts. Only business ones.'

'I meant Dennison in terms of his business interests.'

'I'm not sure what his business interests are . . . were.'

'You play golf with a man for years. You make him your Vice-Captain. No doubt you sit and drink with him. You're a prominent businessman yourself and you say you don't know what Dennison did?'

'I'm not sure what you're getting at. I knew he was involved with one or two companies who are clients of my bank, but I keep business and golf separate.'

'Is Mbayazi Estates a customer of yours?'

'Listen, Odhiambo, I don't like the way you're talking. If you want to know about the bank's customers you take it up with the *bwana mkubwas* of the bank. I'm a small boy.'

'I hope I'm not interrupting. I understand someone was looking for me.'

Odhiambo looked around but he had immediately established the identity of the voice behind him – the pompous voice remembered from the previous evening.

'Ah, Mr Hill-Templeton. Yes, I wished to ask you some questions.'

'About Dennison, poor chap. Dreadful business. I expect Mr Matavu has told you that we don't see any connection with the club as such. His death, I mean.'

36

'Mr Matavu has told me very little as yet.'

Hill-Templeton looked as if he found that reassuring.

'No doubt because we have little to offer. Perhaps you would care to come into my office Mr . . . er . . .?'

'Odhiambo. Chief Inspector.'

Odhiambo rose, as did Matavu. They followed the stiff back of Hill-Templeton into an office that was small but pleasantly furnished with a good dark-wood desk and upholstered chairs and an Indian rug. Two functional metal filing cabinets were against one wall. Behind Hill-Templeton's chair the obligatory portrait of Kenya's President looked down benignly on to the desk, uncluttered except for two trays, a telephone and a smart pen set mounted on a green onyx base. No personal touches that Odhiambo could see. No family photographs, no personal trophies, no pot plants. Hill-Templeton probably regarded such diversions as sentimental trivia.

Looking at the two chiefs of the Royal Ngong, Odhiambo thought you couldn't wish for an apparently better pair of pillars of society. Hill-Templeton, tall, erect carriage, slacks and blazer carrying the club crest, and Matavu, with that solid look that conveys the impression of athleticism rather than density, soberly clad in banker's grey lightweight suiting. Why then had he taken an instinctive dislike to both of them? Hill-Templeton was the easier case to answer; he oozed colonial arrogance. Matavu emitted no discordant vibes, but somehow Odhiambo sensed a suppressed hostility in the man.

Hill-Templeton gestured to his visitors to sit and then walked around his desk to his own chair. Seated, he pressed the tips of his fingers together and looked at Odhiambo with a supercilious air.

'Now, Inspector, what is it you wish to know? The club is grieving this terrible loss and we wish to comfort his family and friends. But, of course, we stand ready to assist the police.'

Odhiambo decided on shock tactics.

'What did you mean last night when you said to Mr Matavu that Dennison might be prevented from becoming Captain here?'

'What on earth do you mean?' Hill-Templeton seemed to have forgotten his outburst when he caught sight of Dennison's body. 'I cannot imagine what you mean. It's, quite, quite – '

Matavu intervened as, Odhiambo recalled, he had the previous night.

'Francis and I had been talking over a drink. He said my year as Captain was passing quickly and Jim's time would soon be upon us. I said there's a lot to do yet in my year before I pass responsibility on. That's all. A casual remark that turned out to be unfortunately timed.'

Did he give Hill-Templeton a warning look, or was it a normal glance at the man whom he was naming? Perhaps I'm too suspicious, thought Odhiambo.

Hill-Templeton was quick to pick up his cue. 'Yes, yes. I see. That's what you are referring to. Good heavens, man – a chance remark, that's all. No connection with the fellow's death. How could there be?'

'So you were discussing Mr Dennison shortly before setting out to view the body?'

Matavu was not attempting to disguise his intention to act as lead respondent. 'Only in the context of the forthcoming golf events and club functions. We didn't know he was dead.'

'And who told you we were on the course?'

'The nightwatchman told us.'

Hill-Templeton was determined to show his intention of full disclosure. 'Actually, John, he told the steward, who told us.'

Odhiambo addressed Hill-Templeton directly. 'Mr Matavu has told me that he was not a close friend of the deceased. Were you?'

'What? What? What a strange question. I mean, I know all the members here. Or nearly all. I've known Dennison for years. Good chap. Steady golfer. But he wasn't a particularly close friend, no.' Then the pomposity was given full rein as he leaned across to lecture Odhiambo. 'Mustn't play favourites, eh! Treat all members the same. Course, Dennison and I have had more to do with each other since he became Vice-Captain. John, here, would invite him to join us if we were discussing some problem or other.'

'So who were his friends? You know everyone, as you say. Who did he play with most often? Who did he drink with?'

Hill-Templeton started to stutter a response, but Matavu gently took over once more.

'Francis will tell you he was widely known. Particularly by the older members. Mainly white.' Hill-Templeton tried to look disapproving. 'I assume you'll be interviewing his wife, Anne. She would be the one to ask about their closest friends.'

Odhiambo changed tack.

'The ground where the body was buried. It was being constructed, was it? The tee or whatever it is.'

Hill-Templeton visibly relaxed, his hands, which had gripped the arms of his chair, letting go and settling in his lap.

'It's a new eighteenth tee. Add some yards to the hole. Yes, they were laying the topsoil on Monday. Then the turves were laid on top.'

'Was anyone working on it yesterday – Tuesday?'

Hill-Templeton considered a moment.

'I see what you mean. Could be important that, what? Actually, I don't think the greenkeepers did do anything to it yesterday. I'd need to check, but I believe they had something of an emergency problem to deal with regarding the pond on the eleventh.'

Matavu had also seen the point. 'You haven't established when Jim's body was put there. Could have been any time yesterday, is that it?'

'He didn't have one of those houses near there, did he?'

'No. The Dennisons live several miles away.'

'Was he friendly with any of the residents of those houses behind that tee?'

A long hesitation by both his interviewees. Hill-Templeton, after an uncertain glance at Matavu, eventually ended the pause.

'A member called Silent lives in one. He is a friend of the Dennisons, yes. But Dennison couldn't have come to grief there. Silent was here last night with Anne Dennison.'

It was Odhiambo's turn to allow a pregnant pause to develop. Then he switched subjects abruptly once more.

'Is Mr Aramgu a member of this club?'

Hill-Templeton gaped in surprise, but Matavu's face tightened.

'The former Regional Administrator, you mean? I understood you knew him, Odhiambo. Wasn't there something between you over that other dead *mzungu*? Why would you ask . . . Aha. I see. Mbayazi Estates. Odhiambo, my friend, take my advice. Go and find Jim's murderer but don't try and drag this club or me into politics. You savvy?'

'Is he a member?'

'No. Damn it, Odhiambo, I've listened to one damn fool question after another. What has all this got to do with your job?'

Odhiambo allowed himself a small smile. Matavu was show-ing signs of strain. At a guess he knew more about Dennison and Mbayazi Estates than he was saying. Well, let these two birds stew a little.

'OK. That's all for now.' To Hill-Templeton: 'I guess I can find you here if I need you.'

He got to his feet and they reacted as he had expected. Both men looked surprised that he was going. Then they recovered and quickly rose to their feet in case he changed his mind.

Outside the clubhouse he gave instructions to his driver where to meet him, then retraced his steps, but turned around the front of the clubhouse to gain access to the golf course itself. It seemed largely unoccupied, at least the part Odhiambo could see, which consisted of three lengths of well-cut grass separated by trees. Two of the well-cut strips culminated in an even more mani-cured area with a flag flying from a small hole in each. These Odhiambo knew would be the so called 'greens' where the golf ball finally arrived to be putted into the hole. That was about the extent of his knowledge on golf.

As he got his bearings and located the eighteenth green and fairway he imagined curious eyes viewing him from within the clubhouse. Without turning he set off up the side of the fairway in the reverse direction heading towards the tee where Dennison had been found. The eighteenth was curved, bending away to Odhiambo's left as he walked it in reverse from green to tee. A golf ball landed in the fairway in front of him, bounced and then rolled towards him. A short while later there was a noise in the branches of the trees above him – a second ball had obviously gone astray. On instinct and without rationalising his decision, Odhiambo stepped deeper into the trees. He heard the voices of two golfers approaching and then he saw them, two white middle-aged men, one short, portly and in shorts, the other taller and more athletic-looking in slacks.

'That's what I heard, anyway. Buried in that new tee is what I was told.'

'There's my ball. I didn't see yours come out. Must be under the trees somewhere about here.'

'Can't be the usual sort of robbery and killing. Why bury the poor chap? It's bizarre.'

'Strange sort of fellow, Dennison. Too close to some of those politicians if you ask me.'

'Damn ball must have ricocheted further in. Pity. A five here for a forty on this nine.'

'Yes, you've played well. Too good for me today. You think politics comes into it?'

'Got to be something like that. Ah, here it is. Think I can get a club at it. Politics or his friends. Trouble with either wouldn't surprise me.'

Silence ensued followed by the swish of a club in the short undergrowth.

'Well out. Found the gap. Good shot. Now see if I can get on in two. You mean the group around old Mephistopheles? One hears rumours.'

'There's more to it than rumour. You ask Jack. He was friendly with that crowd once. He backed off.'

Again a silence, then the sound of impact of club on ball.

'Damn. Pulled it. Bunker probably.'

The voices faded as the players moved on. Odhiambo resumed his walk deep in thought.

6

'So, Robert, here I go again. What is it you *mzungus* say? "Dropped right in it." '

'Och, stop your bellyaching, mon. Right up your street, this. Y'know as well as me, you're happier with this than guarding yon courthouse.'

Odhiambo had found his friend McGuiry still ensconced in his temporary residence and was now sitting, beer in hand, in the same chair from whence he had gone forth last night to find the body of Dennison.

'I got a feeling, Robert. An uneasy feeling. This bloody Ngong Golf Club could be more trouble for me than Eagle's Nest.'

'Solve the murder quickly, then. Don't hang about. What's your first impression, or am I speaking out of turn?'

'No. I may need your help, Robert, on this one. Same as the old days.'

'Ask away, James, ask away. Ye ken I'll do what I can.'

'When are you going back to Nyeri?'

'There's no haste, mon. Another day or two is neither here nor there for old trackers like me. What are ye after?'

'I heard two golfers just now as I was walking here. One said "politics or his friends". That about sums it up. Business politics or something to do with his private life. If you went into the club and chatted up the *mzungus*, you could find out more in ten minutes than they'll tell me in a day.'

'Ay. I could see my way clear to do that, mon. Never a hardship to persuade me to have a dram at the bar. He was Vice-Captain there, ye ken.'

'Yes, I've just been interviewing the Captain and Secretary. The two who came out last night.'

'Well, it's no good a man jumping to conclusions so I should spend a bit of time over there first, but, for what it's worth, I gathered last night the stuck-up Sassenach didn't have too much in the way of high opinion of the dead man.'

Odhiambo digested this convoluted statement for a second or two while he sipped his beer.

'That's right. So the question is, what caused his doubts? That would help a lot.'

'And another thing, James. I can tell ye now. I've not been idle all morning. I've made a few discreet enquiries. There are five houses in this row along the edge of yon course. This is the second, starting from the Karen road. First is owned by someone called Mtenzi, something to do with the government is all I was told. Then this one. Next is a *mzungu* called Smith or rather Smyth – Smith spelt with a y, can you believe. Dinna have much on him except one thing.' McGuiry paused like an old ham actor milking the audience for a good line. 'Yon Smyth is the brother-in-law of the good Secretary at the club.'

'Is that right?' Odhiambo was interested. McGuiry had realised that Dennison might have been killed in one of the houses that flanked that of McGuiry's absent friend. 'You have been busy, Robert.'

'Och, I dare say your chappies have got the details for ye. But I thought my gossiping with the local houseboys might give me a glimmering your bobbies would miss.'

'Quite right.'

'Well, after yon Smyth comes another *mzungu* called, strangely, Silent. Plays golf. Bound to have known Dennison. And up the end of this lane, nice and secure, fence and all, is the last and biggest – owned, would you believe, by our old friend Ambassador Aramgu.'

Odhiambo felt a frisson in his nerve ends; he was a man who trusted his instincts and they were telling him now that when the same names became involved when looking at the case from different directions it was time for him to pay attention. The problem was that there seemed to be multiple name connections independent of each other.

'That's interesting, Robert, very interesting.'

The old Scotsman's eyes were still keen and it was these which told him more than the spoken words. His words were dry.

'Interesting? That's all, James, is it? Fancy you're thinking more than you're talking.'

Odhiambo hesitated, but he owed McGuiry at least a measure of frankness.

'I said just now, Robert, there's two main angles, Dennison's business affairs and his social circle. Take business. Dennison was a director of Mbayazi Estates which is really owned by Aramgu. You told me Aramgu is back in Kenya and now you tell me he lives right next to where we found Dennison.'

'Maybe you got a fixation on Aramgu, James. You bested him once, but I've a fancy you're hankering after a rematch.'

'You're the one keeps bringing his name up every time.'

'Now you want me to go after who his friends were.'

'That's it. And you've a lead there too. I don't want to prejudice your enquiries, as they say in the training manuals, but the name Silent has been mentioned to me before today as a *rifiki* of Dennison; by two people as a matter of fact – including the club Secretary. We definitely need to know more about Mr Silent.'

'Plus the laddie Smith or Smyth. Don't forget, he's related to Hill-Templeton who didn't like our man.'

'OK. So there's your angles. Go and have a lunch-time drink at the Ngong bar. I suppose you can get in.'

'Och, I know a few names I can bandy about as an introduction. And I'm a white man, after all. They don't ask white men to leave places like the Ngong.'

Odhiambo grinned and drained his beer.

'If you're starting on your racist talk, I'm off. My driver should be outside if he found his way here from the club.'

'Right you are, James. You leave the Ngong to me.' McGuiry followed his guest to the front door. The police car was indeed there, the driver in conversation with the houseman who was, no doubt, recounting how he had found the body of the dead *mzungu*. 'Cheers then, James. The only resident of this road who isn't connected is Bwana Mtenzi. According to the books I read that means he must have done it.'

Between them Odhiambo and his driver managed to misdirect themselves to the Dennison home, but eventually they found the road and the house. There was a guard at the gate who retreated at identification barked at him by an irate Odhiambo. Outside the entrance to the house stood a sleek and powerful-looking sports car. It was an unfamiliar sight in Nairobi where luxury tastes seemed exclusively centred on Mercedes-Benz saloons, but Odhiambo's months in Europe had familiarised him with the individual shape of a Porsche. He looked at his watch – it was lunch-time. Did Mrs Dennison have a visitor? She would scarcely be entertaining a guest to lunch – presumably it was a friend providing her with a measure of comfort. Unless this was the Dennison car, but somehow Odhiambo, for no conscious reason, did not believe it was.

His hunch proved correct when a servant ushered him through into the lounge. Rising to meet him was not a distraught new widow but a short, slim man immaculately clad in a black roll-necked shirt that shouted silk and smartly creased black slacks. Had the man dressed for a funeral, Odhiambo wondered? Or was this his normal style – if so, an eccentric one in the tropics. The face was lean, slightly sunken cheeks surmounted by well-defined bone lines below eyes that seemed almost feminine with prominent eyelashes and narrow, curved eyebrows. A thin but pleasantly shaped mouth below a slender nose completed an impression that Odhiambo had seen in paintings of aristocratic Englishmen – well-bred but effete.

'Mrs Dennison's servant said you are the police. A Chief Inspector . . .?'

'Odhiambo. And you, sir?'

The man's voice was light and elegant, but with that edge of superciliousness which Odhiambo was used to hearing from other old colonials.

A slim hand with a large jewelled ring on the middle finger waved Odhiambo to a chair, but Odhiambo stood his ground.

'Silent. Michael Silent. I am a friend of the Dennisons. I am here to provide a shoulder for Mrs Dennison to lean on.'

Was there a subtle warning there? Odhiambo felt an instinctive antipathy to this man. It seemed to be his day for forming immediate dislikes. So he had confirmation that Silent was in Dennison's social circle and his house adjoined the tee in which the body had been found.

'And where is Mrs Dennison? I don't wish to trouble her too much today, but there are certain things I need to know.'

The elegant head inclined in sympathy.

'I understand. Mrs Dennison is taking a shower. She will be with us in a minute.'

A shower? Funny time of day to take a shower, and with a visitor in the house.

'I see. How is she taking this dreadful event?'

'As well as can be expected, I believe the phrase is, Chief Inspector. As well as can be expected. What news do you bring her? Of the circumstance of her husband's death.'

It was effortless, the way this man assumed a position of dominance. Odhiambo revised his earlier assumption. Silent would never be in someone else's social group, the others would be in *his*. There was a magnetism about the man that was like a physical force. Odhiambo ignored the question and put one of his own.

'I understand your house is close to where we found Mr Dennison's body. Was he at your house yesterday?'

'Yes. Not the least puzzling feature of a very puzzling situation. I refer to the location of the body. No. No. Jim and Anne were often welcome guests in my house, but not yesterday. I myself was at the Ngong with Mrs Dennison when we were told the terrible news.'

Odhiambo heard a noise to his right. The lounge formed the lower part of a split-level room, and was comfortably but not extravagantly furnished. A comfortable-looking settee and chairs covered in a beige decorated material formed the main furniture with side tables and a waist-high bookcase against the wall facing Odhiambo as the main extras. To Odhiambo's left a large glass window gave a view of the garden and the Ngong hills in the distance. The noise emanated from the upper level that appeared to be a dining area dominated by a large polished wood table. A woman had come through a door hidden from

Odhiambo's view by the intervening wall dividing the two levels. She stood now at the top of the two steps. She was an attractive woman in her forties, Odhiambo guessed. Blonde hair damp where it framed her face. The woman came down the steps, one hand briefly reaching out to touch the wall as if to steady herself. As she approached him, Odhiambo could see that her eyes were red. Could be tears for a dead husband, or could be alcohol. Odhiambo had a confident feeling that the 'shower' Silent had referred to was a soaking of the face in an attempt to sober up.

'Mrs Dennison? I'm sorry to intrude at this difficult time.'

'This is Chief Inspector Odhiambo, Anne. He's leading the . . . er . . . investigation.' Silent had slipped in his intervention quickly. Odhiambo felt irritation at the way in which he was attempting to protect the widow, shielding her, giving her time. Now he had intercepted her approach towards Odhiambo and steered her gently towards one of the armchairs.

Odhiambo tried once again.

'Mrs Dennison, there's a few questions I need to put to you. Can I speak to you alone for a few minutes?'

'I think Mrs Dennison would prefer if I remained to give . . . er . . support.'

'Mrs Dennison? Are you ready to answer a few questions?'

Anne Dennison looked briefly at her male guardian and then transferred her gaze to Odhiambo.

'I am still shaken, Inspector. But if it's urgent . . .'

There was just a discernible slurring, but she seemed well composed, hands together demurely in her lap. The portrayal of the grieving widow was taking shape nicely. But Odhiambo was sure he was watching a performance. A performance directed by the man sitting opposite her who watched her intently as she settled into her role. Odhiambo refused to become part of a play.

'Who were your husband's enemies, Mrs Dennison?'

'What . . . what do you mean? Jim was . . . was popular. No one . . . I mean . . . that's ridiculous.'

'As a company director. Mbayazi Estates. Was he having problems in his business dealings?'

Silent's voice was smooth, unruffled, but with, to Odhiambo's ear, a hint of menace. 'I don't think it's appropriate to question Mrs Dennison on her husband's business affairs. I'm sure your training tells you that a woman in shock should not be subjected to intensive examination.'

'Mr Silent, I'd be grateful if you would let Mrs Dennison speak for herself. She seems perfectly capable to me.'

'I . . . I don't know much about Jim's work.' Anne Dennison glanced over at Silent as if seeking approval of her delivery. 'I cannot think why poor Jim was . . . was . . .' A sniffle and Silent was beside her, handkerchief in hand. 'Oh, Michael . . .'

Odhiambo swore to himself.

'OK, Mrs Dennison. Tell me this at least. When did you last see your husband?'

Again the glance at her companion.

'Why, I'm not sure . . . It's all confused. I suppose it was yesterday morning. Yes. Yesterday morning.'

'At what time?'

'Oh, I don't know. After breakfast. He went off with his driver . . . To work, I suppose.'

'His driver?'

'Yes. Omar. His chauffeur. Jim uses a company car for business.'

'What about lunch-time?'

'No. I was playing golf . . . Ladies' comp. But he doesn't usually come home for lunch.'

'And later?'

'No. No. I told you. I didn't see him after he went in the morning.'

'What about yesterday evening? Did he play golf?'

'I keep telling you.' The fingers twisted and untwisted in her lap as she spoke, seeming almost breathless. 'I didn't see nothing of him all day nor last night.'

Odhiambo noticed how the voice had become coarser and her grammar careless as her agitation grew.

'You were at the Royal Ngong. Were you there all day? Did you come home at any time?'

'After . . . after leaving the club I went with Gianna to Nairobi. In the afternoon, I mean. We had tea at the Norfolk.'

Silent had resumed his seat, watching his friend closely. Now he turned to look at Odhiambo.

'Gianna is Mrs Iocacci. Her husband is a prominent business-man. Luxury cars.'

Odhiambo remembered the Porsche in the driveway and his colleague Ntende's introduction of the Iocaccis' possible involvement with drugs. He returned to the question the bereaved woman had failed to answer.

47

'Did you come back here, Mrs Dennison? And if so, when did you leave?'

In their recent exchanges Anne Dennison had ignored her companion, but now as if reminded by his voice of his presence she looked once more at the man next to her. He laid a hand upon hers and Odhiambo gritted his teeth to bite back his rising bile. Finally, she deigned to look back at her questioner.

'Gianna dropped me off about . . . oh, I don't know. Sixish. Michael picked me up a bit later. After I'd changed.'

'Was there any sign that your husband had been home before you?'

'Sign? Whaddya mean, sign? I don't go around looking for his footprints.'

'Clothes left out, or a cup or glass. Was there a houseboy on duty?'

'Of course. If Jim had been home Amir would've said so. I mean, how often do I have to tell you? Jim left to go to bloody work in the morning and the next thing I know is he's buried in the . . . in the . . .'

Once again Silent was ready with the handkerchief. Odhiambo gave up the struggle and decided to go for a source who might give him a coherent reply.

'Mr Silent, when you came to collect Mrs Dennison, were you expecting to find Mr Dennison?'

Silent's lips stretched into a smile of sorts without revealing his teeth.

'Of course, Inspector. Jim and Anne were joining me for dinner at the Ngong, together with my other guests.'

'You were surprised when he wasn't there?'

'Naturally. We waited a while, but decided he was unavoidably delayed in the city. He knew where we would be so we went on, expecting him to join us later.' A slight pause as if he was inviting the obvious question but Odhiambo remained silent. 'He failed to arrive, as you know. Tragically he was found dead by your people later in the evening.'

'Outside your house.'

'The tee in question is adjacent to some properties, yes, including mine. But if you're putting the same question to me as you put to Mrs Dennison, no, there was no sign Jim had been in my house yesterday. Not surprisingly as I would have known if he intended to call.'

48

'And your other guests?'

'The Iocaccis, Stefano and Gianna. We've spoken of them already. And a lady friend of mine.'

Odhiambo suddenly felt very tired and dispirited. He would let it go. It would be easy enough to find out who Silent was referring to.

'OK. Thank you, Mrs Dennison, and you, sir. We will keep you informed, Mrs Dennison, and please accept my condolences.'

It was with a sense of relief that he emerged into the warm air. He didn't like being deceived and he was sure that the couple he had just left had been treating him as if he was an imbecile. Silent would bear a close look. Ntende might know more – after all, he was supposed to be an authority on these descendants of the old Happy Valley sets. He climbed into his car.

'Back to the station and try to avoid that Porsche on the way out or I'll have that bugger around my neck for ever.'

The driver said nothing. He'd heard that the Chief Inspector was a strange man. He turned, giving the sports car a wide berth, and headed off towards Nairobi at a speed he hoped could not be criticised for being too fast or too slow.

7

Robert McGuiry sighed with pleasure as he relaxed in a chair on the verandah of the Royal Ngong clubhouse. The sun shone on the green below him, but he was shaded by the thick-leaved wisteria canopy that had extended over a trellis laid above the stone-paved verandah. The air was full of the scent of the wisteria mingled with that of the hibiscus which flanked the steps down to the course. Looking beyond the green the tree-lined course stretched away in a panorama of parkland beauty. All in all a pleasant and relaxing setting, particularly if one had a glass of good whisky to hand and no intention of spoiling the enjoyment by hitting a little ball about.

The Secretary had signed him in as a guest, expressing pleasure at having an old legendary 'white hunter' on the premises. McGuiry was sure, however, that Hill-Templeton's welcome was based as much on curiosity as on fond recollections of colonial Kenya and it was, therefore, with no sense of surprise that he saw the tall, erect figure approaching him from the direction of the clubhouse.

'Everything all right?'

'To be sure. You've got a fine little set-up here, mon. Good of you to let me take advantage.'

'You're very welcome. As I said, your reputation goes before you. May I join you?'

McGuiry gestured at the empty chairs flanking the table on which his glass lay.

'Will ye join me in a wee tipple? Or do ye no drink on duty?'

Hill-Templeton chuckled as he lowered his frame into the chair.

'A golf club secretary who didn't drink? That would be a novelty.' A white-coated steward had appeared at his elbow in response to some signal unseen by McGuiry. 'No, you have one with me.' He turned to the steward and switching to Swahili ordered a replenishment of McGuiry's whisky and a beer for himself.

Whilst they waited for the order to be delivered, Hill-Templeton enquired after his guest's current involvement with the game in the Aberdares and his likely length of sojourn in Nairobi. McGuiry sensed that this was a polite overture to the real questions to come. The drinks came; Hill-Templeton sipped his beer reflectively, settled back in his chair, then, after a pause which McGuiry allowed to extend, he cleared his throat and got down to business.

'Er . . . hem. Coincidence you were staying in Malling's house just when this unfortunate business occurred. Don't expect to look after a friend's house and find bodies more or less in his garden, what?'

'I'll have a few wee words when he returns. Man should be more careful. Mind you, he might be minded to say he canna help what happens when he's gone.'

'Quite. Terrible business. Bizarre's the word.' Hill-Templeton shifted uneasily in his chair and reached for his glass. 'Stranger still, of course, that you were entertaining a detective at the time.'

''Tis a strange world right enough.'

'How long have you known this . . . er . . . what's his name . . . the Chief Inspector?'

'Odhiambo? Ach, James and I go back to the Eagle's Nest business. You must remember that?'

'Well, vaguely. Bad business, too. I don't know what's going to happen. All this violence, I mean. So Odhiambo was the man in charge of that investigation, was he?'

'True. Did a braw job in solving it, too. Despite efforts to stop him.'

'And you became friends?'

'I can tell a good man when I see one.'

'And you've kept in touch, obviously.'

'Not really.'

This was greeted with a sceptical silence as Hill-Templeton took another sip of beer while he collected his thoughts.

'The point is, McGuiry, the point is, I'm anxious . . . that is, the club is anxious, or concerned, yes, concerned about this dreadful business. We don't want any scandal. The fact that the body was on the course had nothing to do with his death. I'm sure of that.'

'Ah. So ye ken more than you're telling.'

'No, no. I didn't mean that. What I meant . . . Well, it can't be anything to do with the Royal Ngong. I mean, Dennison was Vice-Captain.'

'Some would say that points the finger at ye, mon. Vice-Captain found dead on course.'

'This is not a joking matter, McGuiry. Dennison was very popular. There'll be a big turn-out at his funeral.'

'Who were his closest friends? The Captain? You?'

'No, not exactly. John and I . . . well, I mean we knew him well and so on, but we were not part of his social circle.'

'Who was?'

'Actually, there's a little group.' Across Hill-Templeton's face flashed a brief grimace that did not escape the eyes of the old hunter. 'Chap called Silent. Funny sort of name, you're thinking. Dennisons. Italian couple. Another woman, good golfer – more than you can say for the rest – apart from Dennison himself. That's what makes it odd, really. Not his sort, you would say.'

'Not quite the right class?'

'No, no.' Hill-Templeton's tongue seemed now to have got a firm hold. McGuiry wondered how many drinks had preceded the one which he now drained in a long swallow. 'Almost the reverse, as it happens. Silent comes from sound stock. And Iocacci, I understand, is almost aristocracy in Italy. If you accept

51

Italy as having genuine aristocrats. Pauline, also, Old Kenya family, whereas Jim, well, you know.' The waving hand had produced the steward who nodded at the gesture indicating another round. Hill-Templeton waited until the steward retreated. 'Just a bit sharp, some would say.' Hill-Templeton tapped the side of his nose.

'In business, you mean?'

'Well, you know how it is. Sort of man you keep an eye on. Whether it's business or pleasure.'

'Cheated at golf, did he?'

From Hill-Templeton's reaction, McGuiry thought he had gone too far. The Secretary sat up, back straight, chin jutting. McGuiry could almost feel the man's hair bristling.

'I say, McGuiry, no call for that. Never suggested the man cheated.'

'Och, forgive a cynical old Scot who never played the game, will ye? I was going to ask ye how come he was made Vice-Captain if there were all these doubts?'

There was a silence, broken by the arrival of the steward with fresh glasses. He poured Hill-Templeton's beer and moved softly away.

'Only drink beer when I'm on duty. Couldn't work if I joined you on the spirits at lunch-time. Cheers . . . Fact is, I would have to say, between you and me, it was a bit of a surprise when John picked him. That's John Matavu, the Captain. Captain's prerogative, you know. Didn't know they were associated in business and they didn't seem to mix much socially.'

'Surely a Captain just canna pick any old soul?'

'Oh, the nominee is put to the AGM, of course. But if the chap was a real bounder a quiet word would be had sooner. No, must not give you the wrong impression. Dennison was popular enough. Not beyond the pale by any means.'

'You were saying about his social group.'

'Yes, well, the Dennisons seemed to be round pegs in square holes there. Mustn't take a lady's name in vain, but Anne Dennison would not be your choice of close companion for the other women . . . And . . .'

'There's something else?'

Hill-Templeton leaned forward almost conspiratorially. McGuiry was sure now that the man was quietly inebriated. He wondered if the claim to drink only beer at lunch-time was adhered to in the privacy of his office.

'Tell you the truth, McGuiry, there's something odd about Silent and his friends. You know as well as I that in the old days there were a few who overstepped the mark – what's the word the writer fellow used? Decadent, that was it. Well, Silent could have fitted in well enough.'

'But not the Dennisons?'

'No, that's the funny thing. Shade vulgar, perhaps, but not trendy, if you know what I mean. Square. Old-fashioned. Call it what you will. Not the orgy type. Course, that's my opinion and I've been known to be wrong before.'

'You think his death may have – '

Hill-Templeton interrupted his guest with a hand raised and waved in front of McGuiry's face.

'No. Enough said. Too much perhaps. Point I'm making is the opposite. Nothing special about Dennison, but nothing odd either. His death can't be anything to do with anyone here. Better tell your policeman friend to look elsewhere. Business deals. You know what's happening in Kenya today. Some strange goings-on. Look at Dennison's business associates, that's my advice to you – or rather Mr . . . er . . . Odhiambo.'

McGuiry considered a moment. It was time to change tack.

'Coming back to my temporary digs: I gather my next-door neighbour is a relative of yours.'

'What do you mean? Next-door neighbour? Oh, by the eighteenth where you're staying. Yes. Chap called Smyth.'

'And he's a relative, someone said?'

'Well, by marriage. He's married to my sister. Or rather he was married to my sister. Separated now.'

'There didn't seem to be any lights on last night. Away, is he?'

Hill-Templeton looked at the other man as if examining the question for hidden implications.

'Yes, he's away. At the coast, I think. Haven't seen him for some time. My sister went back to England and he pushed off. He's got an interest in some land around Eldoret as well. Bit of a shiftless sort, actually.'

McGuiry looked at Hill-Templeton's glass and raised an eyebrow and a hand, but suddenly his companion seemed in a hurry to leave.

'Must get back to work. Stay as long as you like. Perhaps see you later. Must get on.'

*

John Matavu drummed his fingers on his polished mahogany desk top as he waited for his secretary to make the call he had requested. He had given the matter considerable thought; Odhiambo's questions had added to his worries. It was bad enough that through Dennison's body being buried on the golf course, he was inevitably drawn into the matter. But if Odhiambo pursued the Mbayazi Estates connection it was likely that he would have difficulty in concealing the fact that he had appointed Dennison because of his intimate knowledge of Aramgu's business affairs. In these troubled times it was better not to be linked in others' minds to either camp. He swivelled in his chair and looked out of his window across the busy street scene of Kenyatta Avenue. The sun shone, the tourists were plentiful and the street hawkers were busy. No sense of danger except for the occasional bag snatcher, but that problem existed in European capitals: in Rome, Matavu had witnessed the passenger on a scooter cut the strap of a woman's shoulder bag and snatch it in the brief time it took the driver to manoeuvre alongside, slow momentarily and then accelerate away. No, tourists were safe enough in Nairobi if they took reasonable care – but for how long, Matavu wondered? Trouble was on the way and approaching fast. It wasn't the tourists that concerned him – they would probably be inconvenienced at worst – it was his survival that needed to be assured.

His eyes lit idly upon the building across the avenue from his office and to his left – the Metroarcs building. He had heard talk of Odhiambo's wealthy wife and the enquiry into the Omuto affair had brought her name into the papers. She was an executive with Metroarcs, he remembered. Her father had given evidence against Kiwonka. Did that mean Odhiambo was in the camp opposed to Kiwonka and his allies, including Aramgu? There had been that other business involving the murder of a tourist: hadn't there been trouble then between Odhiambo and Aramgu?

The intercom on his desk let out its over-loud buzz; he must get the damn thing fixed.

'Yes?'

'Mr Mantebe is on the line.'

'Hello, is that you, Matthias? John Matavu here.'

'Afternoon, Bwana Captain. You're going to tell me you've given me a good draw for the medal on Sunday? Or is it banking not golf today?'

'Well, neither exactly. Or, perhaps, a bit of both. Have you heard that Dennison is dead? Murdered, it seems. His body was left by the eighteenth tee.'

'Buried in it was how I heard it. Yes, very strange business. And inconvenient.'

'Inconvenient! I'd put it a bit stronger than that, *bwana*.'

'I meant in terms of his work. He worked for us, you know. I'm going to have to put in some time until we sort things out.'

'The question is, why was he killed?'

'Presuming it wasn't someone he beat on the course, I have no idea. Are you about to tell me?'

'No. How the hell should I know? Listen, Matthias, I've been interviewed by the detective, Odhiambo, you know who he is. He's high profile.'

A chuckle came from the telephone causing Matavu to grimace. This wasn't a laughing matter.

'Yes, I know of Chief Inspector Odhiambo. A mutual friend still has a score or two to settle there.'

'Exactly. That's my point. Odhiambo is in charge of Dennison's murder.'

'What exactly is your point, John?'

'Odhiambo was asking me about Dennison's role with Mbayazi Estates. He's going after his business connections as the reason for his murder. And I don't have to tell you that Dennison's body was found more or less outside Mr Aramgu's house.'

'But he wasn't there, John. Let's not get excited about this.'

'How do you know? I'm not saying he was. I'm just saying that I think Odhiambo has made the connection and I don't want to be dragged into it.'

'OK, John. Thanks for calling. I'll bear it in mind and I'll let the *bwana mkubwa* know of your concern. But there's no reason for you to get worried. Just because we bank with you, doesn't make you our man. I assume your only connection with Dennison was the Ngong?'

'Yes, and I want the club kept out of any scandal over this. But he must have been killed for some reason. Was there any problem with the way he ran the accounts of the Mbayazi exports?'

Again the annoying chuckle.

'John, my friend, you worry too much. Relax, run the Ngong and keep your books straight.'

'You haven't answered my question.'

'You insult me, my friend. Are you accusing us of murdering one of our own executives, because he was taking a cut of the money? Is that what you're saying? Dennison was trusted by the big man. No problem. So get such bad thoughts out of your mind.'

'I didn't imply –'

'OK. Let's leave it at that. See you on the course on Sunday.'

Matavu replaced the telephone and stared at it, thinking hard. He was getting nowhere. When he was treated with amused contempt by the likes of Mantebe, the manager of Mbayazi Estates, it was more than irritating. How could he try and find out what was going on? Should he make another telephone call? He knew it would not be well received, and what were the chances of getting any truthful answers? Better, perhaps, to sit tight and hope for the best. By the gods of Mount Kenya, how he wished he'd never heard of Jim Dennison.

John Matavu was not the only one disturbed as the result of a phone call. Chief Superintendent Masonga stubbed out his cigarette angrily as the deadly voice of his caller continued to echo in his head. It was seldom that Price-Allen wished to talk to him and Masonga wished it was a rarer event even than that. Masonga remembered the days when it was possible to be a policeman, even a homicide detective, without being interfered with by other sources, whether political or security. Nowadays, interference was becoming the norm. The reason he found Odhiambo's sensitivity to interference so provoking was that he agreed with him, but could not say so. But there was interference and there was gut-loosening interference and a conversation with Price-Allen fell definitely into the latter category. In his mind's eye he saw the slim figure of the dreaded white man, dapper in his old-fashioned colonial white shirt, shorts and long socks; not tall, not short, nothing to make him stand out in a roomful of people except these pale blue eyes that seemed somehow dead, as if behind them lay not a human soul but the mind of a devil. Masonga had met many murderers and in his experience they were usually a pathetic bunch, who had become killers through family passions, greed or mental instability. When he first met Mr R.D. Price-Allen, gazed into those eyes and remembered the stories he had heard, Masonga knew that he was in the presence of a killer who had chosen his own path to damnation.

Masonga lit another cigarette and noticed the tremor in his hand. He must be getting too old for this job if a phone call could cause his nerves to jump. However much he disliked Price-Allen the fact remained he was the unofficial overseer of the State Security Unit and a man with the ear and confidence of the President. Masonga had heard something of the incident in Uganda, but it seemed Price-Allen was back in Nairobi none the worse for his adventures. The conversation ran through Masonga's mind one more time.

'Masonga. Price-Allen. I am given to understand our mutual friend Odhiambo is in charge of the investigation into the murder of the white man.'

'Yes, that's correct.' Given to understand, indeed. Masonga had received his orders from State Security and that, he assumed, meant Price-Allen.

'Tell him to come to see me. Urgently. I will be in my private office until some time this evening.'

'I'm afraid Odhiambo is out seeing witnesses. I'm not precisely – '

'It's comforting to know the CID are not all sitting around. Naturally he's out, as you put it. I assume it's not beyond your capacity as a senior detective to find one of your own men. I shall expect him.'

And that was all, yet the match had trembled as it reached his cigarette. Masonga cursed to himself, rose out of his chair, crossed the room and opened the office door. There was his clerk, a crippled former policeman who gave abiding loyalty to his boss; a valuable asset in the leak-ridden Nairobi police station.

'I expect you know who that was?' A nod, indeed, a nervous nod gave Masonga his answer. 'He needs to see Odhiambo. Find out where he's supposed to be. If necessary get people out to the possible addresses. Find him and get him back here *pace sana*.'

'*Ndio, bwana.*'

Masonga turned to re-enter his office then turned to face his clerk once more.

'If necessary get someone to that bar he uses. He likes to think over a beer, especially when his wife's away.'

57

A thin smile acknowledged the confidence. It was not often that Mr Masonga would speak of another officer to a clerk. It made him feel good to be trusted. The problem he was left with, however, was how to find Odhiambo.

8

Felix Aramgu by physical presence alone was wont to dominate any gathering of which he was a member. He was taller than most, but his height was not what impressed at first acquaintance, rather it was the overall package: his upper chest was barrel-like, a suitable base for a huge head, now balding which somehow added to its impression of size. Someone behind his back had termed him the black Mussolini, but in fact he was a magnified as well as a darker version of the Italian Fascist. Nor were his other parts out of place. His arms were long and thick culminating in hands that could individually totally encompass a large orange. He was in fact tossing such an orange from one hand to the other as he appraised the four men in the room who had been awaiting his arrival.

'Welcome, Ambassador Aramgu.' The man who spoke was the physical opposite of his guest: small, greying, thin, wearing a Western-style suit that looked two sizes too big for him. 'You do my house honour.'

The great head bobbed briefly in acknowledgement of the greeting. Aramgu had no great regard for this quiet financier of his political endeavours – he felt uncomfortable with the man's air of culture, the pedantic English and the perfect diction. When one of Aramgu's aides had told him that Kentui was thought to have cancer, Aramgu had replied, 'We'd better bleed the old beast of his blood while it's still warm' – a reference to the Masai custom of draining blood from the necks of their animals as an ingredient of their diet. But they had certainly benefited from copious draughts of blood from this old bull. He had used his considerable fortune without stint in the services of Kiwonka and Aramgu and their ambitions to rule Kenya.

Aramgu wasted no time in further niceties.

'The time has come, my friends, time for you to take the oath and deliver yourselves to the cause.'

'We are all committed men, Aramgu. Our blood is already mixed and shared.'

The speaker was in civilian clothes, but in stature and bearing looked what he was, the Colonel of the crack paratroop battalion.

'Good, but what news of others? Have you secured the loyalty of your colleagues?'

The Colonel frowned. 'I have said before. I am no pimp. I will declare myself when the time comes, let others decide then whether they will follow me.'

'You speak like a fool, Lijodi. I am not interested in futile gestures. It is organisations that will win us this day.'

'Be careful who you curse, Aramgu. I tell you true, it is not to your spear that I and my men will come. We are on the same side for one reason and one reason alone, to put the nation's destiny back in good hands. I am a Kiwonka man not an Aramgu slave.'

'Come, come.' Their host intervened to prevent these two bull elephants from facing each other down. 'We are as one in a noble cause. Aramgu, my friend, you know Sasaweni and Kitwa?'

The two men he indicated were considerably younger than the others in the room, but the man named Sasaweni, although dwarfed in stature by both Aramgu and Colonel Lijodi, somehow seemed best suited to a meeting of conspirators. He alone had remained seated when Aramgu entered, languidly at rest in a floral-patterned armchair, one leg draped carelessly over one of its arms. He had about him an aura of menace. He looked now at Aramgu with an almost insolent smile. My God, thought the ailing Kentui, is it possible those men will keep away from each others' throats long enough to achieve our purpose? He had warned Kiwonka about the flaws in the characters of the inner team. The reply had been resigned. 'Kentui, my old friend, we must make our house with the straw and earth in our *shamba*. It is how well we bake them into bricks that will matter.'

Aramgu looked down on Sasaweni.

'Are you sure you have enough people you can trust around State House and the other places?'

Sasaweni's smile grew wider, but only to take on an even closer resemblance to a smirk.

'I am ready. I have my pieces laid out as I wish them to be.'

'You're sure that bloody *mzungu* has not got wind of it?'

Sasaweni unhitched his leg from the chair-arm, sat forward and shrugged.

'Price-Allen knows little. But if he did, who cares, he will be crushed. Do not fear the white man, Aramgu.'

The giant figure seemed to swell with rage. He loomed over the seated man.

'Crushed, you say. You make it sound as easy as killing a cockroach. From what I hear, you have made one attempt to drown him rather than crush him and he spat in your face.'

'It was not well organised. They thought they saw a chance and tried to take it. The message from your man came too late for it to be planned properly. Next time will be different.'

'They! They! What do you mean by "they"? You are supposed to be the *bwana mkubwa* in State Security. Our headman anyway. You mean your men make their own decisions?' Sasaweni shrugged again without speaking. 'And having made a camel's ass of it your people let Price-Allen get the idiot involved and torture him to get the story. He may know everything.'

'You think that boatman knew anything much? What do you think we are, Aramgu? I tell you – you look after your affairs, I'll not fail with mine.'

'Enough.' This time it was the Colonel who intervened. 'Come, we are about to fight together. No more arguments.'

Aramgu snorted, but forced himself to stand back and adopt a less threatening attitude.

'OK. It's true. But I am right to be concerned.' He turned back to the State Security officer, who at last had got to his feet. 'OK. No *shauri*. But tell me this. Never mind the boatman. What about Dennison? How much did he know?'

Sasaweni laughed aloud. 'I was going to ask you that question. After all, he was your man in Mbayazi Estates. He knows, or knew, the people in Uganda. The message he passed on would have meant little. Anything else he knew he learned from you or your people. I'm assuming no one would be so foolish as to reveal our plans to a *mzungu*. Your neighbours may not be all they seem, Aramgu, but I hear they like their orgasms with some variety. I'm assuming he was strangled as part of some perverted sex activity that these white people enjoy. Why can't they enjoy a woman without all this nonsense?'

'OK. You may be right. My men tell me some of the things that

60

go on are beyond our experience. Maybe when our business is over I will experiment more. But Dennison was my man. I wouldn't want to find out, Sasaweni my friend, that someone had decided to shut his mouth without asking me.'

Their host, who found salacious gossip distasteful, bought them back to business.

'Let us go downstairs and run through the details. We hope, Aramgu, you bring us the one decision we need.'

Aramgu let out a sudden and unexpected laugh that seemed to rumble up from his considerable belly gaining resonance and amplitude as it rose. His mood swings were legendary and suddenly his jovial side came to the fore. He clapped Kentui on the back with his huge hand, causing the ailing man to stagger and cough a dry hacking cough of a man whose lungs were no longer able to take in much oxygen.

'Sorry, Kentui. Forgot you're not the man you were. But yes, I have good news, we set to work in just over two days. Saturday morning. Early hours of Saturday. The pre-dawn move, Lijodi, my friend.'

There were murmurs of approval. The long wait and the growing tensions would at last be ending. As they followed their host towards the stairs and down to what he liked to call the 'map-room', the other of the younger men spoke for the first time.

'The Colonel may consider me a pimp, but I have taken soundings. The barracks at Nsimina may wait a while, but they will not jump in on the wrong side. Once Colonel Lijodi raises his flag they will come out and salute it.'

'And the air force?' Lijodi, despite his earlier bravado, had his concerns. 'Have you any indications there?'

The civil servant Kitwa paused as if in doubt. Then he shook his head. 'Nothing definite as yet, but the Minister said there was no cause for concern. He says they will do nothing without orders.'

For a moment, Aramgu's good humour was dispelled. He turned from the head of the stairs.

'Minister? Isn't that Nlemi now? That man doesn't have the brains to worry. And I promise you this – when the spear shows blood, Nlemi will be hiding with the cattle.'

Kitwa, like a good civil servant, looked suitably embarrassed. Aramgu's great laugh boomed out once more. He clapped a huge arm around Kitwa's shoulders.

61

'Don't tell me you didn't realise that, my boy. Never mind, when Saturday is done perhaps you can give the orders from the Ministry, eh? After all, you are a blood relative of the next President.' He raised his hand, holding the orange that he had taken from a bowl of fruit as he entered the house. 'My friends, on Saturday we will squeeze this country's oppressors like this.' The thick fingers closed around the fruit and tightened. The orange split and disintegrated in his hand, the juice dripping through his fingers to the floor. Again, the laugh boomed forth. Fortunately for Kitwe, Aramgu did not see his grimace of distaste.

9

Despite his superior's suspicion that he might have sought comfort in a bar, Odhiambo, in fact, was diligently pursuing the friends of the murdered man. He had endeavoured unsuccessfully to find his colleague Ntende to see if further inside information was available, and had now located the Italian's car business in Mabendu Street, one of the streets leading off Kenyatta Avenue towards the civic square containing the Parliamentary building as well as the court where Odhiambo had spent so much time in recent weeks. It was a street of mainly modern buildings, a shop with up-market and overpriced carvings, semi-precious stones and other artifacts aimed at the tourist, a women's dress shop that Odhiambo knew was used by his wife, a bookshop with a large window display of glossy books of photography of the landscape and animals of East Africa, an airline booking and ticket office, and a large plate-glass window behind which, artfully arranged, were three European luxury cars, including one Porsche.

Odhiambo ordered his driver to pull into the kerb, got out and opened the door to the showroom. A white woman was about to reach the door on her way out, so Odhiambo held the door and waited for her to leave. The woman was in her late thirties, he judged, clad in a business suit of light material, short blonde hair shaped around her ears. She was not beautiful, almost plain, but Odhiambo's instincts signalled her presence: there was about her an aura of sexuality which the businesslike appearance could not entirely conceal.

'Thank you.' A pleasant, educated voice and a brief smile. Odhiambo nodded acknowledgement of her thanks as she passed and went to enter the showroom. Suddenly, however, the woman stopped and turned back to face him. 'Excuse me. Are you, by any chance, Chief Inspector Odhiambo?'

Odhiambo looked at the woman more closely. No, he was sure he did not know her. 'Er, yes. Yes, I am. Have we met?'

'No.' The brief smile reappeared and went. Smile or not, Odhiambo thought her face was showing signs of strain. It was mainly the eyes, he could almost see the nervousness, even anxiety, reflected in them. 'I saw your photograph in the paper – the *Standard* – a week or so ago. In connection with the Omuto enquiry.'

Normally, Odhiambo would have muttered some platitude and looked to move on, but he blamed the attraction that she seemed to exert like a magnet for his stumbling and silly response.

'Did you? Well . . . I mean . . . I'm flattered you should remember. I mean, you know what newspaper photos are like.'

'Oh, it was a good likeness. Perhaps you're a little more handsome even than the photograph.' The smile was full now and although it didn't quite reach her eyes it transformed her somewhat heavy features. My God, thought Odhiambo, I'm being seduced out here on the street, and feeling as awkward about it as a schoolboy. 'The point is, Chief Inspector, someone told me you were involved in Jim Dennison's death – the investigation of it, I mean.'

Odhiambo managed to pull himself together.

'You are a friend of Mr Dennison, a relative . . .?'

'Oh, only a friend. My name is Florislow, Pauline Florislow.'

'You have some information regarding his death?'

'I don't know. Perhaps nothing. But again there is something you should know. Look, here's my card. I'll be in my office until six or so. We can't talk here. I hope I'm not wasting your time. Maybe I shouldn't . . . Oh dear, I don't know quite what I mean.'

The woman was clearly under tension, but Odhiambo believed that normally she would be a pretty cool customer. His interest was aroused in both the professional and personal sense.

'Thank you. I've got one or two interviews to get out of the way, but then I'll come to your office.'

The smile once more lit up her face then went out, leaving the shadows behind the eyes. She turned and hurried off up the street. Odhiambo glanced at her card. 'Marketing Consultant', it said. The address was on Kenyatta Avenue. He watched her blend into the eddy of tourists, hawkers and other shoppers. Something was troubling her and it was almost certainly to do with Dennison's death. He didn't think she was a hysterical woman who fantasised her worries. It was with a more determined stride that he now sought his original quarry.

Stefano Iocacci was in his well-appointed office on the second floor, to which Odhiambo, after a quick telephone enquiry by the Kenyan in the salesroom, was conducted. The office was not cluttered, but each piece declared its presence and gave evidence of careful selection: the desk was antique, polished, light brown wood with an inlaid top of intricate design, bare of papers, except one file, but containing an elegant art deco glass pen stand. A coffee table consisted of a glass top supported by moulded brass legs and frame. Odhiambo knew nothing of furniture, but the quality was obvious to the ignorant eye. He guessed correctly it was a classic Italian piece. The carpet was Chinese and in the bookcase forming one wall one shelf was devoted to bronze sculptures consisting of pairs of bodies entwined in what seemed to be strange manners of embrace.

'Mr Odhiambo. Stefano Iocacci.' From behind the desk came a slender man about six feet in height, full head of dark hair clearly shaped by a hair-drier and spray, clad in a smart white shirt with tie, tight light blue trousers that hugged his narrow hips and black elegant shoes. If Odhiambo's instincts had warmed to Pauline Florislow, they reacted coolly to the smiling Italian.

'Mr Iocacci, I'm investigating the murder of Mr Jim Dennison. I'm sure you know that his body was found on the Royal Ngong golf course yesterday. I understand you were a friend of his.'

Iocacci gestured to the chairs, low, embroidered seats, and carved legs, which flanked the coffee table.

'Please. Let us sit. A horrible tragedy. Yes. I knew Jim and his lovely wife, Anne. They are friends of ours.'

'Ours? You mean you and your wife?'

'Yes, of course. Gianna. That's the name of my wife.'

The voice was a light tenor, the English fluent but spoken with a slight inflexion.

'When did you last see Mr Dennison?'

If there was a hesitation it was barely a microsecond. The eyes maintained their steady hold on Odhiambo's.

'We were together on Monday evening. A social gathering.'

'Where? At the club?'

'No. I have forgotten my manners, Mr Odhiambo. May I offer you a drink? Coffee or a whisky?'

'Nothing, thank you. Not at the club?'

'Pardon. Oh. No. A Mr Silent invited us to his house. The Dennisons were there together with others.'

'And this was Monday?'

'Yes. Monday.' Iocacci opened an ornately carved wooden box that lay on the coffee table. He gestured to Odhiambo, but receiving a slight shake of the head helped himself to a cigarette and lit it with a gold lighter extracted from his shirt pocket. He inhaled deeply. 'When did Jim die, Mr Odhiambo? Was it yesterday evening?'

'And you were with Mr Silent and Mrs Dennison again on Tuesday, last evening?'

'Yes. We dined at the club. Michael – Mr Silent – had arranged it. We were expecting Jim, of course.'

'You spend a lot of time together you, the Dennisons, Silent. Who else is in your group?'

'I . . . I would not term our social, what do you say, *e non il gruppo* . . . we meet on social occasions, we do not form a society.'

For the first time, Odhiambo sensed he had pushed Iocacci off balance. He pressed his advantage.

'Whatever you call it. Who else is usually present at your get-togethers? Monday, for example. In Silent's house. You and your wife, the Dennisons, who else?'

'It was a small dinner-party if I remember. Let me think.'

'Come, Mr Iocacci, we're talking of this Monday not some date last year. Less than fourty-eight hours ago. Was Mrs Florislow there?'

'Miss Florislow. Signorina, no? At the moment. Yes, Pauline is another friend. She was there.'

'That's six. Who else?'

'We were eight. There was another couple. Tim and Amanda. I do not recollect their surname. Recently arrived. Michael wanted to make them welcome. He thought they might be amusing. To be truthful I found them to be shallow and dull. They left early.

Forgive me, but why so much interest in our dinner on Monday? Jim was certainly alive yesterday morning.'

'You saw him?'

'No, no. Anne said he had not come from work in time to join us at the club. She would have said if he was missing the night before. *E vero?*'

There was a small film of sweat on the Italian's upper lip and the fingers holding the cigarette were unsteady enough to cause the smoke to rise in an erratic spiral.

'Do you know if Mr Dennison had any business problems?'

'I have no business with him. Not even a car sale.' Iocacci laughed. He seemed relaxed at this turn in the conversation. 'He was a director in one or two firms – I think he had interests in land in the Rift or somewhere.'

'Did he seem worried or preoccupied recently? On Monday, for instance.'

'No. He was as usual.'

'Did he drink?'

Iocacci laughed again. 'Drink? Alcohol, you mean. We all drink here in your country, Inspector. We foreigners. You know – the sundowner. Jim usually drank lager. The local beer.'

'What about drugs?'

Odhiambo almost smiled at the great effort it took the Italian to maintain his composure. He looked at Odhiambo for a moment as if he had been struck a blow, then nervously he wiped a hand across his mouth and chin.

'Drugs!! Whatever do you mean?'

'Did he use narcotics socially? Is that a practice in your little circle of socialisers?'

Iocacci considered his reply during an extended pause covered by his stubbing out of the butt of his cigarette.

'Mr Odhiambo, I consider your questions very strange. We are respectable people. We do not abuse the hospitality of your country. I know nothing of Dennison's personal life which is of relevance in explaining his death. I cannot be of help to you in this.'

Odhiambo took a shot in the dark. 'There are traces of substances in his body.'

Iocacci threw up his hands in a very Mediterranean gesture.

'I am not responsible for Jim Dennison, what he ate, drank or anything. I played golf with him occasionally. His wife and mine are good friends. We met on social occasions. He was a respectable man. That is all I can tell you about him.'

Odhiambo got to his feet.

'Very well. Thank you for your co-operation. Oh, one last thing. Miss Florislow was here just before me. Is she buying a car?'

'She is thinking. She is difficult to persuade.' Again the hands spread and the mouth turned exaggeratedly down. 'I keep on trying. I am a salesman, no?'

'Is that what she came to see you about today? Or to discuss the circumstances of Mr Dennison's death?'

'What is it you say, Inspector? Of course we speak of Jim's death. Is that not natural when a friend dies – particularly in such a bad way. You think we do not mention it?'

'But she told you nothing about it, that you didn't already know?'

'*Exacto*. Sure. We, what do you say, consoled each other, no?'

As Odhiambo descended the stairs he thought it interesting that Iocacci had not asked how he knew the Florislow woman. He was certain in his mind that Iocacci had watched his encounter with her from his window.

Back in the car beside his driver, Odhiambo considered his next move. There was Pauline Florislow, but for some deep-seated male instinct he didn't wish to appear to have rushed around to see her at the earliest opportunity. No, he would first pay a call at an address he had looked up in the directory on a street leading off Kenyatta Avenue in the opposite direction. As he turned to the driver he was surprised to see him looking somewhat apprehensive as if desperately summoning up the courage to speak. Odhiambo gave him his prompt.

'Yes? What is it?'

'Ah. Inspector. While you were inside, radio here call me. I think station trying to speak to you.'

'So, what is the message?'

'Ah, there be the big trouble, Inspector. Just as I answer and say you are in building the radio he go die. Lot of noise but no sense.' As if to reassure Odhiambo that he was telling the truth the driver turned the switch, filling the car with the ugly sound of static. 'This is right frequency but I try all over. Radio no good.'

Odhiambo shook his head resignedly.

'I never expect the bloody things to work. Ever since they filled the cars with radios supplied by Arum Patel. Nice little deal, that one. These are all East European rejects.'

'So we go back to station to find message?'

The driver was right, of course; that was the correct thing to do, but Odhiambo was always inclined to avoid taking the orthodox or the procedurally correct approach. It was probably some stupid administrative query. Let it wait.

'No. First drop me at this office.' Odhiambo dug out of his pocket the address he had scribbled down and passed it to the driver. 'While I'm in there you go back and find out what they want.'

'*Ndio, bwana.*' The driver turned the car across the road, using his siren briefly to gain himself the priority.

'And switch that bloody thing off. What with that and your radio you're making me deaf.'

The driver grinned. He had rapidly learned that Odhiambo's bark was worse than his bite. As officers went, Odhiambo was an easy ride.

The unpretentious office building that Odhiambo entered a few minutes later was older than the ones in the street he had just left. It was in an area developed by Indian businessmen in the forties and fifties, close to one of Nairobi's landmarks, the McMillan Memorial Library, a solid stone building with steps and columns of a Victorian design. The street was narrow and bustling. Most of the buildings were two or three storeys only, with shops on the ground floor and miscellaneous small painted business logos on the windows above. The shops were still run mainly by Asian families. Odhiambo often thought how odd it was that within a few minutes' walk you could go from a side street of banks and brokers where white faces predominated, through Kenyatta Avenue thronged with all shades but clearly revealing now that it was the heart of an African city, to an area which would not have been out of place in Bombay. He was prepared to believe that it was this melting pot of entrepreneurs that gave Nairobi and, indeed, Kenya the economic vibrancy it still had. But he sensed it was fading, and it was the Indian population that was likely to suffer most when scapegoats were sought and questions were asked as to where their loyalties lay. He hoped Kenya would not treat them as Amin had treated the Asian businessmen in Uganda, expelling them without warning to the great detriment of the economy.

A clipped metal sign on the dirty green-painted wall claimed that Mbayazi Estates was to be found on the second and top floor, so Odhiambo began the climb of two flights of stone stairs, also in need of a good scrubbing. The first landing contained two doors with signs attached. The first indicated the location of 'A. A. Singh, Lawyer', the other was more opaque in meaning, stating merely 'Stasec Hlds'. The sign for the lawyer's office amplified the minor question that had been in Odhiambo's mind since he looked up the address. Asian names in the building were what one would expect, but an African-owned firm like Mbayazi Estates would normally be found in a more prestigious address with a less dingy ambience. On the top landing, two more doors presented themselves; 'Mustapha Bros. Valuers' announced one and, on the right, was Odhiambo's quarry, 'Mbayazi Estates'. His clenched hand hovered at the door then, changing his mind, he dropped it and tried the old-fashioned round handle. The door opened, exposing a cluttered area containing a steel desk with typewriter, filing cabinets and a small plywood waist-high counter behind which sat a messenger or guard, currently fast asleep. Beyond this reception area there were two offices with windows to the street, of which the one directly opposite the door where Odhiambo stood contained two people in a classic male boss dictating to female secretary tableau. Both looked up at the sound of Odhiambo's entry. The female, short, plump and past the bloom of youth but wearing what seemed like an orange wig, got up and, coming towards Odhiambo, addressed him in Swahili.

'What do you want?'

Odhiambo replied in English.

'Police. Criminal investigation. Who is in charge here?'

The man in the office spoke past his secretary.

'Ah. The police. I was expecting. I am Mantebe. Come in.'

The man at the counter had woken at the sound of Odhiambo's voice and seemed to be intent on shrinking lower behind the counter as Odhiambo passed him and the secretary who moved, somewhat grudgingly, aside.

'Odhiambo. Chief Inspector, CID. I'm investigating the death of a Mr Dennison. He worked here?'

Mantebe waved Odhiambo to a chair and then attempted to put on a sorrowful face. This was difficult as he possessed a round, fat-cheeked face that seemed designed to convey cheerfulness. He was short, overweight, and his shirt was working its way loose from inside his trousers.

'Tragic. Very bad. Of course I have heard no details. These are bad times. Too many bandits around. Somalis, Ugandans. You people need to do more to protect us, Odhiambo.'

'I asked you if Dennison worked here. He was a director of Mbayazi Estates?'

'Yes. Yes, he was. But he didn't work in this office. He had his own office. He had interests other than our company.'

'You run this office?'

'I am the office manager, yes.'

'And this is the head office of Mbayazi Estates?'

'It is the Nairobi office. The main office is in Nyeri.'

'Where Mr Aramgu lives. He owns Mbayazi Estates, not so?'

'Mr Aramgu is the chairman. There are others . . .' Mantebe waved a hand as if the directors were a scattered and anonymous lot. 'Mr Dennison was the executive director. You would like some *chai*, Odhiambo?'

Odhiambo realised that the sleeping man had now risen and was hovering at his side responding to some signal that Odhiambo had not detected. On his feet, he seemed a figure of more significance; something about his posture and balance made Odhiambo think of a boxer. He shook his head, a gesture mirrored by Mantebe causing the third man to slide away.

'What exactly did Dennison do as a director?'

'Executive director.' Mantebe made the correction as if Odhiambo had slighted the dead. 'He did what most executive directors do – he was responsible for ensuring that the decisions of the chairman and the board were carried out.'

'And what exactly do they make decisions about? Mbayazi Estates is what, other than a land-holding company?'

'Ah, Odhiambo, do not dismiss us because we are African company. We own large farms around Nyeri and in the Rift. Coffee mainly in Nyeri and wheat down in the Rift.'

'So you're farmers?'

Mantebe nodded, a cherubic smile regaining possession of his lower face although the piggy eyes remained watchful.

'*Ndio*. We follow His Excellency's orders to till our native soil to feed the nation and export for prosperity.'

'Farmers do not usually have offices in town.'

'Exporters, Odhiambo. More than just farmers. Exporters of

70

coffee, wheat and some tea. We need to keep in touch with our foreign buyers. It is not easy, this business.'

'If you have to keep in touch, as you say, with representatives of foreign firms, don't you need more glamorous offices than these?'

'You think we are too humble? But you are right. But that is where Mr Dennison was useful. His offices are smart. He looked after the, what do you call it, front of house, PR side of things. And the Nyeri offices are very new, very smart. That is where the directors meet important clients.'

'So Dennison was your contact man with these buyers?'

'*Ndio*. That describes him very well. He handled our dealings with these people. And he was responsible for big purchases of machinery, bank financing, things like that.'

'And you?'

'Ah. I am a small boy, not so? I look after the workers, wages . . .' Mantebe waved his hands in the air to indicate the range of worker-related issues. 'Plus the paperwork, licences, contracts, shipping documents. There is too much paper, Odhiambo, is it not so?'

'Do you know if Dennison had any enemies in business?'

'Enemies! Of course in business you are not always friends with everyone, not so? But if you mean someone wanted him killed, no, no. Odhiambo, this is not gangster business.'

'Jealousy? Someone else in the company who thought it was time for the white man to make way?'

Mantebe's eyes bored into Odhiambo's. If the eyes were the windows of the soul, Odhiambo thought, Mantebe's was in need of confession. He held the stare until Mantebe turned his face to the window, giving a short unconvincing laugh.

'Oh, Odhiambo. I hope you are not arranging the bones to point at me. We needed men like Dennison. He was useful. The chairman trusted him. No, no, Odhiambo, you must look to his white *rifikis* for jealousies and hatreds. Read your history, man. You know what these *mzungus* are like when they squabble over women; especially when they have taken too much *pombe* or sniffed a little powder.' Again the gesture with the arms to indicate the existence of other stimulants. 'Dennison's death is a trouble to me, not something to make me happy.'

'What women?'

Again the arms gestured.

'Why do you ask this of me? Go to his club and ask. I'm sure you know by now who his *rifikis* were. Men like Silent and the Italian. Now the Italian's woman, there is something for men to fight over.'

'Was a Miss Florislow a friend of Mr Dennison's?'

'Miss Florislow? I do not know of her. Wait, I think I have heard the name perhaps.' He shrugged, the giveaway shrug of the man who is being less than frank. 'She is in business perhaps.' He looked at Odhiambo as if aware he had not convinced. 'Yes. Now I think about it, she has an office in the same building as Dennison. That's all I know.'

'Is that right? Does she work for Mbayazi Estates as well? She wants to see me about Dennison's death. Can she tell me more about your exporting business?'

'No, no, Odhiambo. I've never met her. Nothing to do with us. May have been a friend of Dennison, eh?' He winked. 'Nothing wrong with having a woman available when you're at work.'

'You seem to know a lot about Dennison's friends. Are you a member at the Royal Ngong?'

'*Ndio*, Odhiambo. I need the exercise.' Mantebe patted his ample stomach. 'I am member, yes. But I am not one of smart set. Dennison and me, we nod. Sometimes he buy me a drink if we are standing at bar. Once we are drawn together in competition. But I was not one of his *rifikis*.'

Methinks he doth protest too much, thought Odhiambo, remembering a snatch of Shakespeare from his Nairobi boarding school days.

'What about Matavu? Are you one of his *rifikis*?'

'Ah, Matavu is a *bwana mkubwa* at the club. He is Captain and good golfer. Too big and too good for me.'

Odhiambo spent some more time questioning Mantebe about the details of the business he was running. It was clear that Mbayazi Estates had sizeable land holdings both in Nyeri District and on the plains of the Rift Valley. This was not, however, unusual for a senior politician like Aramgu and Odhiambo soon became bored with talk of tonnages of coffee and the internal market for wheat.

There was little more to get from Mantebe, it seemed; at least not until he had more facts to trip up this glib servant of Aramgu. Odhiambo took his leave, the door held open for him by the erstwhile sleeper. The face was familiar. Odhiambo paused and turned to face him.

'Did you once box? For Kenya?'

The man's face broke into a smile.

'*Ndio, bwana*. In 1976 Games. I am Mbele.'

'Lightweight or middle, right?'

Mbele nodded without specifying which.

'I was smaller then. Now the *ugali*, it makes me bigger.'

Odhiambo smiled and completed his exit. As he descended the stairs he wondered why Mbayazi Estates, if it was such an honest company, kept bouncers on the door.

10

His driver greeted Odhiambo's reappearance with relief. He had been debating with himself whether to leave the car and go in search of his quarry or stay behind the wheel. He was grateful to be spared further indecision.

'The message, it was for you. You are to go to Bwana Price-Allen. He is waiting.'

The driver knew little about Price-Allen, but such as he had heard confirmed that if you were summoned to him you went like a villager called to his chief. To his surprise the Chief Inspector after a brief curse seemed to be undecided.

'I want to see that woman before she leaves her office. What the hell does that man want?'

The driver shook his head, partly to indicate his ignorance but mainly in disbelief that Odhiambo supposed that Price-Allen would confide in a mere driver.

'The station said he wanted you very much.'

'Shit. Ah well, I suppose I'd better see what he wants. Do you know where he is?'

'They tell me he is in office in the Conference Centre. They no tell me where in there.'

Odhiambo was now in the car and the driver set off, almost colliding with an Asian on a bicycle as he swung the car out from the kerb.

'Watch where you're going, you idiot. All I need is for you to get me involved in an accident.'

Odhiambo fumed quietly for the remainder of the short

journey and the driver was relieved to be spared further assault. When the car stopped by the main entrance to the tall office building that stood adjacent to the low conference auditorium built to resemble a traditional African hut, Odhiambo ran up the steps and pushed through the door. He was stopped in the foyer inside, but having identified himself he received confirmation of Price-Allen's office on the fifteenth floor. The lifts arrived crowded with workers heading for home, but Odhiambo was alone in the ascent. As he knocked on the door, which gave no clue as to its occupant, Odhiambo noticed the small snooper camera in the angle of two walls. Price-Allen liked to be doubly sure of the identity of his visitors, it seemed.

The door opened and there was the dapper man he remembered. He remembered too those eyes, pale, penetrating in their stare, but somehow conveying the sense of the ruthless mind behind. He was wearing a suit, but an African-style suit, fawn in colour, with tunic-style jacket that buttoned to the neck and lay looser around the hips than a normal jacket.

'Chief Inspector! Come in.' He scrutinised his visitor with apparent amiability. 'You have put on some weight. Cornish cream and American hamburgers perhaps.' He smiled sardonically at his references to Odhiambo's international travels. 'We need to give you some decent work to get you back to fighting trim.'

Price-Allen's office was spacious, particularly as there was no superfluous furniture occupying the space. A desk, steel, modest in size, a leather chair behind it, two filing cabinets, a wooden round table with four plain chairs, that was it. The only luxury, a Persian carpet that occupied the space between the door and the desk. Odhiambo knew nothing about Oriental carpets, but he could tell that this one was old and special.

Price-Allen returned to his chair and gestured for Odhiambo to take one of the chairs from beside the table and bring it to the desk. He did so, feeling like a native servant in the presence of the colonial master. He sat facing Price-Allen and made a deliberate effort to put an arrogant note into his voice.

'So. You wanted to see me. Here I am. You have taken me away from my enquiries, so I hope it's important.'

Price-Allen smiled, a thin-lipped sardonic smile, but with a hint of genuine humour.

'Prickly as always. What a pair – you and your dear wife.'

'If you think I owe you anything for looking after my father-in-law you kid yourself. If it wasn't for you he wouldn't have been in trouble.'

The smile lingered, now mocking.

'I care not one fig for your misguided hostility. In fact it amuses me. But I did not tear you away from your tedious interviews for old times' sake, but to assist you in your enquiries, as you put it. As usual, I fear you are blundering about.'

'You mean you know something about Dennison's murder?'

'Dennison works for Mbayazi Estates, which . . .'

'. . . is owned by Felix Aramgu. I know that already.'

'What I was about to say was, which is a cover for his real role of Aramgu's money man and fixer. His body was found near Aramgu's house, I understand.'

'It was just as near several others. Are you saying Aramgu killed Dennison?'

Price-Allen swivelled his chair in order to gaze out of the window behind him. There was silence for several seconds before Price-Allen spoke, his head still turned away from Odhiambo.

'Look out there, Odhiambo. A peaceful scene. Workers queuing for their *matatus*. Footballers practising in Uhuru Park. You may not see it much longer.'

Odhiambo fidgeted in his chair. 'You think I'm stupid, then talk plainly. How do you expect a stupid man to understand you?'

The chair swivelled back and Odhiambo found himself fixed by that hypnotic stare.

'Shortly, very shortly, Kiwonka will make his move. He has to now that we have nailed him with Omuto's murder. Kiwonka skulks in London, but his man here is ready. That man, of course, is your old adversary, Aramgu.'

'What can he do?' Despite himself, Odhiambo felt the power of Price-Allen's presence. 'And what has that got to do with me and the murder of Dennison?'

'There will be an attempted coup, Odhiambo. That is what he can do. It could be a very bloody business.'

'A coup!' Odhiambo tried to snort derisively, but it sounded unconvincing to his own ears. 'You're fantasising. Where's his support for a coup, for Chrissake?'

'You were never very politically attuned, Odhiambo. Take my word for it. I do not waste time in fantasies.'

'But . . . but . . . if you know so much, you can move in and

75

stop it. Arrest Aramgu and his conspirators. Cut the head off the snake.'

Price-Allen shook his head wearily.

'I am not all-powerful, whatever you may think. Never mind the politics, Odhiambo. I do not need you to play the big game. I tell you this for two reasons. First, to explain Dennison's death and second, to show you the need to act fast.' Odhiambo bit his tongue. Price-Allen was about to show his hand; interrupting him would only delay matters. 'Dennison knew too much. Probably, he was not intended to know about the plotting. He may have learned what he learned inadvertently. No matter, the important fact is he knew and he was uneasy. Making money for Aramgu, building his empire, all well and good as long as some of it stuck to his fingers – but overthrow of the government was more than Mr Dennison had signed up for. So what should he do? Tell someone he trusted and hope to stay out of the picture? That is what he intended, but Aramgu got to him first.'

It was the longest statement Odhiambo had heard Price-Allen make. He was normally terse, incisive – a man of few words. It must be serious for Price-Allen to become loquacious. He tried to concentrate. Price-Allen's talk of coups had distracted him. Could it be? What would happen? Thank God, Cari was out of the country. But she'd be back soon. Stop it. Concentrate on the matter in hand.

Price-Allen watched the internal battle as if he could read it all in Odhiambo's expression. He smiled again and waited.

'OK. So you're saying Aramgu killed Dennison. Or had him killed. And you want me to arrest him now, which will prevent him leading a revolution.'

'How simply and clearly you put things. It is one of your traits I admire.'

'Never mind the crap. You're right, I've got a simple mind and my simple mind tells me I don't have any evidence against Aramgu. Sure, I'm looking into Dennison's connection with Mbayazi Estates; what you've just said may be your theory, but where's the proof?'

'I have a witness for you. He was a lesser assassin. An assassin's mate, perhaps. He was there and he places Aramgu there.'

'So where is he? In one of State Security's nice little cellars somewhere while you beat his story out of him? Give me a name and an address.'

76

'You try my patience, Odhiambo. I give you the means to solve your case and still you are hostile. The witness will be secured and available by tomorrow. There are complications. But here am I, a trusted servant of the government, giving you information it is your duty to follow up. This evening Aramgu and I are due at a reception at the Muthaiga Club. Algerian Independence Day, or Liberation Day or some such nonsense. You, Odhiambo, will arrive with a warrant and arrest the good Ambassador on suspicion of murder. You should enjoy interviewing him. Who knows, you may not need my witness by tomorrow.'

'And where does the warrant come from?'

'From this drawer here.' Price-Allen reached a hand below the desk top and opened a drawer. His hand reappeared with a folded document. 'All correct and signed by your superiors.'

Odhiambo stared at the proffered document as if he expected it to sting on touch. He looked up and Price-Allen, a man who prided himself on his judgement of men, was surprised to see genuine hate in the eyes of the policeman.

'I've made it clear to you before – I'm nobody's small boy, particularly yours. I'm not doing your dirty work for you. Next you'll expect me to become one of your thugs to make people vanish. That's what you're known as, you know – the man who orders not punishment but vanishment – no trace unless an animal unearths a bone or two in the Ngong hills or somewhere.'

Odhiambo rose and turned towards the door, leaving Price-Allen still clutching the offending piece of paper.

'Odhiambo!' The voice was unchanged, calm, matter-of-fact, not raised in volume, but the authority was unmistakable. 'You think Aramgu has forgiven you for costing him his job over the Eagle's Nest business? You think he enjoyed being sent to Algeria? He had you, you remember? Then your wife came to me. You think he doesn't know he owes his downfall to your wife? You need me to spell out his plans for you both?'

Odhiambo turned back and pressed his hands on Price-Allen's desk as he leaned towards the seated man.

'I don't frighten easily and I won't become your *toto*. If you've got a warrant for Aramgu, get uniformed officers to go and bring him in. When I've got the evidence and not before, I'll go after him.'

He turned for the door once more, so – fortunately for his already troubled mind – missing the flash of malevolence in Price-Allen's eyes.

Odhiambo tried to gain control of his anger as his driver headed once more for the town centre. How he had got out of Price-Allen's office without throttling the man he was not sure. Now, as sanity returned, leaving behind a core of anger like a throbbing abscess in his mind, he tried to order his thoughts. He had always known that sometime he would have to face down Price-Allen and that when it happened his own days would be numbered. You did not cross Price-Allen and live. He had more than once woken in the night wondering if he would have the guts to stand his ground when the moment came: he was surprised how easy it had been in the sense that his reactions were instinctive in the same way you drew back when finding a snake on the path you trod. If he had accepted the warrant it would have been as if he had grasped the mamba's head. But now it was done, what next? What would Price-Allen do? And when would he do it? Cari was safe for the moment. That of course was what he should do, try and get out before Price-Allen's goons came for him. Join Cari in Washington and become a full-time dependent of his highly salaried wife. And hope that Price-Allen's tentacles did not reach that far – but that of course was the problem, he knew from recent experience that they did. Nowhere was safe, so there was only one thing to do, pick up a stone and squash the snake before it could strike. He sneered at himself. Big words, but what were they worth?

As far as his immediate plans were concerned, the truth was he had none. Should he seek out his boss Masonga and hope for his protection? There was, of course, the chance that if Price-Allen was preoccupied with – what had he called it, the big game – he would be too busy to swat an annoying insect like Odhiambo. This might give him some time. But time for what? He sighed. Whatever he should be doing it ought to be something more useful to his survival than carrying on with his normal round. He had given his driver the address of the woman's office while his mind was still incapable of rational thought, but now he could see the ludicrous irrelevance of his intention to continue as if nothing had happened. Price-Allen had chosen Aramgu as the murderer so that was that. For the first time he considered the possibility, probability even, that Price-Allen was right. Dennison got too close to Aramgu's political machinations so he had to go to keep the plan secret. He was in no doubt that Aramgu was perfectly capable of filling the role. So why didn't he take the goddamn warrant and do what Price-Allen wanted? And the answer remained the same – he couldn't bear to be manipulated, to be despised as someone's tool, to lose his self-respect and the respect of his Luo forebears. He sighed again and leant forward to speak to the driver, suddenly aware that the car had halted in Kenyatta Avenue, but short of his destination.

Odhiambo looked past his driver's head through the wind-screen. Traffic was being diverted from the side road that his car was in back to the central lanes of this main Nairobi thorough-fare. The reason for the diversion was a blockage some forty yards ahead – a knot of people and a vehicle sitting broadside across the road. As Odhiambo focused he realised the vehicle was a police car. He felt a wave of nausea wash over him and clutched the back of the driver's seat for support.

'*Bwana* – we can no get to – '

As the driver spoke, whilst turning his head towards his rear passenger, he was interrupted.

'I'm getting out. Pull in somewhere and wait.'

Odhiambo straightened after ducking out of the door. He still felt sick. He knew, as certainly as if he had witnessed it, what he was about to find. The policeman redirecting traffic hesitated as Odhiambo approached, obviously intending to stride past.

'Excuse me, sir, but – '

'I'm a detective. Chief Inspector Odhiambo. What's going on down there?'

'Oh. I'm sorry, sir. This woman she go fall from up there.' The policeman gestured vaguely at the tops of the buildings. 'She be dead. A white woman.'

Odhiambo strode the remaining distance and pushed through the line of curious onlookers. A policeman was kneeling beside a body and on the body's other side, also kneeling, was a middle-aged African in a suit fussing with the body in the manner of someone with authority and experience. A second policeman was holding the spectators at bay as best he could. Odhiambo looked down at the body. One leg was bent at an unnatural angle, the other leg exposed to the thigh with a skirt rumpled around the waist. One shoe lay a foot or so from the body, black patent leather with a significant depth of heel. The patterned silk blouse was spattered with blood, but most of the blood lay around the smashed head. It was the side of the skull that had taken the first impact on the pavement; the face was damaged but recognisable. Whatever his intentions, he would not be interviewing Pauline Florislow.

The man who looked like a doctor noticed Odhiambo's stare and, as if realising the indelicacy of the dead woman's posture, pulled at her skirt to cover her thighs. The policeman looked up.

'Odhiambo. Chief Inspector. When did this happen?'

'Only just now, Inspector. We were driving over that side.' He gestured in the direction of the main roadway. 'Someone waved us to stop. Maybe five minutes since.'

'And you?' Odhiambo looked at the other man.

'Dr Sang. I was passing just a minute ago. There is nothing to do. She is quite dead.' His hand still tugged ineffectively at the woman's skirt. For some reason Odhiambo found this offensive.

'Don't interfere with the body. Leave it alone.'

The doctor withdrew his hand as if he had been accused of assault. Then pride reasserted itself and he rose to his feet.

'I have only done what is necessary to check whether any help should be given. I do not think the cause of death will be too difficult for you to establish.'

'You think so? You go and do your doctoring and let me do the detecting.'

Sang opened his mouth to speak, then shut it again as the wail of a siren heralded the arrival of an ambulance. He walked towards it, glad for an excuse to leave with dignity.

'Where did she fall from? The roof or a window?'

The policeman, also now on his feet, gestured at one of the bystanders, a youngish man still clutching the fake elephant hair bracelets he had been selling at his pavement stall.

'This man say he see her fall out of window. That one, up there.'

Odhiambo looked up. The building was modern and air-conditioned. The day was hot. Only one window was open, a window on the sixth floor. Odhiambo fished the business card out of his pocket and looked at it. Yes. Pauline Florislow's office was shown as 602, Interglobe Building, Kenyatta Avenue. He looked again at the surrounds of the body: no sign of a handbag. He knelt and with some difficulty found the pocket of the dead woman's skirt. A small handkerchief, nothing else. He looked at the vacant eyes.

'What was it you wanted to tell me, Pauline? Goddamn it, what was it?' He became aware of two new arrivals. He looked up. These were the ambulance men. He stood up and sighed. 'OK. Get the body to the hospital and the mortuary.' He turned to the policeman. 'You go with it. You say Chief Inspector Odhiambo wants a full check and post-mortem. You got that? Right. Make sure you do it. Say it is a suspect murder victim.'

He left the policeman, mouth agape, and headed for the main entrance of the pride of Interglobe.

11

'So, Robert. I'm on the run. At this moment Price-Allen and Aramgu are glaring at each other in Muthaiga Club and I was supposed to be there to pluck Aramgu out of circulation.'

McGuiry watched his friend as he sat on the edge of the armchair, elbows on knees and fingers kneading his cheeks. He had never seen Odhiambo so tense. He knew better than to ask why Odhiambo had not just carried out Price-Allen's instructions: Odhiambo, he knew, would take even the question as an insult – he was a proud man and McGuiry liked him for it.

'Let me get ye another bottle, man. Just sit a while. Gather your wits. Mebbe yon Price-Allen will get another body to do his dirty work and forget about it.'

Odhiambo watched glumly as McGuiry disappeared towards the kitchen, reappearing quickly with a bottle and opener in hand.

'I shouldn't have come here, Robert. It could be dangerous.'

'Och, here, get this inside your stomach. You're sounding like some frightened ninny. Now there's more to the tale, you said. Stop your fretting about me, I want to hear the rest.'

'There's a woman who was said to be part of Dennison's circle with the chap two houses up from here, Silent, and an Italian pair. Florislow, Pauline Florislow. I met her accidentally and she said she wanted to see me about Dennison. Like a fool I delayed going to her office. Went to the Mbayazi Estates office instead. Then Price-Allen sent for me. After my *shauri* with Price-Allen I went to see her although to be truthful I was in a bit of a mental daze. I found her all right: dead on the pavement. Fell from her office window.'

'Mother of God! What are ye saying? Someone pushed the poor lassie?'

'What do you think? Whatever she had to say to me is lost now. Air-conditioned building. No other window open. And if that is what happened to her, it's down to me. She asked me to come and I was too late.'

'Pauline Florislow. That Secretary chappie said she was in with that crowd. Too good for them, he thought. Leastways for the Dennisons. You had a look in her office?'

'Yeah. I got the building manager's key. No sign of a break-in or disturbance. Slight scratch on the window-sill. I called the station and told them to fingerprint it, but . . .' Odhiambo's voice tailed off and he drank two large swallows from his glass.

'It's no good blaming yourself. No way you could have known. I'm no detective, but a question comes to mind: who knew she wanted to see you?'

McGuiry was pleased to see the first glimmering of a grin on the face of his friend since he had arrived back at Karen some half an hour earlier.

'You know, Robert, you're learning fast. You'll be a detective yet. Fact is, hardly anyone. I'm trying to remember – it's possible I mentioned it when trying to get something out of the Mbayazi Estates man in his office earlier, but he didn't seem to know much about her and I thought I could tell when he was lying. He wouldn't have had much time to organise anything. No one heard her talk to me on the street where I met her, but I have a strong feeling the Italian car salesman was watching from his window. She had just left him when she spoke to me as I was going in.'

McGuiry felt that the worst of Odhiambo's mood crisis was over. He was functioning again, concentrating on the puzzles facing him. It was important to keep him focused.

'From me own amateur efforts I can confirm that our wee neighbour Silent has his tight little circle including the Italians, the Dennisons, your lady Pauline. Hill-Templeton thinks they're an odd bunch. Ill-matched, I suppose would be the word. Might have been some queer goings-on with that little lot.'

'And now two of them are dead.'

'So what do ye reckon then, James? A killer loose amongst their wee gang?'

'Possibly. But there's the other angle. Dennison was some sort of middle-man for Mbayazi Estates which meant he might have known all sorts of things. He handled exports: we know what fiddling can go on there – foreign exchange dodges and so on. The Florislow woman worked next door.' He saw McGuiry's eyebrows rise. 'Yes. I checked that when I was there. Mbayazi Estates is Aramgu. According to what you said last night and Price-Allen confirmed this evening, Aramgu is cooking up some mischief. Dennison knew too much and the woman knew something too – either from Dennison or in some other way. Aramgu needs secrecy so they had to go.'

'But Price-Allen seems to know all about it. He's the laddie I'd be troubling my mind with if I were yon Felix . . . I wouldn't be planning a coup while Price-Allen was still in me way.'

Odhiambo drained his glass. He didn't know why, but he felt better although he knew he was in a very deep hole. He looked at McGuiry.

'Well, at least I've disproved your fear last night that I'm a Price-Allen stooge. Unfortunately, I've overdone it. I'm likely now to be a Price-Allen victim.'

'Ah, don't start going morbid on me again. Another bottle? Don't shake your head like that, it's no convincing. Wait here.' Once again the ritual was repeated and Odhiambo found himself pouring his third bottle of beer into his pint mug while McGuiry added some whisky to his own glass. 'I'll tell ye what I canna follow, James. Why does Price-Allen need you? And why pick him up at the stuffy old Muthaiga Club?'

Odhiambo stared at the empty floor space.

'The second question may have an obvious answer. Aramgu will have his men around him, particularly if he's plotting a coup. A diplomatic do at the Muthaiga might be the opportunity to snatch him while his goons are outside the gate. And why me? I think it's a typical Price-Allen set-up. Get rid of Aramgu and he may short-circuit the coup. But he doesn't want to show his hand, so I do his dirty work, pick up Aramgu, some sort of incident occurs staged by Price-Allen, Aramgu is killed, maybe me too. Price-Allen issues a statement saying unfortunately the arresting officer had a previous run-in with the victim that led to their unfortunate demise. He's cut off the head of the snake and got rid of me at the same time.'

'De ye ken what I'm thinking, James? It's a braw time to take a

83

little holiday – visit the old folks in Kisumu, go and look at the lion in the Mara, whatever. Stay out of the way. When two predators like these two go at it, better for the rest of the world to keep out of the way.'

Odhiambo got to his feet and walked across to the french windows. He gazed into the darkness in the direction of the eighteenth hole of the Royal Ngong. McGuiry watched and waited.

'It's not that easy, Robert. If it was just Dennison, well, perhaps. But a woman died this afternoon because she wanted to speak to me and I delayed going to see her. I owe her something.'

'Och, don't talk daft, mon. There was no way of you knowing.' McGuiry saw the angry shake of the large head. 'Granting you're right, which you're not, what good will it do the woman if Price-Allen or Aramgu get to you?'

Odhiambo turned back and looked at his host. McGuiry was surprised to see the change in his demeanour: there was a glint in the eye and the mouth, although determined, was no longer down-turned.

'I'm going to have to go undercover, Robert. That at least gives me more freedom. I'm going to have a few words with that Italian and the Mbayazi man which might go further than official police procedure allows. If I can get to the bottom of this I might be able to stop the coup without walking into Price-Allen's pit.'

'Ach, you always were a bloody fool. Still, if you're set on your way, then I'll be with ye.'

'No. I don't want you mixed up in it. Go back to Eagle's Nest. Stay out of trouble. Even in a coup you'll be safe there.'

'Don't tell an old man what to do. Dinna they teach you respect for your elders in your village when you were a bairn? Truth is, I'd sooner be mixed up in your crazy schemes than having to be polite to another load of tourists. Look, you go and grill Aramgu's man and I'll pay a visit to our pasta-eaters. Or my neighbour, here. As you wish.'

The argument continued for some time whilst glasses were filled and drained one more time, but Odhiambo was both nervous and tired. He was not at his best in resisting the stubborn old Scot.

The Muthaiga Country Club remained much as it had in the white settler days of Lord Delamere. A club for gentlemen rather than businessmen, public schoolboys rather than bachelors of commerce, Christian rather than Jew or Muslim. It was no longer as exclusive as it had been in colonial days, but it still reeked of a strange combination of English country-house gentility, upper-class prejudice, and delusions of grandeur. New money and business were no longer so despised and colour was no longer a bar as long as the applicant fitted the (unwritten but well understood) concept of a suitable club member. It was still impossible, thought Price-Allen, as he gazed around the ballroom, to be in any doubt where you were. Other clubs might have their individual touches, but were basically interchangeable. Muthaiga was unique, as if its old settler heritage and the raffish characters that had boozed, copulated and even plotted murder within its portals had left an indelible aura which had permeated its walls.

Price-Allen despised the club and its membership, but tonight this displeasure was more narrowly focused. Across the room, dominating his immediate entourage, was the huge figure of Felix Aramgu. The room was full of politicians, senior government figures and diplomatic figures, although the real upper stratum of government and ambassadors was missing. Price-Allen could detect an undercurrent of tension amongst at least some of the gathering. Things were coming to a head and if it hadn't been for the stupid pride of the wretched Odhiambo he, Price-Allen, could have precipitated matters tonight according to his own programme. He liked his chess games to be intricate with variations on the set pieces of attack and defence, and he liked his real-life plots to be the same. He would have enjoyed snatching Aramgu out of this setting and then the attempt to rescue him on the way back into the city. The death of a famous detective in the ensuing gun battle providing the excuse for imposing martial order. Aramgu forced to name his associates in one of Price-Allen's safe houses where his cries of pain would not be heard, nor his location known. Now, through the arrogant pig-headedness of one man, he had been forced to reconsider his next move. The trouble was he was engaged in a game of chess where some of his own pieces were masquerading under a false colour. He could no longer trust the loyalty of the State Security officers and because of that his influence over the other organs of government such as the police was slipping. Within State House itself there was an air of complacency that drove Price-Allen to the verge of apoplexy; the Big Man's inner group were now so remote from reality that they could not see what was going on under their noses and, as Price-Allen knew, one or two of that group were traitors who were fostering the inclination to ignore the warning signals.

Back his thoughts came to Odhiambo. It was essential he die in an attempt to arrest a murderer despite the murderer's elevated rank. Although Odhiambo himself did not seem to realise it, out there in the streets his recent adventures had made him a symbol of rugged independence from corruption and manipulation. And he was a Luo. His death could be made into a martyrdom and swing certain influential factions against the Aramgu camp. If Odhiambo would not volunteer to be a martyr then he would have to be a reluctant conscript. Annoyingly he seemed to have disappeared – a watch on his house had revealed no activity and he had not reported to his superiors. Price-Allen, however, had, as usual, arranged for a back-up plan and this had now been activated. Even if Odhiambo was not in his possession by morning his wife would be and the possession of one would quickly ensure the possession of the other.

'RD. Don't often have the pleasure of your company in dos of this nature.' Price-Allen looked to his left at the ingratiating face of one of the white economic advisers to the government. Another pompous ass worthy of his contempt. He allowed himself a thin smile.

'Occasionally it is instructive to observe the ritual dance of the blind and privileged.'

'Yes. Know what you mean. But, er, I thought you might have been too busy these days. One hears of alarums and excursions. I suppose it's gossip really.'

'My dear Allsop, if such warnings penetrate even to your ears deep in your economists' haven they must already have run their course. There is little to keep me busy these days.'

'Oh quite, quite. Probably spoken out of turn. I just hope that when the required economic belt-tightening is announced we don't have certain politicians trying to agitate the masses.'

'As long as you don't raise the price of maizemeal, do raise the pay of the military, and smooth the feathers of the chiefs of the Kikuyu, you may rest assured your theories will not upset our stability even if they wreck our economy.'

Professor Allsop gave an embarrassed giggle. One was never sure where one was with Price-Allen.

'Always the . . . the cynic, eh, RD? Well, better circulate, I suppose.'

Price-Allen watched him sidle off with scarcely concealed contempt. These professors from minor British universities were the curse of Africa, using their opportunity to test their half-baked socialist theories and too dim to recognise the failure when it occurred. Turning back to scan the room once more, he found his line of vision largely dominated by Felix Aramgu.

'So we have the rare opportunity to see the *mzungu mkubwa*, the big white chief. I hear you have been on safari in Uganda.'

It took a lot to disconcert Price-Allen, but Aramgu's effrontery did momentarily achieve it, although nothing revealed itself on his face.

'Ambassador Aramgu. It is good to see you joining the celebration of the country to which you are Kenya's representative. I understand Algeria has seen very little of you of late.'

The laugh rumbled up from the depth of the vast belly and emerged with a volume and resonance that attracted the attention of a considerable audience.

'One's first duty is to one's country. There are matters to attend to, including making His Excellency the President aware of the false tales some of those who are not true Africans are whispering into his ear.'

'I thought perhaps you would be mourning the death of one of your loyal staff. He died just by your house, I understand. Perhaps he had been visiting.'

Aramgu stared at Price-Allen with his mouth slightly open, sucking noisily at his teeth to dislodge a piece of meat stuck between two of them.

'Dennison. You mean Dennison. By my ancestors, you are surely not putting his death at my door? He was my man. I want to know who killed him. I hear that Luo donkey of yours is in charge. You know what that tells me, *mzungu*?'

'It should tell you to be careful, Ambassador. That Luo donkey has blocked your path before.'

The great head bobbed.

'I have not forgotten as I have not forgotten who his master is. I hope to have a talk with him soon and with you too.'

'It may be sooner than you think. I understand his investigation is going well.'

Aramgu opened his mouth to continue the verbal sparring, but a third man chose this moment to join them.

'Ah, Monsieur l'Ambassadeur. Pardon. Permettez-moi de vous présenter . . .'

Price-Allen slipped away, leaving Aramgu to grapple with a language he had not begun to understand despite his responsibility for diplomacy in a French-speaking country. He left the club and retrieved his Peugeot car from the car-park. If only he knew when Aramgu was going to strike. It was imminent, that much he knew. He must get his hands on Odhiambo by tomorrow. He could risk no longer delay than that.

Aramgu, having managed to extricate himself from the linguistic and diplomatic toils of the North Africans, found one of his aides at the bar.

'It is time to go. There is work to do. Get word to the others. Our programme is to be advanced.'

The aide went off to locate Aramgu's driver. He cursed his luck. It sounded as if he was in for a night of labour. If Aramgu had followed his original intention, the next step would have been the Equatorial Moon night-club and after Aramgu had made his selection of girls there would have been pickings enough left for humbler men.

12

Gianna Iocacci groaned as she splashed water on to her face. She was hungover and her head throbbed. It wasn't that she had drunk a lot more than usual last night, it was the fact that she drank while under stress. It was her belief that hangovers were correlated with one's state of mind rather than volume of alcohol. Relaxed, she could drink and feel none the worse the next morning. Stressed out, half a bottle of wine was enough to start a headache. She looked at herself in the mirror – was there just a sign of a sag to the breasts and a hint of spare flesh on her ribs? She didn't eat a lot so it had to be the booze. She would have to cut down. Easier said than done in this Equatorial outpost. Her hair was still lustrous as she combed it, but she needed to be careful about her eyes: they were her striking feature, but the large, wide-eyed, dark brown look that could summon a man with only one glance was being hurt by those nights at Michael's. It was time to make some changes to their lifestyle; she must have it out with Stefano. She sighed as she left the bathroom – after all, she had had this conversation with herself before.

Ten minutes later she descended the stairs of the house and found her husband sitting at the breakfast table on the patio. The sun was well up although the coolness of the night had not yet been finally extinguished. The patio had a view across their back garden to the plains of the Nairobi National Park. It used to worry her that lions could get close to them with only a fence to stop them reaching the garden. She had heard the old tales of a lion walking through the centre of Nairobi. Now she rarely thought about it. Truth was, she rarely thought about very much: she blamed the Equatorial sun, it sapped one's mental energy. Stefano, she could tell, was in bad humour. Like all handsome Italian men his face was expressive of his mood. He was eating, or rather toying with, a plate of sliced mango and paw-paw.

'*Buon giorno*, Stef. It is early, no?'

'It is not good, no. The news is bad.'

Gianna Iocacci sat down opposite her husband and reached for the jug of fruit juice. As she poured some into her glass her hand slipped and a small amount of juice spilled on to the table-cloth. She could feel Stefano's glower without looking up.

'I'm sorry. The handle is slippery.'

There was a muffled snort of derision, but it seemed he didn't want to make an issue of her minor accident. That was the good news, but what was the bad?

'You don't seem very curious.'

Gianna looked at her husband almost in supplication.

'Oh, please. Yes. I am. You say there is bad news. I thought we had all the bad news we need with Jim's death. Is that what you meant?'

'No. It gets worse. Michael called me earlier. Pauline is dead. Apparently she fell from her office.'

The make-up recently applied could not disguise the sudden pallor in the woman's cheeks. She swayed in her chair.

'Pauline! *Mama mia. E non possibile.* How, how could she fall?'

'How should I know how she fell? The point is, she's dead.

That's two dead in two days and one at least murdered. I mean, the police might think she committed suicide, or anything. The point is, they're likely to put us under the grill. You too. You understand?'

Gianna gaped at her husband. Her brain was racing, but was not making much sense.

'You mean, they'll ask me about Jim and Pauline? But I – '

'Not just about them. Don't you see? They were both in our group. Michael's group. Our nights at his house. Think, woman. We do not want the police interfering in our private affairs. *Capisce*?'

Gianna almost giggled.

'You mean our sex parties? You think they wouldn't understand?'

'Michael was right. You're too stupid to be trusted. Pull yourself together, you silly bitch. Taking cocaine is illegal, did you know that?'

'But it doesn't have anything to do with Jim's murder, does it? Or Pauline? Oh, poor Pauline. I can't believe it.'

'Why not? Jealousies within the group. Someone threatening to tell the police about Michael supplying cocaine. Who knows what the police may think?'

But his wife's mind had gone off on another tangent.

'When did Michael phone? I didn't hear – '

'Before you were awake.' Stefano Iocacci did not intend to tell his wife he knew of Pauline's death when he arrived home last night. She was too drunk to be told then and he had not thought matters through. 'It doesn't matter. What does matter is what you tell the police. Now, are you listening . . . ?'

Robert McGuiry walked the short distance from his temporary home to that of his next-door neighbour bar one. Leaving his driveway he passed the high hedge of the absent Mr Smyth. The gates were steel rather than the normal vertical rods. Mr Smyth clearly believed in security when in town. The next hedge was shorter and better tended, recently pruned and allowing a sight of the house it sheltered. What was more, the gate was open. Turning into the driveway McGuiry saw a gardener who, although watering the flowerbeds, seemed to be keeping an eye on the entrance. A Porsche was in the driveway; early though it was, it seemed that Silent had already been out and about.

McGuiry's use of the brass knocker produced a quick response in the form of a uniformed house servant whose height and stature took McGuiry by surprise. Glancing back he could see that the gardener, who had straightened from adjusting his hosepipe, was similarly built. Silent might have a more relaxed attitude to perimeter security than his neighbour, but he had a serious home guard in the form of a couple of strapping Masai. To find members of this nomadic and proud tribe acting as domestic employees was unusual in McGuiry's estimation. It added to the mysterious reputation of his intended quarry.

The servant evidenced no surprise at the early visitor and showed McGuiry through the hall to a spacious room with large sliding windows that formed most of one side, allowing a feeling of light and space to be accentuated. Seated on a sofa were Michael Silent and Anne Dennison. Hiding his surprise, McGuiry responded to the surprise of his host as revealed by the arched eyebrows.

'A bonnie morn, is it not? Apologies for disturbing ye so early and I dinna know ye had a visitor. You remember me. Robert McGuiry, house-warming a couple of doors along. We met Tuesday evening at the club after the dis . . . when we came with the sad news. Mrs Dennison, my condolences once again, ma'am.'

Silent got to his feet and waved in the direction of a leather armchair, which to McGuiry's eye looked old and special. He glanced around, confirming his impression that the room was furnished with both taste and age. The furniture, including an elegant writing-table and a grandfather clock, was clearly made up of collector's pieces.

'McGuiry. Of course we remember. We were just having a coffee. Will you join us?'

'That's hospitable, but I'm disturbing ye, perhaps?'

'No, no. Mrs Dennison is with me because, on top of the tragedy of her husband's death, we have heard other terrible news.'

McGuiry looked at the woman. She had aged since he first saw her less than thirty-six hours ago. The red, baggy eyes indicated both grief and lack of sleep, but McGuiry's overwhelming impression was that the woman was frightened. He sat himself down in the armchair, the leather sighing softly as his weight was accommodated.

'Would that be the news of Miss Florislow's fall?'

Again the eyebrows arched as Silent settled himself back on to the sofa, with a little more distance between himself and his female guest than was the case when McGuiry entered the room.

'Yes, indeed. You know . . . knew Pauline?'

'No. But you did, not so? She was also with you Tuesday. One of your party.'

'Absolutely. A valued friend. But if – '

'How did you hear about her death?'

'A mutual friend called me last evening. But I was about to ask you the same question.'

Silent had poured coffee into a cup while he spoke and, leaning forward, placed it in front of McGuiry indicating the jug of cream and bowl of sugar.

'Black is fine, thank ye. I also heard it from a friend. Who was at the scene just after the lassie fell. James Odhiambo. Chief Inspector James Odhiambo. He's staying with me over yonder.'

There was a gasp from the woman, who was staring at McGuiry as if hypnotised. Silent placed a hand on her trousered knee in an avuncular, sympathetic gesture.

'Ah, yes. I think I heard that you knew our local detective. He's become quite well known, I understand.'

'Ay. He's a good man and a true bloodhound. Likes to get to the bottom of things.'

'Good. Well, the sooner he gets to the bottom of poor Jim's death the better. Then Anne can get on with getting over it all.'

There was a silence which stretched uncomfortably as each man waited for the other to make the next move. Finally, Silent continued, forcing the issue. 'And to what do we owe this visit, McGuiry? Just a neighbourly call?'

'Would you say Miss Florislow was depressed by Mr Dennison's death? I mean, more than one would expect?'

'My dear McGuiry, what are you suggesting? That Pauline was upset enough to jump from her window? What a preposterous idea.'

'Not much more preposterous, it seems to me, than falling out of it by accident.'

The woman had listened to these exchanges with signs of growing stress. Now she suddenly found her voice.

'What are you going on about? Pauline depressed about Jim enough to commit suicide? You're out of your mind. And what's it gotta do with you, anyway?'

'I don't think the police think she committed suicide either. In fact, James was on his way to her office, because she had something to say. Seems odd that, do ye no think? I can tell ye, James finds it odd.'

Anne Dennison's mouth opened and shut but no sound emerged. Silent, however, was quickly into the breach.

'Are you suggesting that Pauline was . . . was murdered?'

'Do you know any reason why she might have been? Or Mr Dennison?'

This time Anne Dennison's vocal chords responded successfully.

'Michael! What would Pauline have to tell the police? What's going on? First Jim, now her. It can't involve – '

'Now, Anne.' The hand that still lay on the woman's knee now gripped it and pressed. 'Don't allow this man to upset you further.' Silent turned back to his unwelcome guest. 'Now look here, McGuiry. I don't know what all this has to do with you, but this is not a suitable time to humour your curiosity. I must ask you – '

'How well do you know the Italians?'

'What? The Iocaccis, you mean? They also are friends of mine. But – '

'The dead woman was last seen leaving Iocacci's office. She then wants to talk to the police. Next she's dead. Don't you think all this is getting a bit close to home?'

'I must ask you to leave. Now.'

Silent was on his feet. Although his face maintained a disciplined passivity, the anger was palpable. McGuiry rose too and turned to acknowledge the Dennison widow, but she was staring at Silent and her face revealed clearly the fright and, yes, suspicion.

'Michael! What the hell's going on? I don't like it. How come every bastard seems to know what's going on 'cept me? It's my husband who's dead.'

'Anne, I will explain once we get this . . . this gentleman out of my house. I don't wish to discuss our personal affairs in front of him. You understand?'

'I don't understand. That's the bloody point.' She turned to the older man. 'Now, you, whoever you are, don't talk in riddles. What do you know about Jim's death and now the – the other?'

'Mrs Dennison, it is widely known that Mr Silent has several of you as his close social friends. Two of the group are dead. The police are going to want to know everything that goes on in your group. If there's something you know you should tell the police quickly. Odhiambo wants to find your husband's killer, not concern himself with your social habits. Unless there's a connection.'

'That's it. McGuiry, you have abused my hospitality. Go now. And if your police friend is still with you tell him if he wants to ask questions to request an interview in the normal way. This is intolerable.'

McGuiry could see no basis for further outstaying his welcome. He had achieved more than he and James had hoped for. The presence of Anne Dennison, which could have scuppered his plan to shake Silent's complacency, had served to demonstrate that the Silent group had something to hide: the expression on her face removed any doubt in his mind. He headed for the front door with Silent at his heels. As he opened the door, Silent spoke.

'You've overstepped the mark, McGuiry. I shall consider complaining to the authorities.'

'I'm not an official, only a neighbour.'

'But you're doing this for your detective friend. Tuesday night you said he happened to be with you. Is he still there? If so, tell him I want to see him.'

McGuiry thought for a moment. It might be worth a little deception. He spoke with voice raised enough to reach back into the room he had just left.

'Not at the moment. Out and about. But yes, I'll tell him when he comes back. Canna miss him, he's big enough. I'll tell him. But don't do what Pauline did, keep something hidden. You might not live to regret it.'

The manager of the Mbayazi Estates Nairobi office had spent the night with one of the girls from the Equatorial Moon in her dingy room at the back of the night-club. His own farm was near Naivasha with his wife and sons in charge. Here in the city he enjoyed a footloose existence with a cheap flat in the poorer area as a base, but often sleeping with whichever girl he happened to be enjoying on a temporary liaison. Matthias Mantebe found his lifestyle most acceptable. He was paid well to look after Aramgu's company in terms of domestic arrangements, while Dennison had looked after the international side. He had land, he had sons, and he had his freedom here in Nairobi: a man could not ask the gods for much more than that. Just when everything was proceeding placidly and agreeably, the sound of distant drums warned of disruption. Mantebe was not party to Aramgu's political dealings, but he was close enough to know more than he should, it was necessary to maintain status after all. There might be some advantage for him in the aftermath of any change in the political situation, but there would be serious harm if Aramgu failed in his bid for power. On balance, Mantebe regretted the uncertainty, he would have preferred life to continue along on its previous pleasant path, but unfortunately small men could not control the giants: the best one could do was to try and avoid being trampled on. Now on top of uncertainty came disruption to his work caused by the death of Dennison. It was bad enough that Dennison was dead with Aramgu expecting Mantebe to handle his work while his attentions lay elsewhere. How could he be expected to cope when no one had ever explained what it was exactly that Dennison did? But on top of everything, the police were trying to connect Mbayazi Estates with Dennison's murder. And not just the police, but specifically Odhiambo, a policeman who was not Aramgu's friend – indeed, Mantebe knew enough of the Eagle's Nest business to assume that Aramgu had a grudge to settle. All in all these big men made life difficult for peaceful men like himself.

As he dressed he looked at the woman whose bed he had shared. She was stupid and somewhat lacking in passion, simulated or otherwise. And she snored. But she had a young body, she was inexpensive, available and incurious. These were all qualities that Mantebe valued more than the skills of a more experienced whore who tended also to be cunning and inquisitive. She was good enough to have slaked his physical needs and allowed him a restful sleep, but now as he buckled his belt his mind returned to his preoccupations. Should he find an excuse to leave Nairobi and visit his family? Keep out of the way until the dust settled? Or would Aramgu regard that as disloyalty?

The knock on the door startled him. Who would that be at this early hour? The night-club proprietor didn't normally interfere with his girls until midday. Had she got an early morning client? Mantebe found that thought amusing. There was a chain on the door, insubstantial, but a sufficient deterrent to prevent a casual intruder from making an inconvenient entrance. Mantebe opened the door with the chain still in place – it never did any harm to be cautious. He was dumbfounded to find himself looking at his visitor from yesterday.

'What . . . what are you –?'

'Open the door,' said Odhiambo. 'You've got one or two questions to answer.'

Instinctively, Mantebe tried to shut the door, but it hurtled back into him as Odhiambo's foot, driven with his full weight behind it, forced the door open, snapping the catch for the chain as if it was a thread. Mantebe staggered back, his leg caught the edge of the bed and he fell back on to his bedmate. The noise and falling weight brought the snoring to an abrupt end as the girl awoke.

'*Nimi maana ya* – '

'*Lala chini*,' Odhiambo snapped at the girl and obediently she lay still and waited for the situation to clarify. 'Mantebe, events are moving fast and I need some answers now.'

Mantebe managed to pull himself to his feet and attempt a show of offended dignity.

'This is outrageous. What do you mean forcing – '

'Shut up and listen. I haven't got time for your whining.' A whimper of fear from the girl was ignored. 'I need some honest answers and I intend to get them with or without force. You understand?'

'But why me? I know nothing.' And then, his curiosity conquering his fear: 'How did you know I was here?'

'I have friends, and your habits are not exactly a secret. Now, no more small talk. Who did you speak to after I left your office yesterday?'

Once again Mantebe tried to assert himself.

'This is not how police should behave. I must – '

Odhiambo's large hand shot out and grabbed Mantebe by the throat.

'My friend, I am acting on my own without rules. You want to know what that means then try lying and find out.' The voice was chilling in its understated ferocity. Mantebe's throat was released. 'Now who did you speak to?'

'I don't understand. Nobody . . . Well, not about anything we spoke of. I . . . I think I made calls on business, coffee sales.'

'Let me aid your recollection. We spoke of Pauline Florislow.

You knew she had her office next to Dennison. Said she might be his girlfriend. Shortly after I left you, Miss Florislow falls from that office of hers before she has a chance to speak to me. Now who did you mention our conversation to?'

Mantebe stared at Odhiambo with every appearance of genuine astonishment. The girl on the bed whimpered again and huddled further under a blanket.

'Fell? But it's a long way . . . You mean she's dead?'

'*Ndio, bwana.* And when I say fell I didn't say she jumped or slipped. You understand?'

'Oh, my God. Listen, Odhiambo, this woman, she means nothing to me. You talked of her and I told you all I knew. I have no connection with her.'

'Who did you talk to, Mantebe? To give a summary of our conversation and just happen to say I was interested in the woman. Who?'

'No one . . .' Mantebe paused as Odhiambo's hand came out threateningly. 'Look, I didn't. I mean, I didn't mention the woman. I didn't think it was of any importance. I spoke to Mr Aramgu's personal assistant. Told him you had asked me questions about Dennison.'

'When was that?'

'In the evening. Six or seven.'

'Not as soon as I left?'

'No. I swear it.'

'Who else?'

'No one. Well. Yes. One more. John Matavu. He had called me earlier. He's worried about Dennison being killed on his golf course and some of Dennison's official transactions for Mbayazi Estates go through him. So I called him, told him you had been and there was nothing to worry about. In my view Dennison got mixed up in some personal *shauri* with his odd friends.'

'Including Miss Florislow.'

'No. I didn't mention her. I may have mentioned that man Silent.'

'And when was that?'

'I don't know. After I spoke to Aramgu's man. I know that.'

Odhiambo, felt ever so slightly foolish. Mantebe, in his judgement, was one of those whose lies were transparent because his body language gave him away. Conversely, he was inclined to believe him when these signs were absent. Here he was, guilty of breaking and entering, using threatening behaviour, and nothing to show for it, except that if Mantebe was not the source then Iocacci must be.

'OK. I hope you're telling the truth, Mantebe, or I'll be back. Now you and your playmate here keep quiet about this. I'm after a murderer and I need him quick. I won't allow anyone to get in the way. You savvy?'

'Odhiambo, I told you right before. Look at Dennison's *rifikis* not his business associates. Just because you and Mr Aramgu are old enemies.'

'Don't start speaking about me and my motives. Don't talk about me at all.'

'Are you . . . are you in some sort of trouble?'

Odhiambo snorted.

'No more than we all may be soon. Right, remember what I said.'

The girl on the bed had overcome her worst fears as she listened to the final exchanges. Now emboldened she asked, 'What about my door?'

Odhiambo looked at the door leaning drunkenly on one hinge as if he was seeing it for the first time.

'Ah, the door.' He fished his hand into his trouser pocket and retrieved some crumpled notes. 'Here. I'm sorry. Get it fixed.' He tossed the notes on to the bed. 'And keep your mouth shut.'

The girl quickly snatched the notes and reached for her purse under her pillow. She was growing in confidence by the minute.

'That's all very well, but it's not good enough . . .' As she looked up she saw she was wasting her breath – the big man had gone. She turned her attention to her lover. 'What are you –?'

'Shut your mouth. Now listen. You do what he said. Say nothing to nobody. You leave the matter to me.'

The girl decided to stay mute. Mantebe now sounded nearly as frightening as the bigger man.

McGuiry was not at home when the visitors arrived, but he had warned the houseman of what might possibly occur. Two vehicles unmarked with official signs and without government number plates disgorged men whom the houseman had no difficulty in classifying.

'Inspector Odhiambo? He is not staying here. Yes, he was here last night but he left. No, the *mzungu* is not in. I don't know when he will be back.'

They went through the house, inspecting every room, and when they finally left after grilling the houseman once more, two men seemed to be interminably engaged in inspecting a culvert at the corner of the cul-de-sac. The houseman smiled to himself and at the agreed time he dialled the number he had memorised.

13

The Boeing 747 lumbered slowly the last few yards before coming to a halt, neatly positioned to allow the passenger tunnel to be attached to the door like an umbilical cord. Cari Odhiambo, sitting by the window in the business class section, watched the process with the half-concentration typical of the dislocated mind of the long-haul, multi-time-zone-crossing passenger. She had been participating in the meeting in New York when the message came, via the Metroarcs head office, that she was needed urgently back in Nairobi as a major deal she had been instrumental in putting together was coming apart. She had called the manager of the Nairobi office, one Omuto-Ogali, who stressed the need for her to be present to work diplomatically on one of the recalcitrant key players who was unwilling to talk to anyone but herself. Omuto-Ogali assured her that he had tried to contact her husband to give him advance warning but he was out of town on a case. Cari called their home number so as to inform their servant that she was on her way home and for him to get a message to James, but the Nairobi operator informed her that her number was temporarily unavailable. One more call to a mutual friend, who said she hadn't seen James but would try to forward a message, and then she was on her way with Pan Am to London, there to connect to a British Airways flight to Nairobi. Now here she was, only half expecting to see James awaiting her, but assuming that at least Ali the office driver would be there to drive her home for a much-needed bath and change of clothes.

As she reached the exit from the plane the purser came forward and, pointing to a uniformed man in the tunnel, said that a member of the ground staff was waiting for her. This man now approached and indicated that Cari should leave the tunnel by a side door and descend the steps.

'There's a car waiting for you, Mrs Odhiambo. Give me your luggage tabs and I'll collect it and have it delivered.'

If Cari had been at full mental alertness she might have questioned whether Metroarcs, far less her husband, could pull enough weight to get her top VIP treatment, but long-haul travel takes its toll. She did have the presence of mind to query the need to pass through immigration control.

'No problem,' came the assurance, 'that will be done as you leave the closed part of the airport.'

Only when she was in the dark saloon and had digested the presence of two men who had State Security almost stamped on their foreheads did Cari realise she had been had and was now a hostage for God knew what purpose.

'It's that bastard Price-Allen, isn't it?' she said to one of the watchful heavies. 'This time I'll have his balls for ornaments.'

Brave words, but as the car headed for the city the true state of her predicament and its implication for the well-being of her husband sank in, and she was hard put to control the trembling that attacked her.

'James, I think we've both taken leave of our senses. Hiding out like this. It's like one of these stories you see people reading. It's not real.'

'If we were still in your place, Robert, we'd be in one of Price-Allen's safe houses by now. Or worse. You were right, your neighbour Silent must have put in a call as soon as you left.'

The two men were sitting on the verandah of a modest house on the fringes of the city on the road to Thika and thence to Mount Kenya. It was owned by a Luo friend of Odhiambo's who, when contacted the previous night and given a partial explanation of Odhiambo's need to go undercover for a day or two, had opened his door willingly. Odhiambo knew that his friend was a passionate opponent of the ruling party, but he nevertheless felt guilty at bringing him into the possible orbit of State Security.

McGuiry had joined Odhiambo at their temporary base after each had completed his first assignment.

'So your Mbayazi man dinna produce the goods? That seems to point the finger at the Eyetie. That's if someone did push that poor lassie out of the window. We still don't know that, ye ken?'

Odhiambo was still digesting the news of the raid on the Karen house as relayed by the houseman's telephone call of a few minutes earlier.

'Silent turning us in is not the significant fact in his behaviour, Robert. You can guess the questions I have.'

McGuiry shook his head. 'I don't follow, James. What are ye driving at?'

'How did he know who to call? And how did he know Price-Allen's goons were looking for me?'

'Och, ay. I see what you're getting at. I thought he might turn us in; but you're right – how did he know there was someone to turn us in to?'

'So what have we got? Let's take stock. One possibility is that Dennison's murder is connected with his work for Aramgu and Mbayazi Estates. Florislow was working with Dennison, so she went for the same reason as Dennison. This is what Price-Allen believes, or at least, wants me to believe. Evidence for this theory – very little. The theory that Aramgu is plotting some sort of coup and Dennison got to know about it is based on nothing but Price-Allen's views. OK, rumour is rife about Aramgu, but even if true it doesn't mean Dennison had inside knowledge. Mantebe claims Dennison was not connected with Aramgu's political interests, only his financial affairs through Mbayazi Estates. True, Dennison's body was found near Aramgu's house, but equally it was near Silent's house and it was on Matavu and Hill-Templeton's golf course so that proves nothing.

'The second theory is that Silent's little social group were into sex parties with drugs. My colleague Ntende says this is true. So a decadent group get stoned out of their minds and Dennison gets strangled in some perverted sex act. The group panic and take the body out on to the golf course and hide it. They then go to the golf club and pretend nothing's happened. Next day Pauline Florislow has second thoughts now the drugs have worn off. Iocacci sees her talking to me, tells Silent, and between them they push her out of her window before she tells me what she knows. Still, Silent is worried I know too much so he tips State Security off as to where I might be. This implies he knows someone who in turn knows that Price-Allen has put out a call on me.

Could be he's a buddy of Price-Allen and Price-Allen is protecting him by pointing me in the direction of Aramgu. Evidence for all of this is circumstantial, but there's a lot of it. If Mantebe is not lying it's only Iocacci who could have known that Pauline had spoken to me briefly. What's more, she'd been to see him, perhaps saying she wasn't happy about covering up Dennison's death, so whether he saw her speak to me or not, she had to go because they couldn't trust her.'

McGuiry had been inclined to the theory just expounded ever since he heard of Silent's inner circle and assessed the type of man he was, but he saw one huge problem with the case as Odhiambo set it out.

'James, I like it by and large. Silent and yon Price-Allen are just the sort of bastards who would be chummy with each other. But there's something I can't swallow in this and that's Mrs Dennison. If your theory's right Mrs Dennison is protecting her own husband's killers. From what you say and what I saw this morning she's hardly ever away from Silent's side.'

'Well, maybe that's it, Robert. Perhaps it wasn't an accident during some sort of orgy. Perhaps Anne Dennison plotted with Silent to get rid of her husband. Pauline Florislow suspected that she and Silent were having an affair and that Jim Dennison was in the way so they got rid of her too. Perhaps Anne Dennison is the real mover behind this thing. After all, most murders are domestic ones.'

'In which case the Eyeties might know nothing about it.'

'Possible, yes. But somehow I think Iocacci is in it. Although I admit I may be prejudiced because I can't stand drug pushers.'

'So that's it then? Silent and his friends either by accident during some sexual antics or to free the Dennison woman from her husband.'

'There's one more possibility. Golf club politics. Matavu, Hill-Templeton and Dennison are the *bwana mkubwas* of the Royal Ngong. Dennison was the new entry into the power group. He's a financial whizz. He finds that Hill-Templeton and Matavu, who are close as grains on a maize cob, are fiddling the club's books. So they decide to have a new eighteenth tee using Dennison as the base.'

McGuiry shook his head. 'I dunno, James. That's a wee bit too far-fetched for me. I like the sex party.'

'Yeah, so do I. I rang Dr Kisani who's doing the post-mortem

102

on Dennison. He confirmed he was strangled, but it doesn't take a pathologist to tell me that. I asked him to look for evidence of sexual arousal or whatever. That would be crucial to the accident during sex theory. We won't know that until tommorow and by then my access to him may not be so easy. But you're right. That's the one we go with. And the man we've got to break is Iocacci. Or his wife. And we haven't much time. So you drop me at Iocacci's fancy showroom and if he's there you go on to his house and see what you can do with the wife while I have a go at him.'

McGuiry contemplated for a long moment, trying to formulate the right words.

'James, I'm with it all the way as I said last night. But do ye no think you'd be better getting away?'

'We had this out last night, Robert.'

'Ay, I know. But now we know they're after you, it somehow seems different. Time to think again.'

'No. My best chance is to get the killer quick and take the case to Masonga. Then even Price-Allen may have difficulty putting me away.'

'But if Price-Allen is right, there's trouble no too far away which might sweep him and his henchmen away. Why not lie low for the nonce?'

'My Luo instincts, Robert. Price-Allen and me, we've been destined for this ever since he came into my life. Even before that when he tried to get his hooks into Cari. I've got to go on. But you, that's different.'

The old man got to his feet.

'I had to try one more time to make ye see sense, but I'm staying by to try and keep your fool head on those big shoulders.'

Ten minutes later, McGuiry pulled his old Land Rover into the kerb outside the gleaming showroom in which the three exotic cars were on display. Odhiambo got out and hurried inside, only to return within a minute.

'Damn. The bloody man's gone out of town. So Mrs Iocacci's our only bet. Here's the address, Langata. I know the road.'

Their luck improved on arrival at the Iocacci residence. The gateman let them in and a house servant who met them as they pulled up at the side of the house confirmed that the lady of the house was in. They found her sitting in the lounge with a plate of sandwiches and a pot of coffee on the table, which Odhiambo presumed was her intended lunch, but a glass in her hand indicated she was still on her pre-lunch drinks. The ice in her glass tinkled against the crystal as Gianna Iocacci rose to greet the two men.

'Mrs Iocacci? Chief Inspector Odhiambo. I'm investigating the death of Mr Jim Dennison. This is a colleague of mine, Mr McGuiry.'

The fear in her eyes was detectable to both men and Odhiambo's instincts went further: he had an almost physical sense of the vibrations emanating from the woman. She was dark, tanned, slim with a full-lipped sensual face. Normally, Odhiambo thought, she might have communicated sexual overtones, but what his senses picked up today was a woman whose nerves were stretched as tight as a violin string. That plus alcohol should be enough. He almost grinned with confidence. Whatever this woman knew should not be difficult to extract. And there was no husband or Michael Silent to act as a buffer.

The woman stammered her greetings, looked with vague recollection at McGuiry, and invited them to sit. Odhiambo chose an upright chair opposite the sofa where his quarry resumed her seat. McGuiry plumped himself into an armchair on the woman's right.

'Your husband is away?'

'Yes . . . yes. He was intending to stay with me today. I was . . . we both were upset. We have had too much bad news. Then he got a telephone call. I'm not sure who it was, but he said he had to go. To Naivasha. He was angry. He didn't want to leave me. He tried to contact a friend, but he was out. I told him I'd be OK.'

Odhiambo smiled at her, a reassuring, nothing to worry about smile which had often served him well.

'Of course. I can see you're well able to cope. We only want some background information. You don't mind?'

'No . . . no. I don't mind, but I don't know anything.'

'You don't know what we want yet, Mrs Iocacci. You say you are upset by bad news. Would this have been the death of another friend as well as Mr Dennison?'

'Yes, that's right. It's very sad, no? A close friend. You know of this?'

'Pauline Florislow? Yes. I was there.'

'What . . . what happened? How did she fall?'

104

'I'm hoping to find that out. Was Miss Florislow a close friend?'

'Yes . . . yes. Not, what do you say . . . long-standing, but I liked her very much.'

'And news of her death upset you more than that of Mr Dennison?'

'Yes . . . well, no. Jim's death was terrible. He was murdered, wasn't he?'

'When did you last see both Mr Dennison and Miss Florislow?'

'Pauline was with us Tuesday night when the news came that Jim's body had been found. We were at the club.'

'And Jim, when did you last see him?'

'I'm not . . . I'm not sure.'

'Come, Mrs Iocacci. Jim Dennison was a friend. You were part of a social group. Surely you can remember when you last saw him?'

'I think some of us had a drink together on Monday evening.'

'Where?'

'Where? Does it matter where? The club or one of our houses.'

'Mr Michael Silent's house?'

Confirmation was evident in the woman's eyes although her tongue prevaricated.

'It might have been. He's very, what do you say, *simpatico*. He always makes us welcome.'

'Hospitable, is he? A good host?' Gianna nodded eagerly, her dark hair falling forward across her face. She brushed it back with one hand in a casually elegant manner. 'He is, of course, from an old settler family. And you and your husband are clearly of upper society. Tell me, were the Dennisons quite your type? Or Mr Silent's for that matter?'

The question was unexpected and the woman's eyes opened wider in surprise. Then it was as if she was reassured that the conversation was on safe ground. She spoke with greater confidence and animation.

'Oh, the Dennisons are OK. I mean, Anne Dennison amuses me. I like her. She is, what do you say, earthy, no? Maybe she not go to good school but she is good to have as friend. I play golf with her every week. She is much better golfer than me.'

'And Jim Dennison?'

'Oh, Jim. He was OK, too. He was handsome and charming, no?'

'Would you say Michael Silent was the dominant member of your group?'

'I . . . I . . . How do you mean? We are all friends. It is not like a business. There is no boss.'

'Mrs Iocacci, I have met Mr Silent. He has a very powerful personality. One cannot mistake it, even at a first meeting.'

'Yes . . . well, he is, as you say, a great man. He is very smart.'

'You say your husband tried to contact a friend before he left. Was it Michael Silent he called?'

'Yes, yes it was. How did you know?'

'Because all of you turn to him when there are questions to be answered, don't you? Your husband wanted him to come and see you, didn't he?'

'Well, Stef was afraid that the police . . . well, I mean, you would come and frighten me.'

'I hope I'm not doing that, am I, Mrs Iocacci?'

'Well, no. You're very nice. But you know what I mean. Stef was worried.'

'Because Michael Silent supplies the drugs that help you all to perform well in your group sex exercises, is that it?'

The sudden switch from relatively harmless questions to that of her worst fears, combined with the more aggressive tone of voice, left Gianna Iocacci panic-stricken.

'Oh no. What are you saying? I can't . . . I can't speak to you. Please go. Stefano warned me this might happen.'

'Mrs Iocacci, I have no time to play games. A killer has killed twice. Yes, twice. Your friend Pauline was murdered. Thrown to her death. I must, will, have the truth.'

McGuiry managed to bite back a request to be careful. He realised that Odhiambo intended to put the woman into shock. It looked as if he had succeeded: Gianna Iocacci's face had become ashen against the darkness of her hair and she clutched her hands in her lap in an attempt to control their trembling.

'It can't be anything to do with us?'

'It has got everything to do with you. Just yesterday your husband saw me talking to Pauline. An hour later she was dead. She wanted to tell me something. Was it something to do with Stefano or was he protecting you?'

'Stop it! Stop it! This is nonsense. Stefano wouldn't harm Pauline. Why, he was . . .' Her voice tailed off and a hand shot to her mouth. She bit into her knuckle and her eyes were like those of a condemned prisoner who hears the erecting of the gallows. Odhiambo waited. 'You must go and see Michael. He will explain everything.'

'He was what to Pauline? You were about to tell me. He had a relationship with her, didn't he, and you were, are, jealous?'

'No. It wasn't like that.' There was a long pause but Odhiambo waited patiently. The woman was clearly about to crack. 'You don't understand. We meet together and we enjoy each others' company. There's nothing illegal about sharing pleasures. OK, some people may think it's odd, but its natural.'

'And you were sharing those pleasures on Monday night?'

'It was a dinner-party with us, the usual ones, and a new couple. New to Nairobi. They didn't seem to take up Michael's suggestions and left early. I think Michael was cross. His judgement is usually good, no? Anne went too. She has been having doubts lately. You know, about the sex side of things.'

'But you, Stefano, Jim Dennison, Michael Silent and Pauline stayed on? Five in a bed.'

'Don't be silly. You make it sound ridiculous. We use different rooms.'

'But without Anne the numbers were unequal.'

'Well, I looked after Jim and Michael. Pauline went with Stefano.'

'And what drug did you take, Gianna?' The woman went silent. Again the hand went to the mouth, the knuckles between the teeth. 'It's no good stopping now. Michael handed round the powder, or was it a needle?'

'It's not like that. We are not heroin addicts. OK, Michael has some cocaine. It's only for our own use. He doesn't sell it to us, I mean. It's a private thing. We don't do anyone any harm. It helps us enjoy ourselves. You don't understand, do you? Stefano says ordinary people don't understand. We are special, he says. There's no harm in it. If Anne didn't want to join in nobody pressured her. Well, Michael was a bit upset. He told her she was very special – to him, I mean. Oh, I don't know, talking to you makes it all seem unclean.'

Suddenly the tears flowed and Gianna Iocacci fell forward off the sofa on to her knees, beating her fists against her temples. McGuiry with a quick look at Odhiambo got up and knelt beside her.

'Come on, my dear. It's nearly all over. It's better to be honest.

Y'see, James knew more or less what you're saying. Come now, and sit down while I get ye a fresh drink.'

After a few minutes and clutching a large gin and tonic, Gianna Iocacci lay back on the sofa looking exhausted. Odhiambo had not moved.

'Now I must have the important part, Gianna. What did Jim say or do that was unusual?'

'Nothing, really. But he'd had a lot to drink as . . . as well as the other stuff. He wasn't up to . . . well . . . performing. Michael made fun of him. Said something about it wouldn't do if his boss found out. He didn't like men who couldn't handle two at a time. Something like that. And . . . and Jim got angry. Said he could tell Michael a lot about . . . and he named somebody . . . I don't remember. And there wouldn't be time for sex for a while. He had other plans. Michael stopped teasing him after that. Could see he was upset.'

'How do you remember all this if you were high as well?'

'I wasn't. I don't take the stuff. Well, hardly ever. I mean, it's the men who need it, isn't it?'

'And what happened when the party broke up?'

'Stef and I went home. It was two . . . three o'clock, something like that. Pauline was fast asleep in the bedroom and Jim had passed out in the lounge. Michael said he'd look after Jim.'

'Did you see Jim Dennison again?'

'No. The next day Anne asked me what time we left Michael's. I told her and said Jim was still there. I didn't like to ask what time he came home. In the evening she said he was working late. She seemed not quite herself and Michael was talking quietly, whispering really, to her. Then she seemed to relax. And then . . . then we heard Jim's body had been found.'

'And you've been scared ever since?'

'Well, wouldn't you? It is scary. Stef says I'm foolish. Oh, my god, what's he going to say when he comes home?'

McGuiry, who still had an old hunter's hearing, said, 'I think he may be here. I heard a car. Don't worry, we'll speak to him.'

The woman got to her feet and went to the door. There was the sound of a door slamming and hurried footsteps. Stefano Iocacci appeared in the doorway.

'Whose Land . . .' He looked at his wife and then at Odhiambo and McGuiry standing side by side. 'What's going on?' He looked back at his wife. 'What have you been saying?' His scrutiny seemed to confirm his worst fears. 'You stupid bitch, what have you been saying?' He grabbed her arm.

Odhiambo spoke. 'That will do, Mr Iocacci. Leave your wife alone or I'll break you in two.'

Iocacci turned towards the policeman, genuinely startled.

'What the hell do you mean, coming here, threatening us . . .?'

'Shut up and listen. You're in big enough trouble without making it worse.'

Thirty minutes later, Odhiambo and McGuiry took their leave. Between them they had at least half persuaded Iocacci that his wife's explanation had saved him from being arrested. Odhiambo had told him to tell no one, particularly Silent, of what had occurred.

'You may be under his spell, Mr Iocacci, but if you speak to him before I do I'll charge you with conspiracy.'

After he had repeated variants of this threat to the Italian, Iocacci promised silence. One thing he refused to admit was telling anyone about Pauline Florislow's meeting with Odhiambo.

'So, OK. I saw you both outside. So what? I didn't know she wanted to see you later. If she knew anything about Jim Dennison she could tell anyone for all I care. Gianna and I had left Jim sleeping it off. We never saw him again. I didn't see Silent until later that evening when he told me Pauline was dead. I never mentioned even then that I'd seen you outside my office. No reason to.'

'And you didn't go to her office to tell her to keep quiet about your little group?'

'No. I've got witnesses that I was still in my office for at least two hours. She was dead by then, I'm told.'

And nothing would shake him from these protestations.

14

Odhiambo sat next to McGuiry as they headed back towards the city centre. He was thinking hard. On the face of it, the field of suspects was narrowing: if the Iocaccis were to be believed, Jim Dennison had thrown a name and an implied threat at Michael Silent while under the influence of drink and drugs. Despite his repetitive probing of both Stefano and Gianna Iocacci neither claimed to have heard or remembered the name Dennison had blurted out. If the Iocaccis went home, as they said, it left Dennison with Silent and Florislow and nobody seemed to have seen him alive again. Well, only one person, Anne Dennison, but her claim to have seen her husband the following morning could be a Silent-inspired misdirection of the police. Now the woman was dead too it left Silent as a possible killer of both. Did Silent strangle him because Dennison threatened to expose him in some way? And the woman knew something so she had to go too. But if Iocacci was not lying, how had Silent learned of Pauline Florislow's wish to talk to Odhiambo?

Or had Dennison blurted out something that would have hurt his boss, Aramgu? And somehow he had got to hear of it and had Dennison kidnapped later and killed. Was Silent tied up with Aramgu in some way? Was Price-Allen right? Dennison's death was caused by his knowledge of the impending coup. And Florislow's intended meeting with Odhiambo had been passed on by Mantebe, despite his protestations to the contrary.

He cursed himself silently. Somehow he was missing something. He had the pieces but they didn't form a picture. Somewhere in the back of his mind was the nagging feeling that there was a piece he had, but couldn't retrieve, that would tie the rest together. Meanwhile time was running out. Once more he started to run through the interviews he had carried out since yesterday morning. He must make it come together.

Suddenly Odhiambo's preoccupation was shattered by a loud Scottish expletive from his companion. He looked across at his friend. He was braking the Land Rover and staring up through the top of the windscreen.

'What's up?'

'I canna quite see.' Their vehicle was now stationary beside the kerb approaching the first roundabout leading to Uhuru Highway, the main dual carriageway that ran the length of the city. 'Get out, James, and look up. There's a plane up there with a message.'

McGuiry's tone conveyed sufficient alarm and urgency to cause Odhiambo to open the door and jump down rather than ask for clarification. McGuiry started to clamber down somewhat more slowly. Odhiambo scanned the sky – yes, there was a small aircraft towing some sort of banner with an advertisement on it. The plane had passed in front of them but had now turned, leaving the banner at an angle that rendered the writing unreadable. Odhiambo turned to McGuiry who had joined him on the pavement and was also focusing his eyes on the sky.

'What's the matter, Robert? What did it say?'

'I'm no sure. Wait a while, yon plane is circling. We'll be able to see it anon.'

True enough, the plane was clearly making a circuit of the city. Odhiambo saw the concern on his friend's face, but bit back another query and held himself in check. It seemed agonisingly slow, but at last the banner was closer and swung broadside to their line of vision. Odhiambo stared at it, his mind at first uncomprehending. He saw the words made up of big letters:

BACK WITH RD CONTACT PLEASE CARI

Suddenly the words took on a meaning that burned itself into his brain. He swore repetitively and obscenely as he struggled for self-control. He hardly felt McGuiry's hand on his shoulder.

'Steady now, laddie. Keep your grip on things. How d'ye read it? I thought your good wife was abroad.'

Odhiambo stared at his friend, but the words made no impact. His mind was a maelstrom of emotions from which one emerged to dominate his whole being: the urge to place his hands around Price-Allen's neck and twist his head off his shoulders. He turned back to the Land Rover.

'Get in and get me to the Conference Centre.'

McGuiry obeyed, resuming his place behind the wheel and taking the exit off the roundabout on to Harambee Avenue to head towards the tall building already visible.

'Now, James, listen to me. What's going on? You must tell me. What's happening?'

Odhiambo stared ahead, but this time at least he recognised McGuiry's plea.

'Somehow that evil bastard has got hold of Cari. Like he got her father when I was there. RD – that's Price-Allen, he's RD. Price-Allen.'

'But what's that plane doing up there announcing it to the world?'

"Cos he doesn't know where I am. He knows I'm still around and he'll get me sooner or later, but he needs to get his hands on me urgently. So he gets his message up where I'm bound to see it. OK. Stop here.' The Land Rover was approaching the outside entrance to the centre. 'Don't go in. We don't want you caught up in this.'

'But what are ye going to do, James? Don't walk into his trap, mon. That won't do Cari any good.'

'For some reason he needs me to get Aramgu. So I'll do it once I'm sure Cari is safe. Then I'll kill the sod with my own hands.'

'No, no, no, James. I canna let you do this – '

'There's no way of stopping me. Look, if you want to do something useful, go and see Masonga, Superintendent Masonga . . . my boss. Tell him everything. Price-Allen trying to spike Aramgu's plans. Using me for the purpose of linking Aramgu to Dennison's death. And whatever happens to me, the pair of you try and make sure Cari gets out of the country, if he's brought her back here.'

'Now, listen to me, James . . .'

But it was too late. The door opened and Odhiambo was gone. McGuiry watched the large man disappear through the gates towards the entrance to the tall office building. It was his turn to swear long and hard to himself.

15

'Ah, the wanderer returns.'

The two burly men on either side of Odhiambo, as he stood inside the door of the rather ordinary-looking domestic room, quickly grabbed his arms as he started to move forward towards the speaker seated primly on a Victorian-style desk chair that looked as if it was badly in need of repair and refurbishment. The room was sparsely furnished with similar old-fashioned pieces that had seen better days. Price-Allen was seated at right angles to a battered table at which he had been reading prior to swinging his chair around at Odhiambo's entrance.

'Where is my wife? If you've harmed a hair – '

Price-Allen raised a languid hand.

'No clichés, please. The dear lady is in my care in conditions of some comfort, although I have to say she is demonstrating a degree of hostility to me. Understandable, I suppose.'

'I want to see her. Get her here or I'll break your neck.'

'You must try to broaden your vocabulary, Odhiambo. You will see her in a moment. First, you will listen, do you understand?'

'How did you get her back to Nairobi?' Despite his rage, Odhiambo's curiosity got the upper hand. 'If you got those American thugs – '

'Nothing like that. Just a little subterfuge. I knew your tendency to disobedience, you see, so your disappearance was predictable. I'm pleased you saw my message.'

One of Odhiambo's escorts spoke for the first time.

'He came to the office, *bwana*. We were waiting. We bring him here as you ordered.'

Price-Allen looked at his man with unconcealed venom.

'I do not need to be told the obvious.' He turned back to Odhiambo. 'You have tried my patience, Odhiambo. I gave you a basis for arresting Aramgu for the murder you are investigating. I also gave you a national duty reason for acting promptly while his whereabouts were known. You deserted your post, so deserve no consideration. However, I intend to give you one more chance. Unfortunately, locating your quarry may now be more difficult. You have, however, brought that on yourself. There is no time to waste and you had better hope that your Luo gods are with you.'

Odhiambo managed to close the gap between them, dragging his guards a couple of paces before they brought him to a halt once more. He spat at the white man in the chair, but the spittle fell short. He felt a blow in his kidney but ignored it.

'You've screwed me up since we first met. And Cari too. This is it, you bastard. This time it's to the finish between you and me.'

'Oh, stop being so theatrical. You still don't understand, do you? You are here to do my bidding.' He picked up a telephone from the table and gave a brief command. After a short pause the door on the far side of the room from where Odhiambo stood opened and in came Cari Odhiambo with her own pair of minders. She looked dishevelled and angry, but Odhiambo's heart leapt with both joy at the sight of her, and hope, because she seemed unhurt. 'My dear lady, I hope you haven't been causing too much trouble with your tantrums. Here is your husband. I told you he would come.'

A nod from Price-Allen and the Odhiambos were released to come together in each other's arms. Cari had endured a long journey and had been given no opportunity for a shower since her kidnap, but Odhiambo's senses swam at the familiar smell of her hair and the touch of her flawless face, somewhat flushed with anger and frustration though it was. It was Cari who retained her grip on the reality they faced. She pulled away despite his reluctance to loosen his grip.

'James, darling. Sorry to be making your life difficult. I don't know what he wants, but you do what you think best. Don't worry about me.'

'Oh, Cari. God, I'm glad you're all right. I promise you we'll do what you've wanted. We'll leave this place. For good. Once I've settled with this bastard here.'

'Ssh. Don't make silly promises. What's going on? What does he want with us?'

Price-Allen was watching them with an air of sardonic amusement.

'I can, as it happens, enlighten you, my dear. Your husband has a little job to do in the line of duty. Meanwhile, you will continue to enjoy my hospitality. Once he has completed his task you will be reunited and free to go where you will.'

Some chance, thought Odhiambo. He was sure now that he was not destined to return after his securing of Aramgu. Price-Allen was playing one of his intricate chess games in which Aramgu was the opposition queen and Odhiambo the sacrificial pawn. But he had no choice but to obey, then try to forestall whatever Price-Allen had planned in order to get back and somehow release Cari. More out of desperation than hope he tried to set a condition of his own.

'Set her free now, Price-Allen. Set her free and I'll do what you want. You know I'm a man of my word.'

Price-Allen laughed. 'You're always a source of amusement, Inspector. Let's not waste more time. There is no bargaining to be done. Your wife is safe here in this house. In fact, I believe you were here courtesy of Mr Aramgu once. But Mrs Odhiambo will not be in the cellar where he housed you – at least for as long as you do what you're told. I'm awaiting confirmation that Aramgu is back in his house by the golf course. Once that is received you, together with an ample squad of these men, will go and get him and take him to the central station cells.'

'How do I know you will let Cari go?'

'You don't, except for my word.' Price-Allen raised his head to stem Odhiambo's protest. 'Quite so. I have been known to dissemble. But I have never harmed this young lady, even when I could have ruined her over the little matter of the drugs when she was an American student. I kept my word regarding her parents and I will keep it now. There is no advantage to me in harming her.' Odhiambo opened his mouth to continue his protest, but was forestalled by that insistent, compelling voice. 'No more debate. It is time for action. Take her away. Bring him to the basement office.'

'Tonight, Lijodi, you must move tonight. I called you here because the matter is urgent. Rumours are all over Nairobi and what is more the *mzungu* is upwind of them. He is preparing to move against me . . . us. Whatever that fool Sasaweni may think, Price-Allen is dangerous. But Sasaweni says he is ready so you are the man who must now roll the bones. Take the city tonight and declare Kiwonka President before anyone has time to react.'

'When the British trained me in England, Aramgu, they taught me never to jump without checking the parachute once again. This is what I am doing. Going through the plans to make sure everything works. It is not safe to change the timetable now.'

Aramgu snorted. Why did he have to put up with these donkeys? They were once again enjoying the hospitality of the ailing Kentui, who sat now in an armchair, his eyes flicking from one of his heavyweight guests to the other. His face was etched with pain and the eye-sockets seemed to have shrunk into the skull, but the eyes within these sockets still burned with determination to fight the pain and live to see his clan back in its rightful place. He watched as Aramgu took a gulp from his glass of whisky. Lijodi watched the glass also, disapproval showing clearly on his face. Now the big man shook his head.

'To wait is more dangerous, I tell you. By the gods, Lijodi, are you and your troops women? I'm not asking you to jump out of your bloody plane. Just march into Nairobi and take the places agreed and stand with a big chest in front of the television.'

'What you mean is you want me to put the plan at risk because you are worried about your safety. Well, Aramgu, my friend, come with me: my men will look after you well until it is time to move.'

Aramgu heaved himself to his feet. He took Lijodi's words as a threat. Who did this man think he was? Did Lijodi believe that he, Lijodi, had the brains to carry out the coup? Aramgu suddenly had an insight into how military men who are used to front a coup end up with ideas of becoming the President. It was time to put this jumped-up soldier in his place.

A cough from the chair on his left was not very loud, but it served to summon Aramgu's attention. Kentui, with an effort, pulled himself away from the support of the chair-back and sat up, arms extended to the protagonists as if to soften a blow.

'Enough. Read your history, gentlemen, and see what happens to conspirators when they fall out before their task is completed. I must pass on a message from our leader. I took the liberty of contacting him when Aramgu told me of the accelerated timetable.' The speaker saw Aramgu stiffen. 'No offence, my friend, but Mr Kiwonka likes to use me as a messenger sometimes. Colonel Lijodi, your future Commander-in-Chief asks that you accede to the new timetable. He asked me to tell you he has every confidence in you. He will start his journey home tonight and hopes to salute you as a hero at Kenyatta Airport in the morning.'

Lijodi got to his feet and seemed to stand at attention as he received Kiwonka's words. He bowed slightly as Kentui slumped back in his chair as if his energy had been sapped in passing on the instructions.

'Thank you, *mzee*. I am pleased our future President has confidence in me. Tell him I will be there at the airport ready to escort him to State House.' He turned back to the discomfited Aramgu. 'Go home and wait, Aramgu. Take shelter while the fighting men do battle. I will contact you when it is safe for you to come forward.'

The words were said in a level voice, the contempt contained in them given away only by the curl of his lips. Aramgu's reaction was in no way concealed. He let out a bellow of rage and smashed his huge fist on to the small table beside his chair, causing his whisky to leap into the air, fall and smash on the parquet floor.

'You dare to talk to me as if I was a woman? You go too far, soldier. I have been exposing myself to arrest in bringing us to this point, while you stayed happily in your barracks, saluting the Big Man.'

Once again, the old man summoned from somewhere the energy to intervene with his superior self-control.

'Enough, I tell you both. Our lives are all at stake because the cause is great. Our country's destiny. You must not threaten it now because you have the tempers of little children.'

The Colonel did now formally snap his heels and his hand saluted the man in the chair.

'You are right, *mzee*. I apologise to our friend here. Let us shake hands. There is enough work for us all in front of us.'

It was Aramgu's fleshy lips that now started to twist into a sneer, but with an effort of will he clamped them together and took the soldier's hand in both of his. Lijodi might be a buffoon, but for now he was needed.

'Very well, Lijodi. I accept. The next task is yours. Do not let us down.'

A few minutes later Kentui's servant saw the two visitors to the cars which awaited them with their chauffeurs; the cars were their private saloons rather than ones carrying official insignia. Kentui waited for his servant to return to help him to his feet and to his bed. Why should such a cause as his be dependent on such as those two? Of Lijodi he had no great fear. Limited in intellect he might be, but as a leader of his men he would perform. Aramgu was another matter, but with luck his role was nearly over. He had warned Kiwonka that Aramgu would have to be watched. Now he believed that watching would not be enough. Ah well, the gods of Mount Kenya would decide.

Odhiambo sat in the Land Rover trying once more to move his mind into a higher gear and find a solution to his predicament. He was seated next to the driver, but behind him were three State Security men in plain clothes who were there to assist him with the arrest of Aramgu. It was what else they were there to do that concerned Odhiambo. They were parked in the driveway of the house that belonged to Hill-Templeton's relative. The gate had been opened by one of the security men. Odhiambo had asked the senior of the Price-Allen men the reason for the choice, to be told that it was well shielded from the access and convenient because it was unoccupied.

117

'How do you know Aramgu will come here this evening? Perhaps he is with his friends or with a girl at the Equatorial Moon. We could be wasting our time.'

The security man shrugged. 'Others are looking. If necessary we will go elsewhere. But his bodyguards are here, we are told. They are waiting for him.'

'How many bodyguards? They may stop us arresting him.'

A thin smile greeted Odhiambo's concern.

'Let us worry about the others. Your task is to arrest the big man. After all, Odhiambo, you are the policeman here. You are the detective.'

There must be others, Odhiambo thought. Or else Aramgu's men had been subverted. Nothing would surprise him if Price-Allen was involved. But he could see the final act of the script. Aramgu and himself shot by these thugs sitting behind him, the blame put on Aramgu's men for killing a senior police officer, and praise for the killers for not letting Aramgu escape.

The radio crackled; the driver, who was wearing earphones, listened and then half turned to nod at his superior who smiled and leaned forward to speak once more with Odhiambo.

'Your wait is nearly over, Odhiambo. He comes.'

Come on, Odhiambo urged himself. There must be a way out. Call out a warning to Aramgu and his men? What good would that do? And Cari would still be in Price-Allen's clutches. He prayed to his Luo ancestors. Come to my aid and I will give up this life and return to work the land of my fathers by the great Lake. But even in his extremity he knew no spirit would believe him. Then strengthen my arm because I am Odhiambo and I have brought honour to my family and my tribe. He heard as if it was real a mocking laugh in his head and the voices say, 'What honour, Odhiambo? You let others see to your mother's needs while you live on the earnings of a woman who does not know the duties of a wife. A woman who is not of us.'

The man with the radio listened again. He turned once more and announced in Swahili the imminent arrival of their quarry. The man behind Odhiambo barked a command and the driver started the Land Rover and slowly emerged from the drive on to the murram-surfaced lane. The vehicle stopped broadside across the lane, completely blocking it.

'Out, quickly, unless you want Aramgu in your lap.' The State Security man laughed. 'We wait at the gate here.'

118

As he got out, Odhiambo could appreciate the choice of spot. The direction from which Aramgu would come past the house where he had stayed with McGuiry was just around a curve in the lane. Aramgu or his driver would not see the blockade until it was too late. Should he run for it? God! Keep a grip on yourself, Odhiambo! The only reason he was here was Cari. He had to go through with it. He heard a vehicle as it turned off the tarmac on to the earth. He felt his stomach tremble and a movement in his bowels. Get a grip, man. You've looked down the barrel of a gun before. You've been at the mercy of a madman. Don't panic now.

The car suddenly appeared, moving quite fast, too fast for a narrow lane. The driver braked too late; the car skidded, throwing clouds of dry murram into the air, and then hit the Land Rover a glancing blow before ending with its front wheels in the shallow ditch on the far side of the lane. Another car came round the bend, but with more care, the driver bringing it to a halt behind the scene of the collision. Two State Security men were already at the rear doors of the lead car, one each side; they yanked them open and pointed their revolvers at their target who, swearing obscenely, was trying to pull himself upright having been flung into the well between the two front seats.

Four men piled out of the second car and Odhiambo caught sight of machine pistols.

'Right, Odhiambo. There he is. Do what you came to do.' The security officer was slightly behind Odhiambo, who could seng see the pistol close to his spine.

When would it happen? When would the shooting start? Odhiambo walked slowly over towards the crashed car: Aramgu had regained his seat and was now staring at the man guarding the door on Odhiambo's side, spitting out obscenitites which emerged with even more venom as he saw Odhiambo approach. The driver, Odhiambo noticed, was slumped, stunned, over the steering wheel.

The guard at the car door ordered Aramgu out in curt Swahili. Odhiambo, mustering all the authority he could in his voice, given the dryness of his throat, countermanded the instruction in English.

'No, wait. I must speak to him first in the car. The usual caution.' This intervention seemed to disconcert the guard, who looked uncertainly across the road towards his superior.

Odhiambo seized the chance to slip into the seat beside Aramgu, who paused in his invective at this unexpected turn of events. 'Listen to me, Aramgu.' Odhiambo spoke in a low but urgent whisper. 'We are both caught in a trap. Your only chance may be to run for your house. These are Price-Allen's men.'

Aramgu was sweating and there was a smell of fear emanating from him, but he was listening. There was, however, no time for more; the senior security man had crossed the road to deal with Odhiambo's unexpected move.

'What are you playing at, Odhiambo? Get out of the car and bring this man with you.'

His gun was now pointing directly at Odhiambo, any pretence that the policeman was in charge now gone.

'Get the driver out of the car and see what injuries he has.' Odhiambo was desperately playing for time, seeking an opening where none existed. 'See, he's coming round. I wish to speak to the suspect privately. He has information Price-Allen needs.'

The original guard now found his voice.

'He was saying something to him. Warning him.'

'Your last chance, Odhiambo. Out or I shoot you where you are.'

Odhiambo slowly eased his legs out on to the road. Could he make a grab for the guns? No, his main target had stepped back as if reading his intention, and the other man on his side was sheltered by the door. Not to speak of the heavily armed reinforcements from the other car.

'This is not what Price-Allen wants. Aramgu is a suspect, that is all.' Nobody was listening: indeed the only response Odhiambo heard was the click of a machine pistol being placed into automatic mode. He half turned his head to Aramgu who was pressing up against him as if using him as a shield against bullets. 'This is it. Run!' He stepped forward, hands out in a placatory gesture, but as Aramgu rose to his feet he bent forward and headed straight past the guard behind the car door, grabbing his gun arm as he drew level and jerking the man off his feet.

Aramgu was at his heels and Odhiambo had a momentary thought that far from him sheltering Aramgu the reverse was true, for Aramgu's considerable bulk was between him and the gunmen. Now to his senses came the sound of automatic fire – the fast-repeating detonations reaching his ears and seemingly becoming amplified as they passed to his brain which had every screaming nerve alert for the impact of the bullets. But still the sound signals came – the snapping of the cartridges through the firing chamber – and still his brain waited for the nerves to transmit the pain. He could still hear, also, Aramgu's panting breaths behind him. He was at the driveway into Michael Silent's house and dived behind the hedge. But now another set of sounds had been translated belatedly by his fevered brain: the gurgling cries of men in their death throes and the sounds of bullets hitting metal. He turned back as Aramgu went past, stumbling with the effort of driving his massive body forward.

The scene that greeted him threatened to unhinge his mind. One of the two men who had threatened him and Aramgu lay on the ground twitching although much of his head seemed to be missing. The second man, who had been on the other side of the car, was not in his view. The senior of the trio was arched backwards over the bonnet of the Land Rover, blasted there it seemed by a torrent of bullets which had turned his torso into a gurgling expanse of blood and tissue. The windscreen of the Land Rover in which he had arrived was missing and he could see the driver slumped against the door, his head thrown back in a last statement of mortal agony. Behind this scene of carnage were the men with the automatic pistols who had followed Aramgu's car and advised Odhiambo's companions of his arrival. One of these men stepped forward, glancing at the two bodies in his path, but seeking the men who had vanished behind the hedge.

'Bwana Aramgu. Come back. You are safe. And the policeman. Ah, you are there. You too.'

New shouts came from further up the lane, the direction of Aramgu's property. Aramgu had reached the corner of Silent's property, but could get no further because Silent's hedge concealed a steel fence on the other side. He shouted back. Odhiambo presumed that his bodyguards were finally rallying to his cause. Another of the surviving band of killers was running forward, also shouting to the approaching newcomers. Misunderstanding leading to further mayhem seemed the most likely outcome and Odhiambo thought of trying to escape around Silent's house on to the golf course. Unfortunately, the man who had spotted him was now too close.

Aramgu had made enough sense of the various shouted exchanges to have regained a modicum of composure. He looked at the man who had called to reassure him and with a voice which still betrayed some of his earlier fear managed to put a question.

'I have seen you, no? With Sasaweni?'

'*Ndio, bwana*. I am one of Sasaweni's men. Mantuli. We were sent to kill you by the *mzungu*, but he doesn't know that we no longer take orders from him. We have removed your enemies. Now we take you to safe place.'

Aramgu seemed to reinflate himself, straightening his body and dragging in air that a minute earlier he thought he would never breathe.

'Aha. *Asante sana*, man of Sasaweni. He was right to be confident. Now what else have we here: the *mzungu's* boy, the Luo son of donkeys.'

The subsiding noise in the background signalled the establishment of understanding of the new coalitions between new and former bodyguards. The danger of further gunfire seemed to have diminished, but Odhiambo knew he was still in jeopardy – a prisoner now of the man who most hated him.

'I tried to warn you, Aramgu. We were both to be killed.'

Aramgu's spirits were improving by the second. The great laugh of derision, which Odhiambo remembered so well, boomed up from the depths of his belly.

'Do not tell me you are a Sasaweni man too, Odhiambo. I do not believe it. You have been Price-Allen's man too long.'

'I am not Price-Allen's man and never was. He uses me and I am too small a boy to prevent him. He has my wife. My coming after you was the price of her life.'

'Your wife? Bito's daughter? He's welcome to her. Sam Bito betrayed Kiwonka, but tonight he will return and turds like you must be flushed away.'

Mantuli, the so-called Sasaweni man, having listened to these exchanges between Aramgu and Odhiambo, decided to contribute to the debate.

'He speaks the truth, Bwana Aramgu. Price-Allen said he must die with you. It must look like you were resisting arrest and shot him. We would have put a gun in your hand, but after you were dead.'

Mantuli laughed with genuine merriment and Aramgu joined him. Odhiambo glared from one to the other. Their fondness for laughing at their own witticisms was one of the grudges he bore them. Aramgu wiped his eye with a sausage-like finger.

'Ah, I thought he would try some trick like this. But he is too late. Nothing can stop the people now. Tonight and then the new order dawns and Price-Allen and all his slaves I will feed in pieces to the hyenas. Now, man of Sasaweni, there is no reason why part of the *mzungu*'s plan should not succeed. We do not need this Luo shit.'

Mantuli shook his head. 'No, *bwana*. Sasaweni says that we try to keep the policeman alive. Sasaweni wishes to see him. He has work, I think, for the Luo to do.'

'Beware, man of Sasaweni. His man you may be, but I am Aramgu. Aramgu, Kiwonka's agent, soon to be with Kiwonka in State House. Sasaweni takes his orders from me.'

The display of bravado did not seem to impress Mantuli. A typical Price-Allen product, thought Odhiambo, a self-confident killer. He shrugged.

'You must say that to Sasaweni. I have my orders.'

And so it proved. A little more bluster from Aramgu preceded his giving way with such grace as he could muster. He signalled his acceptance of Mantuli's command by drawing back his fist and crashing it into Odhiambo's face. Taken by surprise, Odhiambo only managed to half dodge the blow which split his lip and sent him stumbling. A boot in his ribs completed his fall to the ground. Aramgu leaned forward and spat into Odhiambo's face, then he turned away.

'Right, do what you like. I will see Sasaweni. I will tell him what I want done with this piece of shit.'

16

Cari Odhiambo had known some dark hours, including the desperate last days she and James had spent in Washington, but the past few had tested her mental endurance to its limit. James had agreed to go off on a Price-Allen errand because she was a hostage to his obedience. She wasn't sure what game Price-Allen was playing and James had not had the chance, or, probably, the will, to tell her, but she could read a lot from his demeanour and attitude, to the point where she could claim to be reading his mind – at least that part of his mind he hadn't sealed from the world, including his wife. James had set out on a dangerous task, dangerous enough that the signals told her he was frightened, more frightened than she had ever known him to be, which, in turn, meant he did not believe he was in control of his own destiny. She, herself, had not been harmed – after the meeting with Price-Allen and James she had been locked in a bathroom, odd but practical as a cell and, she supposed, less uncomfortable and demeaning than one of the basement cells that James had described to her from his period of captivity a year or so earlier. Price-Allen was a killer and a sadistic killer at that, but Cari believed he was uncomfortable with women and had a certain old-fashioned reserve about the manner in which he handled them even when he had them at his mercy. This, she believed, explained the bathroom.

It was the feeling of helplessness that was so mentally debilitating. Far from being able to help her husband in some way, she was the cause of his danger and could do nothing about it. More than once she felt hysteria threatening to engulf her, but she fought it off: she had to stay mentally alert to take advantage of any opportunity which might arise. The bathroom was bare of loose objects, but she investigated the cistern of the old-fashioned pull-chain toilet and was able to unscrew the arm connecting one of the internal bits to the ballcock. This gave her a rod which she slipped into the pocket of her jacket: it might not be much of a weapon, but it was better than nothing and it gave her a sense that she had done something, however small, which in turn helped her to overcome the sense of despair.

Price-Allen's men had left her with her watch and repeated glances confirmed the slow painful struggle of the hour hand to advance. Nevertheless, after she had completed her raid on the cistern, another look at her watch confirmed that the day was past. The only window was boarded up on the outside, but she knew that if she could see through it she would find the sky had turned from blue to black.

What seemed like aeons later she heard, at last, footsteps approaching. Were they bringing her food and drink or was the visit more sinister? James had been gone many hours: something must be wrong. Her heart seemed to speed up and then flutter as she contemplated the worst of the possible consequences of error. There was a perfunctory knock and then the sound of the key in the lock. There was a bolt on the inside of the bathroom door but Cari had not come up with any sensible reason for bolting the door shut – for a start, it would be no protection against a forceful boot to the door. The door opened and the bulky presence of one of her guards seemed to fill the entrance.

'Come. The man wants you.'

Cari followed him out of her 'cell' and up the corridor. The second of her guards fell in just behind her. They retraced the route to the main living area, the guard standing aside to allow Cari to pass. Price-Allen was standing, and around him and from adjacent rooms came both the air and the noise of bustle. Something had happened and, although Price-Allen's face was, as always, carefully composed, Cari knew it was bad news. Her heart sank; if it was bad news for Price-Allen it could be terrible news for her. Price-Allen looked at her and she sensed the evil behind the eyes, but when he spoke he somehow maintained the pseudo-courtesy with which he always addressed her.

'Ah, my dear young lady. Matters are coming to a head and I must depart. The question is, what do I do with you?'

Cari was aware of the two men who had followed her in and were now standing a pace or so behind her. She fingered the rod in her pocket: could she reach him before he and the others could react and would the rod if applied with all her strength be sharp enough to impale his neck? She strained for normality in her voice, but it came out, to her ears, as a squeak.

'What about . . . where is James?'

'It seems I've been outsmarted, but not, I hasten to add, by your husband. Some State Security men have turned traitor and have set Aramgu free, killing some of my men in the process.'

Was this a cause for hope or final despair?

'But James . . .?'

'Your husband failed in his task, although in this case he may not have been master of his fate. I don't know where he is.'

'You mean he's not . . . ?'

'Dead? No.' Price-Allen gave a short laugh. 'Or if he is you must blame Felix Aramgu not me.'

Thank you, God, she thought. Oh, let him be safe and I'll never let him get mixed up in murky affairs in this country again. But would he be safe if he was in Aramgu's hands? Despair returned as quickly as it had lifted.

'Then you have nothing to gain by keeping me. I can go?'

'I'm afraid you are out of touch with the news, my dear. It

seems we are witnessing the start of an attempted coup. One regiment has moved to take certain strategic points. A helicopter is coming to take me and my men to where we can organise the government's resistance. There will be, I fear, no room for you.'

'Then let me go.' She struggled for the word, but managed to swallow her pride. 'Please.'

The slight shake of the head caused her heart to sink, but it seemed the gesture was of inward reproach. A thin smile appeared.

'You and your lumbering ox are a piece of unfinished business and I think you know how I deal with such. Yet I'm going to let you go, my dear. Call it the weakness of an old man if you wish.' Cari's look showed her disbelief. Price-Allen gave a short, dry laugh. 'You doubt my intentions, I see, even when I give you what you ask.' He looked at her while he pondered. 'You are an intelligent woman. The position is perilous. Your husband is almost certainly in the State Security building near the Norfolk Hotel. The one signed as "Local Administration". A man called Sasaweni has his unit there. On the very long shot that you get to see your husband, you tell him that Aramgu and Sasaweni have captured the President. Yes, it is true. If he survives the next few hours and by some circumstance sees a chance, it is his duty to do what he can to thwart their ambitions.' Price-Allen smiled. 'He is stupid enough and lucky enough that you never know. Every contribution may help.' He shrugged. 'It is as I say not a likely proposition, but it costs me nothing.'

Cari Odhiambo bit her lip.

'But, how do I . . . I mean, there's no way . . .' A noise from outside the house startled her. After a second she realised it was the sound of a helicopter hovering above them. Price-Allen bent to retrieve a brief case at his feet. 'If there's fighting in town I may not . . . I mean, how do I get there?'

'I hold out no real hope, but at least I give you a chance.' Price-Allen nodded at a key on the desk to his left. 'That's the key of a jeep outside. My men won't be needing it for now. Make sure you return it in good condition.' One more brief, thin smile, a nod to his men and he was gone.

Cari's knees felt weak as she walked to the desk to retrieve the key. She sat for a full minute on the chair beside the desk. She must get her mind working. She had to get to James.

17

Until ten o'clock in the evening, Lijodi had every reason to be pleased. His men had moved into Nairobi with their vehicles and seized most of the initial, priority sites. The airport, television and radio stations, telecommunication centres and main government offices were secured without serious resistance. Incredibly, despite the rumours, little seemed to have been done to provide for their defence. A few soldiers and guards here and there, but no match for the best of his own men. Most importantly of all, the President was in their hands. There remained significant resistance around State House and some of the President's key men were still there, presumably trying to co-ordinate some organised resistance. Sasaweni had not succeeded in bringing all the State Security units on to their side. Those around the President had remained loyal and there were rumours that Price-Allen was still at large with men still at his command. The barracks outside Nairobi were quiet: Lijodi had circled them with tanks and armoured vehicles and negotiations were under way to get the troops there to back the coup, but as yet the officers were sitting tight, trying to sniff the wind. This, however, was not unexpected.

Outside Nairobi the news was only beginning to penetrate. The President's most loyal battalion, other than his personal guards at State House, was in Nakuru, one hundred miles away. Lijodi was confident that by the time they digested what had happened and dared to make a move it would be too late, and that if they were wise men their officers, too, would suddenly discover a previously hidden love of Kiwonka, the new President. Lijodi's only concern was the air force. It had no great aerial power, but a few planes could be the key factor in an attempted counter-coup: more importantly the air force had a significant number of well-trained ground troops. The President, in a classic ploy of keeping his eggs in different baskets, had nurtured these as a counterweight to Lijodi's own paratroopers. Lijodi had never been convinced that a showdown with the air force could be avoided. One of his officers was at their barracks now, but Lijodi had decided that if negotiations had not made good progress by midnight he would attack suddenly with maximum force. The latest news confirmed him in this decision; Price-Allen, it was said, was ensconced in the air force HQ and was making his influence felt.

It was just after ten when he left the studio at the television centre where he had recorded a statement announcing the end of tyranny and the imminent arrival of the Great Liberator, and commanding people to be loyal and stay off the streets. One of his aides was waiting for him in the corridor.

'Colonel, some of the men have got out of control. They are causing great damage in the Asian areas of Westlands and around the city market. Some bottle stores have been broken into: they are drinking.'

'Which unit?'

'It's not clear. But one group, it is said, has killed its commander. They are burning houses and bodies have been seen. Indians.'

Lijodi swore. He had argued with his superiors that recruits in the last two years had been selected for the wrong reasons – nepotism, favours to friends and the like – and then the money to provide a full and rigorous training programme had been denied him. He had assigned such suspect units to the minor role of securing the homes of prominent ministers, senior government supporters and officials, and placing the occupants under house arrest. He would have left them behind if had had a choice, but he needed numbers. Now, he would have to divert others from more important tasks so as to restore order.

'How bad is it?'

'It is not clear, Colonel. I am waiting for more detail. Already fires can be seen. But it is mainly the Indian areas.'

'Don't be such a fool. Drunken rioting will damage our chance of preventing trouble on the streets. If the Indian community are in fear of their lives anything could happen. Get me Kiwanza. I want him to get over there and restore order. Shoot the ring leaders if necessary.'

The aide was reluctant to query what 'over there' was supposed to mean. From what little he knew rampage was spreading over many streets like the fires themselves. Restoring control might not be easy.

'*Ndio*, Colonel.' A perfunctory salute and he turned to hurry away. Another problem occurred to him. Where was Major Kiwanza? He turned back. 'Ah . . .' He stopped. Lijodi was already in conversation with another side. Discretion was perhaps the better part of valour. He'd have to find Kiwanza for himself.

Lijodi headed back for his temporary command post within the complex of buildings comprising the Kenyan Parliament. As he entered his car he looked towards the north-east back in the direction of his own barracks on the Thika road. Flames lit the night sky. He cursed softly but obscenely. A general could plan and lead and deliver, but if the men underneath him ran amok the objective could be lost. It looked bad. How many men could he spare to bring the undisciplined to heel? It depended on the air force coming out on his side or at least staying in their quarters. Curtly he ordered his chauffeur to hurry.

Crossing Delamere Avenue he saw two soldiers wearing his regiment's insignia emerge from a small Asian-owned supermarket clutching bottles in each hand.

'Stop the car,' he ordered. The driver eased the car into the side of the road he had just entered. He looked around questioningly. 'Wait here.'

Lijodi got out. The two soldiers, rifles over their shoulders, were heading towards him. One was already swigging from a bottle. Lijodi marched towards them, drawing his revolver from his belt.

'Halt. I am your commanding officer, Colonel Lijodi. Your names and unit.'

The two soldiers focused on the man who had suddenly loomed in front of them. They were already half drunk. They had been charged with guarding the side road leading to offices housing some embassies of smaller countries. Nothing stirred on their corner and it had seemed like a good idea, now that they were in Nairobi and in power, to help themselves to a drink. They recognised the name, if not the figure. They stuttered out their names and unit.

'Where is your immediate superior?'

'Sergeant Otieno. He is somewhere over there,' said one of the soldiers, waving vaguely towards Parliament Square. He seemed to realise that this might be considered inadequate and made an attempt to pull himself to attention. 'Guarding the government buildings. We are guarding these buildings for the foreigners.'

129

'You are a disgrace to the regiment.' Lijodi raised his revolver, aimed at the speaker's mouth and fired. The soldier's face seemed to explode. The second soldier stared as the body of his friend slumped to the pavement; the sight sobered him but also transfixed him with fear. He saw the gun barrel swing towards him and felt it reach his temple, he opened his mouth but no sound came.

Lijodi's driver had scrambled out of the car at the sound of the first shot and was in time to witness the second. He too stood still, stunned by the unexpectedness of the incident. He saw his Colonel coming back towards him.

'Right. Get back in the car. Hurry.'

Back in the car Lijodi brooded for a while and then, as they neared the Parliament gates, he gave one more instruction to the driver. 'After you drop me find a Sergeant Otieno. Tell him to see me immediately.'

But back in his command post there was other news that took the missing sergeant completely from the Colonel's mind. A young captain approached him with a radio message.

'Colonel, there is news from the air force barracks. It seems your emissary there has been shot. We are told the commanding officer has declared support for the old regime. It is said the *mzungu* with State Security is there and he ordered the shooting of your man!'

Lijodi stared for a long moment at the anxious young captain. He had always prided himself on his clear-sightedness: the incident of the two soldiers followed by this news that he now faced the air force seemed to coalesce in his mind and he saw a vision of his future, an end similar to the one he had just imparted to others. Just for a moment his jaw sagged, then he pulled himself together.

'Pass the order. All officers at central level will report to my office immediately for a revision of our dispositions.'

Cari Odhiambo gingerly steered the strange vehicle with open sides down the hill towards Uhuru Highway. Somehow the sense of a pattern emerging and beginning to go her way gave her hope and confidence rather than the despair which still lurked at the back of her mind. She cursed and braked as hard as she could when a soldier in full battledress stepped out and waved her down as she reached the roundabout where she would cross the highway. She leaned out as the soldier pointed his rifle at her.

'What do you want? I have business to do with State Security.'

The soldier was taken aback. First, he had not expected a woman in the jeep and second, the authoritative tone was new to him when coming from a woman.

'Who are you? Where are you going? There is a curfew.'

Cari did not know whether the soldier represented the rebels or the government, although she guessed he was on the side of the coup leaders. She could see in the night sky beyond the university the glow of fires. It seemed as if the city was indeed falling into the invading hands. She chose her words carefully.

'You have heard of the State Security, no? You know that they are on your side. The office is down there.' Cari gestured across the roundabout. 'I have a message for the man in charge.'

The soldier hesitated, but surely his officers were not using civilian women for important work?

'Get down and give me your papers.'

'I am in a hurry. Stand aside.' Cari wished she was more familiar with the jeep; she could have slipped it into gear and made a dash for it. 'You are delaying affairs.'

But something in her voice now strengthened the soldier's suspicions. He advanced nearer and once more raised his rifle which he had lowered at the first sound of her voice.

'Come here or I shoot.'

Cari eased her trousered legs over the side of the jeep and lowered herself on to the road, shielding with her body the action of her right hand as she retrieved the thin rod from her pocket. To her own astonishment she felt in control of her emotions and physical reactions. She looked at the soldier, lit dimly by the lights of the roundabout: he was young and slight in build, and somehow she felt almost sorry for him, so confident did she feel.

'Please, put that gun away.' She turned towards the soldier, hands half raised in a gesture of submissive innocence. 'Look, here, I have the proof.'

The young soldier, guarding he knew not what, was once more mollified by the woman's body language and voice. He half lowered his gun and came close to this strange woman to see what she was proffering in her left hand: there did not seem to be anything in her hand and he bent forward to peer more closely in the dim light. Cari brought the rod into a striking position in her right fist and brought her hand down with all the force she could muster. Her eye-hand co-ordination had always been good – at her American college she had performed with distinction on the basketball court – but she realised even as she struck that, given the poor light, luck was on her side. The rod caught the unfortunate soldier in the neck just under his left ear and gashed into the soft tissue between his jaw bone and his neck muscle. The blunt rod did not penetrate far but the shock caused the soldier to drop his gun as his hand went spontaneously to his neck: he was convinced he had been stabbed and was mortally wounded. His troubles were not complete; just as he clasped his neck wound the woman's knee made vicious contact with his groin.

Cari surveyed her handiwork with what only later she realised was cool detachment. It was as if she was operating at a level where her mind was isolated from her present environment. The soldier had one hand pressed to his neck and the other to his groin as he kneeled, doubled over, at her feet. She picked up the rifle, hurled it into the darkness and climbed back into her vehicle. Only as she moved forward did the soldier attempt to rise and make an ineffectual gesture for her to stop. Instead, she accelerated around the roundabout and headed down the road past the University of Nairobi on her left. There were a number of soldiers around the entrance to the university grounds, but they made no move as Cari shot purposefully past. She could see now the old building that was her destination. It was framed by a backdrop of flames that lit the sky. My God, thought Cari, this was becoming a full-scale disaster. She had read of coups that took place surreptitiously in the night with a new government in control by the time the populace awoke. But this was a battleground. She wondered what the scale of resistance was. Her thoughts were quickly brought back to her immediate circumstances as she braked at the gate, her feeble headlights illuminating a faded wooden sign that read 'Local Administration'.

Incredibly, if what Price-Allen had told her was true, there seemed to be only a nightwatchman guarding the gates: and a very nervous nightwatchman at that. Seeing the government number plate on an army-type jeep he hastened to open the gates without question or challenge.

Cari shouted at the man in Swahili as officiously as she could while she eased the jeep through the entrance. 'Who is in command here? Sasaweni is here?'

The man was clearly frightened: Cari could see the trembling of his hand on the gate.

'Not know, memsahib. There is too much trouble. I not understand this trouble.'

'Are there government people here?'

'Many go, memsahib. Some not go. I am frightened for my family. There are fires down the hill. That is where my family is.'

'OK. I will see if they will let you go to find your family.'

Cari drove on. No harm in making a friend. He looked as if he was likely to leave his post at any minute, in any case. She braked to a halt and climbed three steps on to a wooden verandah. She had no idea what she was going to do next, but in the absence of a plan she was pressing forward mindlessly: any action was better than doing nothing and going mad, and anyway there was nowhere to go to do nothing in. She tried the old-fashioned round knob on a pair of doors. It turned and she entered a large room with several desks and a working surface down one side. It looked as if it had once been a general office, perhaps for draughtsmen, map-makers or the like. The room was dimly lit by unshaded overhead bulbs. Cari could see three men, two in uniform and one in slacks and open-necked shirt. She addressed the man in civilian clothes as being the one most likely to belong to State Security.

'Is Sasaweni here? I have an urgent message for him.'

The man came closer. He was young, with the blank eyes and lack of expression of a State Security plain-clothes man who listened in public places for gossip that could be construed as seditious. But it was clear that he too was nervous, or, at the least, confused.

'He has left. There is much happening. Who are you?'

Cari ignored the question.

'And Mr Aramgu? Felix Aramgu. Where is he?'

Her air of authority and easy reference to important names made a clear impression.

'He was here. He left with Captain Sasaweni. Some minutes ago.'

Cari was thinking on her feet. It was important not to appear hesitant or her psychological ascendancy over the SS man would dissipate. He must not be given time to think.

'That is unfortunate. My orders are to be given to one of them. Sasaweni or Aramgu. You are in charge, right? You have someone here who must be taken to the *bwana mkubwa*. A policeman – Odhiambo.'

The man's eyes narrowed. 'Sasaweni said he must be kept here until he comes back. He thinks he can be useful in controlling the police. Once the new government is in charge.'

Cari interrupted him with an imperious gesture. 'Sasaweni! Sasaweni is a *toto* in this affair. You know who the main man is, don't you?'

'Yes, Colonel Lijodi. But – '

'No buts. Lijodi. You are right. This man Odhiambo has information the Colonel needs. There is opposition by the police. The same police Sasaweni talks about.'

Her gamble seemed to work. The man turned and headed for a door at the far end of the room. Cari followed. She found herself in a passage. Her guide paused as they neared the far end and pulled a bunch of keys from his pocket. As he inserted one in the lock doubts came to the surface once again.

'And you? Who are you? Where is your authority?'

'This is no time to talk of bits of paper. There's a coup going on, man. Are you that stupid? You think Lijodi's people here printed bits of paper before they attack? Or maybe you want something signed by the *mzungu*, Price-Allen? He's on the other side, for Chrissake.'

The name of Price-Allen and her total air of superiority seemed to do the trick.

'OK.' He unlocked the door and preceded the woman through it. 'He is the only one here. The others we . . . ' There was a slight hesitancy. 'We "removed" before the *shauri* started. Sasaweni said we will need the space.'

Cari found herself in a small courtyard enclosed by low buildings with several doors. There was a smell that made her take a deep breath – a smell of blood and urine, sweat and pain. She struggled to maintain control.

'Where is he?'

But the guard was already unlocking one of the doors. The area looked as if it had been used for storage, but the doors seemed solid. This part of the complex had clearly been reinforced to serve its later sinister purpose. The courtyard was lit by a bright floodlight fixed above the door by which they had entered. Cari spotted a brick lying on the weed-strewn cobbled floor of the yard. She picked it up. The guard had fumbled for the right key, but was now turning the lock.

'Get him out.'

Cari's voice was in his ear. The guard bent to enter the low doorway. The smell that assailed Cari's nostrils grew stronger as the door was pushed open. She brought the brick down with all the force she could muster on the back of the guard's head. He sank to his knees and, biting her lip, she smashed the brick down again and again. She felt sick, not only at the smell, but at her own unaccustomed violence. She stepped over the prostrate body and peered into the dark cell. The light from behind her revealed the figure of her husband kneeling on the foul straw-covered floor with his back to her. His arms were handcuffed behind him and she could see that a chain from a ring close to the floor was around his neck.

The next few minutes she could never recall afterwards. Now that she had found James her mind, which had responded to each demand so well in the last hour, seemed to switch off. Somehow, she found the keys under the body in the doorway and eventually found the ones that freed her husband from his restraints. He collapsed on the floor, his legs and arms deprived of circulating blood, and only then did she see the gag taped across his mouth. She was sobbing now as she ripped the gag away and finally heard the voice she had feared she would never hear again.

Their escape, her husband told her later, was easier than they might have expected. By the time his circulation returned and he was able to walk, one of the two soldiers Cari had left behind had come down the passage to see what was happening. As he came into the courtyard, Odhiambo, a much bigger and stronger man, easily overpowered him and took off him his rifle which had been hanging from his shoulder rather than in his hands. Now that he was armed, the taking of the remaining guard and the handcuffing of the two together took only a few minutes. The jeep was still in place, there was no sign of the nightwatchman who had now presumably gone to check on the safety of his family, and off they went into the night. The whole episode, she was to reflect later, epitomised the incompetence that besets conspirators when things start to go wrong.

18

Robert McGuiry had been left in a state of mental confusion by his friend's decision to walk into the trap set for him. He sat in his Land Rover, his hands gripping the steering wheel tightly, reflecting the tension in his body, until he saw Odhiambo emerge from the building he had entered a few minutes earlier flanked by two obvious security men. It crossed his mind to follow the car the three entered, but when it pulled on to the main road it took off at high speed in the direction from which he had come. By the time he turned the Land Rover and regained the roundabout on Uhuru Highway he had lost his quarry. He cursed, spitting out the words towards the windscreen, feeling himself a failure in terms of assisting his friend in times of need. There remained Odhiambo's own request to him, namely to put the whole story to his boss. Wearily he circled the roundabout once more and headed back into the city centre to the police headquarters.

He waited some time before his request to see Chief Superintendent Masonga was granted, having been told he was not in his office. At last in the late afternoon he was shown to Masonga's office and found there a shortish, thickset, rumpled-looking man, puffing in a harassed manner on a cigarette.

'Chief Superintendent Masonga, I'm a friend of one of your men, Chief Inspector Odhiambo. He asked me to see you.'

Masonga grunted and inhaled deeply on his cigarette whilst looking searchingly at the grizzled white man across the desk.

'So I'm told. So where is he and what's his problem?'

McGuiry launched into his story, starting with the contretemps Odhiambo had had with Price-Allen the previous day and the subsequent events. Even to his own ears the story of the message trailed by an aeroplane seemed unbelievable, but Masonga listened, lighting one cigarette from the stub of another. As McGuiry brought his tale to a close, Masonga rose and paced the small, untidy office.

'I heard about the plane and some message. I didn't make the connection. So you think Odhiambo has gone looking for Mr

Price-Allen for news of his wife? I thought she was out of the country?'

'She is. Or was. I dinna want to tell ye something ye already ken, but yon Price-Allen is bad news.'

Masonga waved smoke away from his face with a petulant gesture.

'I know Mr Price-Allen.' He resumed his seat. 'You met Odhiambo over that other case, didn't you? You're involved with the tourist place at Nyeri.'

McGuiry nodded.

'Ay, that's right. We became friends. He's a good man.'

'Well, thank you for the information, Mr McGuiry. I think the best thing you can do is go home and leave it to us.'

'You realise I'm concerned about him? You'll do your best, I reckon.'

Masonga seemed to be contemplating the smoke drifting from his nostrils. McGuiry waited a few moments more and then rose to leave. Masonga watched him reach the door and came to a decision.

'Mr McGuiry, what I'm telling you is confidential. I have heard of an incident involving Mr Aramgu and officers of State Security in the road where you've been staying. Odhiambo may have been involved. We're looking into it. But Aramgu and Odhiambo, if he was there, seem to have gone off with the other men. I'll do my best but these are difficult days.'

McGuiry looked at the worried policeman with alarm, but also sympathy.

'I dinna like the sound of that, I'll tell ye true. But I understand. No good me clumping about getting in the way. I'll rely on you doing what can be done.'

Masonga gave McGuiry time to leave the outer office and then went to see his clerk.

'Have you tried to get the *mzungu*?'

'*Ndio, bwana*. He is not in his office or his home.' The clerk shrugged. 'I think there is much going on.'

Masonga retreated into his own sanctum once more. He was concerned about Odhiambo. Why did he have to get tangled up with Price-Allen again? No, to be fair, he'd been set up. Price-Allen had wanted to use him in his battle with Aramgu, that much was clear. But Odhiambo's safety was a relatively minor matter compared with the dreadful feeling Masonga had that big, big trouble was now about to engulf them all. Like animals out on the game plains who smell an impending thunderstorm, Masonga anticipated with dread the turbulence that he sensed was upon them.

McGuiry drove towards his temporary home, which seemed to be the epicentre of so much that had happened in the last days. It was not a conscious decision; in truth, he was in a state of mental confusion and indecision. He felt like a cork bobbing along in a river, driven by forces over which he had no control. As he neared the junction where he should turn off the main road it crossed his mind that it might not be safe to return to his lodging. He dismissed this thought; it was, after all, James who was being hunted, not himself. Nevertheless, this thought process, once started, continued to the stage of acceptance that his friend was out of commission and, though he could do nothing to help him directly, he could perhaps continue to act as a Watson to his black Holmes. Decision made, he drove past his turn, pulling off half a mile further on into the drive of the Royal Ngong Golf Club. It was early evening, when one might have expected the car-park to be full, what with those members playing a round after a day's work and those skipping the exercise and slaking their thirst at the bar – but in fact, McGuiry noticed with surprise, there were no more than a dozen or so cars present. Consistent with the evidence of the car-park, the bar was very sparsely populated, but McGuiry's quarry was there, nursing a tumbler of whisky.

'Mr Hill-Templeton. You remember me, I dinna doubt.'

The answering voice was ever so slightly slurred, and the delay in focusing the eye just perceptible.

'Ah, Mr McGuiry. Our temporary neighbour.' A raised finger produced the immediate attention of the barman. 'What are you having?'

'I'll join ye in a wee dram, thank'ee kindly.'

Doubles, McGuiry noted, were the order of the day – presumably the barman knew Hill-Templeton's view on the required size of a tot without instruction. The Secretary seemed to think it necessary to explain the lack of customers.

'Not many here this evening. Neither in here nor playing. There's a lot of rumours around, McGuiry. Good time to stay

138

indoors seems to be the order of the day. Have you heard anything?'

'No, nothing firm – there's some worried faces about, though. My concern is my friend, James, the policeman. I hear he was caught up in some *shauri* near my house this afternoon. Do ye know aught about that?'

Hill-Templeton took a long suck at his glass.

'Yes. There was shooting. Killings. Someone saw it from the course. You mean your policeman friend was involved?'

'So I believe. But what happened to him is the question. I'm worried, I'll tell ye that. I'm afraid he was set up.'

Hill-Templeton tried to express appropriate concern although, in truth, Odhiambo's fate was not a serious worry to him, then he raised his glass once more, drained it and plonked it on to the bar.

'Yes, Sammy.' He gestured at the glasses. 'It's a bad business all round, McGuiry, I'll say that. Killings right beside the course. Police or security people, whatever. It's a ... what's the word I'm looking for? It's a hardinger of things to come. Yes, that's it, hardinger of things to come.'

'Harbinger.'

'Eh, what? Oh – right. Things are going bad, McGuiry, and coming to a head.'

'So everybody says. But coming back to James – the policeman, Odhiambo.'

'Can't help, old boy. Wait a minute, though. Someone said two senior men took shelter in the garden next to yours. One was the chap lives at the end of the road there. Important chappie. He may have been the target, I'm told. Him and a senior officer, the chap said. That may be your friend. In which case he may be all right.'

McGuiry disentangled the information from the slightly slurred tongue and rambling story-line. Perhaps there was hope.

'And what happened to them?'

'No idea, old boy. All the survivors drove off. Later some lorry came to pick up the bodies. Typical. Not civilised really, whatever we say in public.'

Another train of thought struck McGuiry. There was something slightly odd about the way Hill-Templeton referred to the garden next to his.

'Where they sheltered – you said the garden next to me. You mean your brother-in-law's place, Smyth?'

139

'Who? Ah, old Smithie.' Hill-Templeton paused and looked at McGuiry, trying hard to bring his face into better focus. He leaned forward so that their heads were close together. 'Tell you the truth, old man, don't think of it as his really. Never there. My sister's left him, you know. Buggered off to dear old Blighty. Can't say I blame her – bit of a cold fish, he is.'

'So it's shut up most of the time? Garden looks as if someone's looking after it.'

Hill-Templeton again leaned forward in a conspiratorial manner.

'Lends it to friends.' He tapped his forefinger on the side of his nose. 'Special friends. Enough said. Know what I mean?'

McGuiry ordered another round, but Hill-Templeton was now becoming incoherent and sat moodily drinking his fresh drink. McGuiry drained his quickly and said his good-byes. The car-park contained even fewer cars, he noticed. It seemed everyone was scurrying home. Reaching the turn to the lane leading to his borrowed home, he braked and hesitated, but only for a moment. He turned the wheel and sent the Land Rover bumping up the lane that had been the scene of the earlier carnage.

He was barely in the house before he heard the back door open and shut and the house servant came in looking distressed, much as he had done two evenings earlier after finding Dennison's body.

'*Bwana*! You have heard? There is big trouble. Radio he say army take over. President captured.'

'What! On the radio? You're sure? There's a coup started?'

'Some general or big officer is going to speak on radio. They are saying we must stay where we are. Soldiers told to shoot if you go walkabout.'

McGuiry cursed. For once Hill-Templeton and his golfing members were right. The rumours this time were true, Aramgu's *coup d'état*, it seemed, was under way. It wasn't going to make his task of finding his friend any easier.

'Well, you do what they say. Lie doggo. You savvy?'

'Nightwatch, he no come. I think he not coming.'

'Doing the same, I woud'na wonder. But if you're right there won't be many thieves abroad this night.'

'I will listen.'

'You have family with you in your quarters?'

'No, *bwana*. They are at my *shamba* in Machakos.'

'Good. They'll be safe enough there. It's the middle of town that's no the place to be. What about other staff? Do they know?'

'Servant in first house, he told me to listen to radio. But next one here, he be empty.'

McGuiry noticed the sudden hesitancy. It seemed that every time the empty Smyth house was mentioned people's manner changed.

'Is it ever used? Does *Bwana* Smyth use it much?'

'*Hapana*. One, two time I see him. But sometimes other men come. They have keys. Other boys here say it is not good place.'

McGuiry tried to probe further, but the man shook his head, saying he knew no more. McGuiry decided not to push him given the tension that he was under due to the breaking news.

The servant asked if he wanted supper. McGuiry shook his head. 'I may not stay. I must get back to another place before trouble spreads.' He cursed himself quietly. He must be getting senile. The announcement of the coup attempt had driven his main preoccupation from his mind. 'Did you see the *shauri* this afternoon? Was my policeman friend here? Was he OK?'

Again the shake of the head. 'I was in Karen, buying *chakula*. When I came back there were still bodies. But not your friend. But the one who tell me about radio he say your friend was in fight with the big man, Aramgu, then they go with others.'

Further questions failed to produce any more detail. McGuiry decided it was time to get back to the house where he and James had spent the previous night. He might be there or there might be a message. The question was, could he get there if there was a coup in progress?

'OK. You stay here and keep out of the way of any trouble. I must go and look for my friend.'

'Do not go, *bwana*. These soldiers they will not respect you just because you are a *mzungu*. Better you stay. You can do nothing tonight.'

McGuiry knew the man was right. To get to Odhiambo's bolt-hole required him to go through the city.

'I'll wait and see what they say on the radio. So if you make me a sandwich, that will be good.'

The servant smiled. He was glad the old man listened to him. Some of these *mzungus* thought they could go anywhere, protected by the colour of their skin. He hurried off and prepared a plate of cold meat, bread and chutneys. Returning with the plate, he found McGuiry sunk in a chair, clutching a glass, his head bowed in thoughts that he could see were not happy ones.

'The radio saying all is going well for new man. New President arriving in morning from your country. But radio he sometime lie.'

McGuiry roused himself.

'You're right enough there, laddie. And thank'ee for the *chakula*. I'll see if I can get the BBC. Might get something we can believe.'

As he left McGuiry alone once more, the servant hesitated at the door. There were more serious things to worry about, but perhaps he should tell this friend of the policeman or later on it might be they would say he should have spoken.

'*Bwana*, there is something also I hear. Not important. But about that *mzungu* we find buried.'

McGuiry had risen to fiddle with the radio situated with a record player in the corner of the room. He turned to face his companion.

'Dennison? You know something about him being killed?'

'No, no, *bwana*. Not how he die. But in Karen I met boy who work for dead man. He belongs to my clan. He say that he not come home night before we find him. He not see him since Monday.'

'Dennison didn't come home Monday night, you mean? But Mrs Dennison . . . ' He broke off, thinking back to Odhiambo's account of his interview with the widow. Yes, she had said Dennison had gone to work Tuesday morning. 'Is your friend sure of this? That Dennison was not in the house to sleep?'

'That is what he say. He is not very smart man. But he no see him. Memsahib there but not *bwana*. I tell you this because I know you and policeman friend were asking when he die. Maybe he die Monday. Maybe he be in ground since Monday.'

'You did right to speak of this. *Asante*. I will tell my *rifiki* – if I can find him, that is. He will be pleased.'

This time the servant left and McGuiry turned back to the radio. As he twiddled the knob, looking for the BBC World Service programme, he wondered why, if this story was true, Mrs Dennison had lied. Well, if she was lying, McGuiry thought he knew who had put her up to it. Perhaps that's why Silent seemed to keep her under his wing, and why she looked so frightened. James would be interested, but that assumed he was safe and that conditions were such that he was able to carry on in his police work. If Kiwonka and Aramgu took over there might be no future for James. He only hoped that his future hadn't come to an end already.

Suddenly a voice came from the radio speaking English and in an accent that was unmistakably that of a BBC newsreader.

' . . . Mrs Thatcher stated in the House that she did not intend to alter her proposals with regard to trade union ballots and accused the Labour leader, Mr Kinnock, of being a puppet of the union barons.'

'News is just coming in of a coup attempt in Kenya. It is understood that an élite paratroop regiment has stormed State House, where the President is thought to have been, and taken strategic buildings including the airport and the radio and television stations. Our correspondent in Nairobi in his latest dispatch said that it is assumed the coup leaders wish to install as President a former politician called Kiwonka, who has recently been living in England. It is not yet clear whether the coup is being resisted by forces loyal to the government, but a curfew has been imposed.'

'That dinna help me any,' muttered McGuiry to himself. He felt terribly frustrated stuck here, but what should he do for the best?

19

The choice by the air force to stay loyal to the existing President proved to be the decisive moment in the coup attempt. The, admittedly limited, airpower was sufficient to stage an attack on the armour surrounding the Nairobi garrison – the actual damage was minimal, but the besieging forces were startled into seeking cover and, most significantly, it had the effect of bringing the garrison officers off the fence with their own declaration of loyalty. The ground troops of the air force, commandos, trained purposely as a counterweight to Lijodi's best paratroops, moved in the direction of State House and it was in this area that the hardest and most disciplined fighting then occurred as the best units Kenya possessed joined each other in a close quarters encounter. The commanding officer of the Nairobi battalion, with a keen eye for public relations, broke out of his garrison with two platoons in fast transport and with ridiculous ease drove to and recaptured the radio and television stations. Soon the public that was awaiting further pronouncements from Lijodi and a promised message of greeting from the newly declared President Kiwonka heard a somewhat breathless officer declare that the plotters were in retreat, the leaders were being tracked down, order was being restored and the President was not in the hands of the enemy. Most of this was guesswork, but the appearance of being in charge was important. Those in the mainly Asian sections of the suburbs, if they had the opportunity to listen, would have greeted the reference to restoring order with derision because drunken looting and burning had now turned these areas into places of chaos and despair, with many innocents losing their lives.

Colonel Lijodi brought all his training to bear and managed to maintain contact with and discipline in many of his units – indeed, around the State House area his men were at least holding their own into the early hours. At some hour past midnight the major in charge of the captured President asked if he should kill him. Lijodi reminded him that he was a soldier and angrily refused the request to shoot a prisoner. He last saw Aramgu with the repulsive Sasaweni at about this time, but did not mention the matter to them as he had a good idea what their response would be. Before dawn even Lijodi had had enough. Rumour had it that Aramgu had fled the city and then definite news arrived that the airliner bringing Kiwonka back home was diverting to Dar es Salaam. Lijodi gave orders for disciplined surrender with line officers to negotiate their individual arrangements, requested his aides to leave him alone in the office within the Parliamentary building, smoked a cigarette, drew out his pistol, placed it to his ear and pulled the trigger.

Without thinking, Odhiambo headed the jeep in the direction of his and Cari's home: only when they were safely away from the place of his latest incarceration did he manage to get a potted version from his wife of how she had obtained her freedom and expropriated the jeep left behind by Price-Allen.

'But why would he leave you the key? There's no sentiment in that bastard. I'm surprised he didn't leave you to rot, or worse.'

Cari felt as if she had moved her being into some sort of parallel universe. She actually felt exhilarated. The derring-do she had engaged in that night seemed not to have crushed her but rather given her a sense of self-confidence – a self-confidence that, she was still sufficiently in control of the real world to realise, was dangerous. She laughed. It sounded odd to her own ears – a few hours earlier the idea of laughing at Price-Allen would have seemed absurd.

'I don't believe it.' Odhiambo's own mental state was one of exhaustion from his recent painful imprisonment and confusion in terms of the chaos around him. Rather than riding an adrenalin surge like his wife, he was dangerously close to sliding into a depressive breakdown. 'He must have had some bloody plan or other in that pit of a mind of his.'

Cari chuckled again, the sound jarring in her husband's ears. 'Actually he did. It was you he wanted to save. A long shot, he said, but there was just a chance I could get you out, so what had he got to lose. And I pulled it off, big guy. Oh, James, you don't know all the awful things I was thinking.'

Odhiambo stood on the brake of the jeep. He had stayed on the back roads, but was now circling to cut back across the dividing highway to head up the hill towards their own suburb. So far, so good – he had avoided any road blocks. It was his wife's words that made him bring their vehicle to a protesting halt.

'What are you saying, Cari? Why would he want to get me out? Once out I'm likely to hunt him down and kill him, he knows that. And I will.'

Cari was sobering up. She realised James was surviving on his nerves. But it was too late to stop now. He wouldn't let it drop; she knew his stubborn streak too well.

'He knows you better than you think. He told me to tell you that things were bad and if I got you out to remind you it was your duty to protect the government. I was so amazed I didn't laugh in his face. Amazed and scared, to tell you the truth.'

There was silence as Odhiambo tried to make sense of these incredible words. Thinking about them brought him back to a more rational state of mind.

145

'Are you saying he expects me to go putting down a coup single-handed?' It was his turn to laugh, although it came out like a rattle from between his bruised and cracked dry lips. 'He thinks he's Superman, not me.'

'James, I don't think we should be sitting here. It might be better if we found ourselves a safer spot.' She nodded appreciatively as her husband let in the clutch and started forward again. 'I found this thing a bitch to drive. Price-Allen likes chess, he likes thinking several moves ahead for whatever immediate move his opponent makes. Covers the angles, as they say in the States. He was just seeing one possibility of saving a pawn for later in the game.'

To her surprise, her husband once more brought the jeep to a stop. She turned to expostulate, but his words caused her to explode.

'He's right, of course. I am on duty, sort of. I suppose I should do something.'

'Like a pig's ass you will, buddy. I didn't get you out of that hell-hole for you to drive like some black John Wayne into a gun-fight. I've flown thousands of miles, I've been kidnapped and scared stiff, I've had reason to believe you've been killed, I've driven through a city in flames, by a miracle we're free and together, and you give me some shit about doing your duty. Your only duty is to get us somewhere safe and then out of this place for ever.'

Suddenly the euphoria vanished and she fell forward against the plastic window, sobbing uncontrollably. She felt an arm around her, pulling her upright and over so that her head fell against her husband's chest.

'God, I'm sorry, Cari. My mind isn't working. I haven't even thanked you properly.'

The sobs stopped as suddenly as they had started. Cari sat upright and wiped a finger across her cheeks.

'You can thank me properly when we're in a nice bedroom in some nice hotel in some nice safe spot like London. You're very welcome, sir. Now let's get the hell out of here.'

Odhiambo's brain was working again now. As he started forward once more he was thinking aloud.

'But where to? We don't know who's winning this business. If we go home we could be caught again – either by Aramgu or Price-Allen. Then there's McGuiry. You remember him from the

Eagle's Nest affair. Lovely old boy. He's kept me sane these last couple of days – I'll explain later. I left him in the lurch to come after you. He's borrowed a place in Karen. He might have gone back there. We'd be safer there than in Dagoretti. Assuming the road's clear.'

'Are you sure? This isn't some other quixotic gesture?'

'I think it's quieter out this side of town. Call it my Luo instinct. Karen it is.'

But a mile or two along the road to Langata and Karen they encountered what, if given time for calm thought, they would have regarded as inevitable – a road block. It was positioned around a corner so that, although Odhiambo had space to stop, there was insufficient warning for him to turn and retreat. He heard Cari's sharp intake of breath. He reached out a hand and squeezed her leg, but her voice was controlled and authoritative.

'I've got through this already tonight. Keep calm and bluff, James. And for God's sake don't lose your temper.'

Two soldiers in full combat kit quickly flanked the jeep, one machine pistol pointing at each door. A third directed a spotlight first on to the windscreen and then on to the number plate. Odhiambo attempted to address the soldier on his side.

'We have authority to go to Karen.'

There was no reply, only an unmistakable gesture with the barrel of the gun. Odhiambo looked across at his wife; she too had received the same signal from her side of the jeep and was starting to get out. He followed her example and quickly they were lined up side by side facing the jeep with their hands spread on its roof. Odhiambo tried again.

'Who is in command here? It is important we are allowed to proceed.'

No answer came immediately, then suddenly, from in front of the jeep, the beam from a powerful torch was directed on to his face and paused there for a second or two before moving on to that of Cari. Somewhat incredibly to their ears, straining for the ominous sound of guns being cocked, there came a chuckle.

'I thought I recognised that voice. Why are you out looking for robbers this night, Odhiambo? Didn't someone tell you there's plenty other troubles?'

The voice was deep, but with a slight stutter. Odhiambo jerked his head around and half turned, regardless momentarily of the muzzles behind him.

'Who . . . is it . . . I mean, Okelo, is it you?'

Surely the gods were with him. A road block commanded by a captain he knew socially, a fellow Luo at that.

'Business, Odhiambo, or out with a girlfriend? I heard your wife was away. Neither activity to be recommended tonight. Better you find something to do inside.'

'This is no joke, Okelo. This is my wife. Get your light out of our faces and your guns out of our backs.'

'James, is this a friend of yours?'

Cari seemed to be having difficulty breathing; the words came haltingly, between gasps. She had turned to face away from the jeep and now she slid down until her bottom rested on the edge of the driver's floor, bending her head towards her knees.

'Okelo, what's going on?' He remembered his friend was in the air force, not a pilot, but some special support group. 'Where do you stand?'

The commando captain was now at their side, having gestured his men to stand off.

'Where do I stand? What a question for a policeman. Loyal to the government and the country. As I hope you do.'

'I was taken by Aramgu and his men earlier. I've just got away. We don't know what's going on.'

'The paratroops have tried a coup. Backing Kiwonka. But we're fighting back and others are joining us. The worst is over. But there's fighting, plenty fighting. And a curfew. You shouldn't be risking your neck and this lady.'

'We had no choice. I told you, we just escaped – or I did, with Cari's help. We're trying to get to Karen. Somewhere safe. I was held by renegade State Security people.'

'You look as if you've both been guests of Stasec. OK, Odhiambo, it should be safe as far as Karen. Safer than going back anyway. Get somewhere quick and stay there.'

A minute or two later the road block was opened and the Odhiambos drove through. Cari was shaking with post-traumatic nerves. She had held herself together through a long, tough day and, oddly, it was a lucky break that had caused her to feel faint.

'I'm glad I bought a few beers for that guy in the past. I guess the gods are smiling on us, Cari. Could have been any old trigger-happy idiot. Or Aramgu's men. Yes, the gods are good.'

Cari was silent. He could sense her trembling – well, she was

148

entitled to tremble, he had nearly wet himself. He carried on chatting so that she had something to listen to. He changed the topic from their current plight to a summary of the Dennison and Florislow murder cases. As he turned off the main road to McGuiry's temporary residence, he had a nagging feeling that he had almost grasped a fact of significance which had previously eluded him. What had he just said? No, it was nothing more than a superficial recap just to keep talking. It was something else. Something said earlier. It was so close, but, hard though he tried, he couldn't pin it down.

He pulled the jeep into McGuiry's drive. To his great relief he saw the familiar old Land Rover lit by the outside security lights. As he got out he saw a side door open momentarily and then close again. Presumably the servant checking the new arrivals. He waited as Cari slowly emerged from her side. He took her hand.

'We made it. We should be OK here.'

As if in answer the front door opened and there, framed in the light from behind, stood a familiar figure.

'Ah, James, is it? And the little woman, I hope. I was thinking it was taking you a braw time to rescue her. Come on in.'

Another of Cari's sudden mood swings seized her and her laughter echoed round the compound.

'God, James, are all the people you know crazy?'

20

It was the morning after the night before with a vengeance and the evidence of it was clear enough on the faces of the three people seated around a table laid with breakfast in the form of fruit, cereal and toast. Showered they were, but after spending most of the night listening to the radio and sharing their own experiences not one had managed any sleep. The coup had been crushed, the leaders were either dead or fugitives, the President had been freed unharmed and Kiwonka was seeking asylum in Tanzania. Nairobi streets were being patrolled by the troops of the Nairobi battalion, the air force commandos were guarding State House and other important government buildings, and the suburban areas that had suffered most from the fighting, looting and burning were still under curfew. In other areas, only those with essential functions were authorised to emerge on to the streets – although it was unclear how such essential people were to identify themselves as qualifying for free movement.

One such, in his own eyes at least, was James Odhiambo. He was attempting to convince his wife that duty called and that he should drive to the central police station to report in. He had attempted to telephone but the lines were down – almost certainly as a by-product of the coup.

'I've no reason not to go in, Cari. I'm a police officer. It's important the police re-establish civilian control as soon as possible.'

'Civilian control, ha!' Cari's sarcasm was evident in every syllable. 'Listen to him, Robert. Have you heard such rubbish? Civilian control, indeed. What civilians? I'll tell you – Price-Allen, that's who. The man who kidnapped me and arranged your execution. Yes, go on. Knock on his door and say, "Reporting for duty, sir. Where do you want to have me killed next?" '

'She's right enough, James. Ye canna put your head back in the lion's mouth. We were on the run before the coup, remember?'

'Because Price-Allen in trying to stop Aramgu and destroy his reputation wanted him dead and blamed for killing me. That doesn't apply now. Price-Allen will be concerned with re-establishing his influence. Anyway, I'm not going to Price-Allen, I need to find Superintendent Masonga. My boss. Even if it's to give him my resignation.'

Cari banged her fists on the table, causing the milk to spill out of McGuiry's cereal bowl.

'You promised me! Sorry, Robert, but this man aggravates me so. Send him a letter. Or wait a day or two. Price-Allen will not forgive you this time. You need to lie low. And not here. Let's make a run for it. Drive down towards Mombasa and cut across into Tanzania. Catch a plane out of Arusha.'

There was a silence as the concerned woman and the craggy old Scot watched the internal struggle behind the handsome face. Odhiambo sighed and toyed with his spoon.

'We'll go, Cari. I promised and I meant it. But I can't skulk away like a rat. I won't take any risks, but I must do it my way.'

Cari Odhiambo knew her husband well enough to recognise the resolve in the decision. She shook her head.

'God, you're a stubborn man, James. OK, you win. But while you're handing in your resignation, I'll find a phone that works and get us some tickets. Metroarcs will handle it.' She got up, her body silhouetted against the morning sun streaming through the open french windows. Both men watched her transfixed. 'I need some fresh air and relief from listening to your self- justification.' And with that Cari disappeared into the garden.

'Och, that's some woman ye've got there, James. A beauty with brains and determination. Ye'd be well doing what she wants, I'm thinking.'

'Yeah, I'm lucky. I suppose this is it for me in Kenya. But it's not easy, Robert. Cari was raised in the States. I'd never left here until after I met you. That's less than a year ago although somehow it seems a lot longer than that.'

The old man watched his friend with sympathy.

'Ay. I know how you feel. And there's something else bothering you too.'

'What do you mean?'

'The case, mon. The Dennison murder and that woman. You still blame yourself for her. Och, dinna deny it. I can read you like a book, same as young Cari can. You can't stand letting the murderer beat you. You're a proud man, James. Not that that lessens you in my book.'

'You're way off the track, Robert. With all that's gone on, I'd forgotten Dennison.' But the voice was unconvincing. 'Well, I admit, I wish I knew. I have a feeling I've missed some vital clue. It's there but I can't put my finger on it.'

'There you go. You're off. Let it go, mon. Cari's right. Your first duty is to get her to safety – and yourself.'

'It could be Aramgu, of course. Just 'cos Price-Allen wanted to frame him doesn't mean he's innocent. But then there's that creepy neighbour of yours, Silent, and the Italian. They're still in the frame.'

'You're incorrigible. Actually I learned a bit more last even, before the fireworks started.' McGuiry stopped himself. What a loose-tongued fool, he thought. 'Well, it wasna' much. Forget it.'

Odhiambo laughed. It sounded strange – it seemed a long time since he had had cause to do so.

'Too late now, Robert. Out with it. I'm not going to go around detecting. Even I don't believe the morning after a coup is the best time for that.'

'Well, the main thing came from our laddie here. Joseph, the houseman. It seems the Dennisons' servant is from the same village. He told Joseph, Dennison never came home Monday night. I asked him if he was sure. He said yes: Dennison's servant never saw him after he went to Silent's party. Ye ken what that means?'

'The servant was on duty?'

'Obviously. Come on, James. Why would he go around saying he dinna come home if he wasn't there himself?'

'OK. Don't get *kali*. So if your man's right, Anne Dennison was lying. And why would she be?' He paused, but only theatrically before answering his own question. 'Because she didn't want suspicion to fall on her friends. She didn't want us to think Dennison died in Silent's house. That explains why he never leaves her alone.'

'But that means she must have been in on it. Why else would she protect that slimy fellow Silent? Perhaps she and Silent are lovers. Bumped poor ol' hubby off as he was in the way. Wouldn't be the first time that's happened. Wouldn't even be the first time something similar happened here. Remember that Lord Erroll fellow who was murdered here in Karen and the Broughtons? Love triangle again. He got off, of course, and she owns half Kenya – Lady Delamere she is now.'

'The Happy Valley set lives on, you mean. The drugs, the kinky sex, the jealousies and the murders.'

'Anyway, forget it. You dinna want the case in the first place. Out there on the golf course you said, "Not me. No more dead *mzungus* for me." Where are ye going?'

McGuiry was startled as Odhiambo got up very suddenly from the table and headed for the door.

'I wonder if she's still there? In Silent's house.'

'James, this is not the time for more detecting. That's what you just said.'

But Odhiambo was gone. Cursing to himself, and with a guilty look towards the garden beyond the windows, McGuiry laboured after him.

Odhiambo's knocking at Michael Silent's front door produced no response, so with McGuiry now back in contact they walked around the side of the house to the servants' quarters. A sleepy-looking tall man emerged whom McGuiry recognised as the

152

Masai house servant who had let him into the house during his last encounter with the occupant.

Odhiambo's curt demand as to the whereabouts of his master produced only a surly non-committal response. McGuiry thought that Silent probably demanded extreme discretion from his staff and the Masai were inclined to be non-cooperative with officialdom in any case. Odhiambo was getting angry and the servant increasingly stubborn so McGuiry intervened, addressing the startled man in his own ancient language of the nomadic warrior tribe. Initial surprise gave way to doubt, and then suddenly the man seemed to relax as if conversation in his own language placed the questioner and himself in a different cultural context, sitting around a fire on the plains watching for predators seeking to invade the cattle herded into a thorn-protected compound.

Finally, McGuiry said his farewells and turned away, taking his policeman friend by a reluctant arm.

'What the hell was all that about?' Odhiambo's frustrations were ready to boil over. It was humiliating to have a *mzungu* acting as an interpreter in order for two native Kenyans to speak to each other. 'You didn't tell me you spoke the language of the Masai.'

'Ach, I've spent a year or two down in the Rift with yon laddies. Not easy to gain their confidence, ye ken, but no hope at all unless you talk to them in their own lingo.'

'You bloody old colonials, still patronising us. OK, so what did he say?'

'Silent left before your *shauri* here yesterday. And before the coup, of course. He's no been back.'

'And why couldn't he tell me that in Swahili? Stupid bastard.'

'Tut, tut, James. Let's have no tribal animosities.' McGuiry was beginning to enjoy himself. 'He said more than that. Well, sort of implied, if ye get my meaning?'

'I'm going to throttle you in a minute, Robert. You've made your point, now get to the real point.'

'I asked about the white woman. Mrs Dennison, I mean. I asked if she "belonged" to his boss. He almost laughed at me. I get the impression that our Mr Silent may have preferred Jim Dennison to his wife, if you get my meaning. And if you want my opinion, yon Masai is a bit more than a house cleaner. There were precedents for that in the old days.'

153

The two men had reached the road again and were passing the unoccupied house that separated Silent's house from their own temporary abode. Odhiambo's temper had subsided and he was deep in troubled thought.

'Homo or bisexual, it could explain a lot.'

McGuiry was looking at the driveway of the Smyth compound.

'So this is where you and Aramgu got your heads down yesterday. Comrades in distress, sort of. I'll tell ye something else, James. Last even, before things got bad, I was talking to that Secretary fellow. He said his brother-in-law is hardly ever here. But others use it. And he was sort of secretive about it. Tapping his nose. Lowering his voice. All of that.'

But Odhiambo did not seem interested in Hill-Templeton and his relatives.

'Come on, McGuiry, we've got to get over to Anne Dennison's place.'

'Och, you're a stubborn fellow. What's the little lady going to make of this?'

McGuiry was soon to find out for Cari intercepted them in the drive and was not best pleased when her husband indicated his intentions. Odhiambo paused to explain to both of his companions.

'Look, Cari, I have to. It's nothing to do with obsession with the job. Robert here knows. This woman Anne Dennison is protecting the man who might be her husband's killer. Yet I don't think it's because of the usual love triangle. I think he persuaded her that her husband's name would be ruined, and hers too, if she told of their little parties. So it was best not to say that the last place Dennison was seen alive was in Silent's house. She believed that Silent and her other friends had nothing to do with it. But she's no fool. Robert will tell you she was starting to ask questions the last time he saw her. If Silent thinks she now suspects him and the others she'll be in great danger.'

'But why are you more concerned about a lying woman than your own safety?' Cari continued her protest, but the conviction was lacking. 'Why are you the one that has to be responsible?'

'Because it was Robert and I that asked the questions that put the doubts in her mind. And we did it in front of Silent. So we are responsible and we ought to see that she's all right.'

Cari turned to the Scotsman, but with a resigned air.

154

'You see, Robert, it's hopeless. What do you do with a man like this? Anyway, I'm coming too.'

After some argument it was agreed that, as the Dennison house was on the way to Nairobi, they would all go together, check on the safety of Anne Dennison and then proceed to the Odhiambos' house closer to the city where both Odhiambos could obtain a badly needed change of clothes. Abandoning the borrowed jeep they set off in McGuiry's Land Rover. The road from Karen towards the city was quiet. The radio commands were being obeyed, people were staying at home. They were stopped only once and Odhiambo's police pass was sufficient for them to be allowed to continue. Odhiambo directed McGuiry to the side road containing the Dennison house and thence to the house itself. As the Land Rover squealed to a stop beside the front door a figure emerged and hurried to greet them.

'You are police, yes? You come at last.'

'Hold on.' Odhiambo jumped down, followed more slowly by his companions. 'Who are you?'

'I am Amir. I am houseboy for *Bwana* Dennison. Now for Memsahib Dennison. You come quick. It is bad. First the *bwana* now this.'

Odhiambo felt his heart race and his spirits slump. The servant was clearly very distressed. They were too late. He knew what they were going to find.

'OK. Lead the way. Robert, you stay here with Cari while I see what's happened.' He followed the servant back up the steps and through the front door. Amir hurried down the hall and down two steps to the lounge that Odhiambo remembered. He gestured towards the lounge while looking back at Odhiambo as if reluctant to look once more at what lay within. Odhiambo brushed past him and looked around. 'Christ.' The blasphemy was wrung from him for his astonishment was total. He gazed at the settee, trying to get his thoughts in order given this unexpected turn of events.

The body lay half on and half off the settee where it had slumped with the impact of the bullets. Blood had soaked part of the settee and the carpet beneath it. The face was unrecognisable as it had taken at least one bullet square on and central, which had left a bloody mess where the nose and eyes should be. The stains on the front of the corpse seemed to indicate that other bullets had entered the chest area. The coagulation was such it

155

was obvious the murder had occurred some time ago. Odhiambo crossed to the body to feel the skin, but this merely confirmed the obvious: the body was cold.

Odhiambo retraced his steps. Reaching the servant, who stood hand to mouth, he paused.

'What did you say your name was? Ah, Amir. Right, Amir, how long ago was this? Last night? Yes. OK. Stay here. I'll be right back.'

He found McGuiry and his wife waiting hesitantly on the steps by the front door.

'What is it, James?' Cari peered past him. 'What's happened? Is she all right?'

'I don't know. I haven't seen her. But Michael Silent is in there with half his head gone. He's been dead since last night.'

21

Aramgu and Sasaweni had reached one of Aramgu's properties deep in the Rift Valley under cover of darkness before road blocks this far from Nairobi had been set up. The dilatoriness of the Nakuru battalion to take any action whatsoever would be the subject of a later secret enquiry and would cost the officers their jobs and some their freedom. Now this morning, sitting on the verandah, they ate a breakfast of goat-meat and *ugali* and considered their options.

'We must assume they will come for us very soon.' This was Sasaweni. 'And for Price-Allen this will be a personal thing. He will come for us himself. We may have failed due to Lijodi's men, but I would wish to have the chance to finish with the *mzungu*.'

'You're a fool and like all fools you blame the other man.' Aramgu raised a bone to his mouth and tore a chunk of meat off it with his strong teeth. He spoke and chewed simultaneously. 'If your people had killed the *mzungu* as you were supposed to, the opposition might not have been organised. And we were told you'd even managed to lose that Luo policeman: his woman got him away from you. Ha! What people to have! Kiwonka and I deserved better.'

'I didn't see you in the forefront, Aramgu. Don't insult the leopard if you have no claws.'

'Leopard! The only resemblance between you and a leopard is the speed with which you ran away.'

'In order to keep up with you. But enough of this. We must not fight over what has been lost, when we need to join our wits to get out of this alive.'

'My plan is made, Sasaweni. From here I drive through the Masai Mara and into the Serengeti. Once there in Tanzania I go to Arusha. I have friends there. If Kiwonka is in Tanzania we can meet there or in Dar. The *mzungu* will have to wait. His time will come.'

'And the guards in the Mara? You think they will not be watching for us? And on the border.'

Aramgu snorted with derision. He looked at his fellow fugitive with unconcealed contempt.

'You were brought up in the towns, Sasaweni. Like a sewer rat you are blind when put in a field of maize. You think I am a fool? You think I intend to go into the park through the front gate paying my fee and saying to the guards, "I am Felix Aramgu"? No. There are paths used by the animals. One of my guards used to be a ranger here. He will take us where we will not see guards or soldiers. I go this evening.'

'Paths used by animals are no use to your Mercedes, Aramgu. And I don't see you walking through the Mara.'

'Go out in the back, man. You will find a four-wheel drive, small wheelbase. Now I must brief my man to plot our route with care, for our journey and our crossing into Tanzania will be in the dark.'

'One more thing, Aramgu.' Sasaweni sat forward in his chair, pushing his uneaten *ugali* to one side. 'Our plans were betrayed. Price-Allen knew too much. Where did the leak come from, Aramgu? Was it that white man you employed? The one who was killed?'

Aramgu got up from the table, leaned down and grabbed Sasaweni by his shirt, yanking him to his feet without seeming effort.

'Leaks, you say. It was the shambles in your own set-up you should think about. You thought you were plotting against the *mzungu* and your State Security men were with you. Well, many of them stayed with the *mzungu*, didn't they? As for Dennison, I

157

told you this before. He knew little. Only one thing he was involved in. Because of his connections with Uganda, where we send wheat and bring out coffee, he knew certain people. He acted as a courier for your people so that arrangements could be made to feed Price-Allen to the crocodiles. Naturally your clowns bungled it. But this was past. Dennison's knowledge was no good once it was over.'

'Rumour was that Dennison was ready to talk and had to be stopped. Perhaps he had already talked and you were too late.'

'You shithead. You dare to talk to me like this?' Aramgu pulled Sasaweni towards him and them straightened his arm with the speed of a boxer's jab, letting go of Sasaweni's shirt as his arm extended. Sasaweni was hurled backwards, losing his footing and tumbling off the verandah into the dirt below. Slowly he pulled himself to his feet as Aramgu stomped off to look for his ex-ranger. There was venom in his eyes as he watched the retreating back. He spoke quietly to himself.

'Get me to Tanzania, you bloated braggart, and then we shall see whether you should have dared to touch me.'

Price-Allen sat in the office he had established within the air force base from which he had co-ordinated the use of the State Security men who had remained loyal. The President and the government had been saved, but he was concerned that, in the course of the action, figures had emerged into positions of power who threatened to sideline him. He would need to give much thought to the next few months, which were likely to see many fluctuations in the power base and many opportunities to enhance or lose influence. But first there was a pressing matter to deal with. Aramgu and one of his own men, Sasaweni, had plotted not only against the government but against himself. Kiwonka might temporarily be beyond his ability to reach, but he was determined not to let the others escape him. Once again he was pleased with the way he had placed his pawns in readiness. One of his own men had been carefully manipulated into a sleeping agent position as one of Aramgu's bodyguards. Contact had already been established and Price-Allen looked forward to a trip to the game park.

Not a pressing matter, more one of light entertainment, was

the story he had just been told by the trembling wretch sitting opposite him, with a guard standing behind him.

'So, not only are you a traitor, but you are not able to handle a woman. Deceived and knocked out by a woman. Your name will cause shame to your family for generations.'

The man slipped forward on to his knees to beg for mercy, but the watcher behind him leant forward and hauled him back to the chair.

'Only one thing I want. Did they say anything that you heard before they got away?'

The man gibbered his apologies that he had heard nothing. Price-Allen gestured and the former security man left in charge of Odhiambo by Sasaweni was dragged from the room. Price-Allen sat back in his chair, and allowed himself a small, thin smile. What a woman. He really was growing quite fond of her. His whimsical gesture of last night had been seized by her and put to good use. Cari Odhiambo was a woman of resource and intelligence. What a pity she had a lumbering plodder for a husband. Now, where would they turn up again? Odhiambo would be consumed with a burning desire to get even with the man who had kidnapped his wife and arranged for him to die, so he could wait for him to turn up. There would be another score for him to settle, namely with Aramgu and, bizarre though it seemed, Price-Allen believed there was even a chance that Odhiambo would be trying to find Dennison's killer.

Dismissing the Odhiambos from his mind, or rather deferring further consideration of their fate, Price-Allen returned to the main issue of the day, the interception of the leading fugitives. He reached for the telephone; he needed to give instructions to the police and national park authorities to ensure that their men on the ground did not get in the way and alarm his quarry. Also, there were detailed arrangements to make within the Masai Mara. Revenge was only sweet if it was undertaken smoothly and carried out with style. Then one could enjoy the climax as one witnessed the pain.

Superintendent Masonga was still at his desk where he had been throughout the night. The air was so contaminated with cigarette smoke that not only was it difficult to see, it was even difficult to breathe without coughing. He had done his best to keep his men off the streets while the army fought it out. The central police station had been briefly occupied by Lijodi's troops, but apart from informing Masonga that he should await further orders they had not bothered him and soon left – never, as it turned out, to return. He was now trying to re-establish some presence of his men on the streets to look into reported crime, although the major area of looting and even murder was still a no-go area for them, the army having virtually sealed it off. His opposite number in charge of the police stations in the city and its suburbs had disappeared, so, in default of a senior officer, Masonga found himself fielding requests for instructions from junior officers who were gradually re-establishing contact with, and organisation of, these stations.

His mouth and throat felt dry and tasted awful. He needed a Pepsi. Wearily he got up and crossed to the door. Opening it allowed the fetid air to escape, causing his long-suffering clerk to splutter.

'Get me a Pepsi, will you? I need a drink.'

'*Ndio, bwana*.' The clerk got to his feet and reached for his stick, for he had one semi-useless leg, caused by an accident when he was a street officer. 'I was going through these incident reports as you told me. There's this one.' He picked up a sheet from the pile on his desk. 'I thought you would be interested. A houseboy reported early last evening a murder in the house. Not the occupants, but another man. Nobody go yet due to the troubles.'

'Well, get somebody there now. Why do you say it's for me?'

'The servant say he work for Mr and Mrs Dennison. It's the house where the body is.'

'You say what? Dennison. The *mzungu* murdered at the golf club. Whose body?'

The clerk shook his head. 'This report doesn't say.'

'This was Odhiambo's case.' Masonga had sent out an alert to all his men to watch for his missing Chief Inspector. He had also tried to contact Price-Allen, but access to the white man was, it seemed, on a very restricted basis. A dark possibility crossed his mind. It couldn't be . . . why would he be there? The clerk watched as his boss stood thinking. 'OK. Get me that drink, then I'm going to that house. Get someone to join me. And tell me how to get there.'

Half an hour later, Masonga's car pulled up behind a Land

Rover that had seen better days. He jumped out and seeing the front door ajar he hurried in. To their mutual consternation he collided with his subordinate who was on the way out. Behind him he could see Odhiambo's wife and the game ranger who had been to see him to report Odhiambo's disappearance.

'Odhiambo! What the hell are you doing here?'

Odhiambo tried to collect his wits.

'And you? I only called in a minute ago. We came looking for Mrs Dennison.'

'The houseboy reported it last night, but no one could do anything then. But God Almighty, man, this is not the morning for you three to be playing detective. Is it the woman? Where's the body?'

'No time to explain, but I was afraid for Mrs Dennison's safety so we came over. But it's not her. It's another of their circle. A man called Silent. There's no sign of the woman.'

Masonga took the time to view the body, before returning to the matter of his officer.

'I'm getting someone to deal with this. But you, Odhiambo, if you've got any sense or care for your wife, it's time to lie low. What happened with you and Price-Allen?'

'He set me up to be killed with Aramgu, but here I am thanks to Cari. I haven't had time to make plans. Where is Price-Allen?'

'God knows and I don't care. I'm trying to get some order back into things.'

'We need to find the Dennison woman.'

'Why? We'll pick her up in due course. You said she was in danger. Well, maybe you were right. That *mzungu* in there came to threaten her so she shot him. Maybe she can claim self-defence. But this is all for later.'

Cari Odhiambo and McGuiry had been hovering in the wings during these exchanges. Cari decided it was time to put her foot down.

'Quite right, Mr Masonga. Your Super is right, James. This is not the time to worry about your case. I want to go home. Tell him, Mr Masonga.'

There was the sound of another vehicle outside followed almost immediately by the entrance of Inspector Ntende and a uniformed policeman.

'Ntende!' Odhiambo was surprised. 'This is not your sort of business.'

v arrival laughed. 'On a day like today it's no good your job description – especially when the Superin- ants support.'

Masonga was pleased that someone competent had turned up. 'Seal this place and try and get someone to check the body before you move it. And don't take all day – we've got more to worry about than a dead *mzungu*.'

'What body we got in there?'

Odhiambo was the first to answer.

'Silent. Michael Silent. One of the group around Dennison you told me about a day or two ago. Jeez, it seems like a year.'

Ntende whistled.

'There won't be many of that lot left the rate they're going. Mr Masonga, can we go outside a minute, without . . .' He gestured at Cari Odhiambo and McGuiry. 'There's some news you may want to hear.'

Masonga followed Ntende back to the front step. Odhiambo followed, willing to assume, even if erroneously, that Ntende had not excluded him.

'What is it, Ntende?'

'I heard from a contact of mine. In the air force intelligence. They think Aramgu and others are down in the Rift Valley head- ing for Tanzania. Price-Allen is going to go after them person- ally. In the park.'

Masonga snorted. 'Well, I hope the lions get the bloody lot.' He stopped, as if realising his indiscretion. 'Thanks, Ntende. It's useful to know. Right. Odhiambo, this is an order. Get your wife to safety, get rid of your *mzungu* friend and then we'll talk.'

'Yessir. What with you and Cari I'll do as I'm told. But one question for you, Ntende, my friend. Has he gone yet – Price- Allen, I mean? When is he hoping to get them?'

'That's two questions, Odhiambo. No. My man says they're setting it up for tonight.'

Masonga's insistence, Cari's look of anger and McGuiry's look of embarrassment finally did the trick: an uneventful ten- minute drive and they were back at the Odhiambo home. McGuiry, despite his protestations, was persuaded to stay, Odhiambo arguing that the streets were no place for him on his own. After a shower and a change of clothes both Odhiambos joined their guest with a pot of coffee on the verandah. The weather was cooler than it had been during the week and there was a smell of rain as the clouds built up from the direction of Mount Kenya. Cari Odhiambo felt a little better. Perhaps the nightmare was ending and this time she could persuade her husband to come to the States. It did not take her long, however, to feel uneasy again. James was sunk once more in his own thoughts and she could feel the tension growing within him.

'Come on, James, you're ignoring your guest.'

Odhiambo looked across at McGuiry and then sideways to his wife's troubled face. He didn't know how to start. It was as he was dressing that he had seen, with absolute clarity and conviction, himself face to face with Price-Allen. And an inner voice with total certainty had said, 'There is no escaping until you have settled what you owe this man.' And then, trying to dismiss this from his mind as he sipped his coffee, he had suddenly seen, dimly and with many blank areas, a coming together of the recent murders and a possible explanation. His mind, after the stresses of the last days, seemed suddenly to have a laser-like ability to penetrate the confusions that had beset him.

Well, there was nothing for it. He put down his cup carefully, as if it was important to place it exactly in the centre of the saucer.

'Cari – Robert – I'm sorry, but I have to play the story out. It is destiny. I know you'll say I'm crazy, but I've seen the future and I can't avoid it!'

22

Stefano and Gianna Iocacci had bolted and shuttered their house in the hope of surviving the coup without damage to themselves when a telephone call from Anne Dennison caused their minds to revert to their other problem. Since the traumatic interview with Odhiambo, the Iocaccis had been conducting themselves in a strained, artificial manner with neither able to talk over with the other the one thing which both wished to talk about – what was to happen to them and their life in Kenya given their involvement with the victims of the two murders and the circumstances of the murders? They were scared enough to keep their promise to the policeman and refrain from getting in touch with

ilent: what surprised Stefano Iocacci was that Silent
en in touch with them. Silent's likely approach had
m, because he knew that under scrutiny from that
y powerful personality his resistance would crumble
and he would tell of Odhiambo's suspicions. But then as news of
civil unrest reached them, Iocacci felt almost relieved: Silent
would have other things to worry about now, to say nothing of
Odhiambo. At last, he managed to raise something in conversation with his wife that went beyond the trivial.

'We lie low and let these Africans fight it out. We'll be all right
if we stay indoors. There's always coups in Africa. As soon as it's
over we get out. We go and then I'll fix it with the company for
another posting.'

The dark eyes of his wife, set within a face that seemed to have
aged years in the last three days, filled with tears, but tears this
time of gratitude.

'Oh, yes, Stef. Please. That would be very good. I want to get
away from all this. This business,' she gestured to the walls with
her arm indicating her concern with the world beyond them,
'and the group. It has got too much. I . . . I don't mean because of
Jim and Pauline – or not only because of them – I . . . I was having worries before . . . about Michael, particularly.'

The wall that had risen between them had started to fall.
Iocacci started to protest, to defend Michael and their friends,
but he stopped himself. Better to sympathise with her fears, at
least for now. He knew his wife well enough to realise that she
was dangerously near the edge of a nervous breakdown. And
then the telephone rang. He recognised the voice and he could
also detect the hysteria.

'Stefano, I need help. I'm coming round. Is that all right? I have
to leave here.'

'Anne, *cara mia*. There is talk of a coup and fighting has started.
It is not safe to go on the road. You would be safer there. You are
at home?'

'You don't understand. I can't stay here. Not with . . . well, I'll
tell you when I get there.'

'I really think you should not go out. What is worrying you?'

'I cannot tell you on the phone. But it is awful. And I don't
know who to turn to. Gianna is my best friend. Please. Please.'

'Of course you may come, but I am worried for your safety.'

'Yes. I am in danger here. I must get away. I can't bear to look . . .'

164

Iocacci heard the sound of suppressed sobs, then a muffled voice saying something he didn't quite catch, then silence.

'Anne, Anne . . .' He was conscious of his wife, who had risen and moved towards him as the seriousness of the conversation became apparent. The line was dead. He replaced the phone. 'That was Anne Dennison. She sounds scared out of her wits, but wouldn't say why. She's on her way here. I tried to tell her it won't be safe to drive, but she wouldn't listen.'

'Oh my God, Stef. What's happened now? It's a nightmare. I can't stand any more.' She beat her hands against his chest and started to scream. 'Get me out of here. Please.'

Two hysterical women, thought Iocacci. What have I done to deserve this? The trouble was he knew the answer. He should have stayed clear of Michael Silent. There were other groups interested in some wife-swapping and other ways of getting hold of social drugs. He had known Silent was dangerous from the first time he met him.

Anne Dennison arrived safely, heralded by a squeal of tyres. Iocacci had found his nightwatchman and told him to open the gate until one car arrived and to lock it securely afterwards. He waited as Anne hurried up the steps on to his verandah dressed in blouse, slacks and, incongruously, an unzipped golf jacket. She saw her friend behind him in the doorway and rushed unceremoniously past to embrace a startled Gianna.

'Oh, Gianna, I'm so glad to see you. It's terrible. It's Michael . . . He's . . . he's dead!'

The Iocaccis managed to get their hysterical guest into the house and settled in a chair with a large gin and tonic. After a long swallow of her drink, her words became just slightly more coherent. Iocacci probed gently.

'Tell us what happened, Anne. Slowly. Only then can we help. We must know first what happened.'

'Michael was a great support to me since Jim . . . since Jim was found. I thought he was being considerate. I even lied to the police for him. But all the time it was him!'

'What do you mean, "it was him"?'

'He said, "Look, we don't want the police getting into our private affairs. Embarrassing for all of us." He said Jim left his place during the early hours. He didn't know what happened to him afterwards. He must have been still drunk and started walking across the golf course. That's what he said. And then he was

165

r something. So he asked me to keep you all out of it.
I believed him.'

ised and took another mouthful of her drink. Iocacci's
as he tried to interpret her meaning. His wife sat, fist
to her mouth, as if in shock.

'Are you saying Michael killed Jim? Is that what you mean?'

'I believed him when he said he didn't know what happened.
And I told the police that Jim was home the next morning. But he
wasn't. At the time Michael told me he'd gone straight to the
office because there were important things to do. Another lie, of
course. Then when he was found he had the other story. Oh, how
could I have been such a fool?' Once more the glass was raised
and this time it was drained except for the ice cubes. Iocacci took
it from her fingers and crossed to the bar.

'Go on. You haven't told us how he was involved. And what
has happened now.'

'He told me how difficult it would be if I told the police Jim
didn't come home. And he made sure I wasn't alone. But then
you, Gianna, told me there'd been a row earlier. And you two
had left Jim and Pauline behind. Then some man came around to
Michael's house when I was there and as good as accused
Michael or both of us of killing Jim and Pauline. Michael was
angry. Very angry.' She took the fresh drink from Iocacci, but
now seemed intent on her story. 'I started to think things over.
Then Michael went out. He told me to stay. He'd be back in an
hour, he said. I decided to find the man who had come to
Michael's house. He was supposed to be a neighbour. I went
next door. It was all locked up. I mean, it seemed as if there was
no one living there. But when I went round the back to see if
there were any servants, I caught sight of something glinting in
the drain. It was a tie-pin. The Ngong bloody Golf Club Commit-
tee pin. I had a good look through the french windows. Nothing
to see inside. But then at the bottom of the windows there was a
peculiar stain. Doesn't take a genius to figure it was blood, Jim's
blood.'

Iocacci stared at his guest bemused.

'What are you saying? Michael took Jim next door to an empty
house and killed him? Mary, Mother of God! Why would he do
it?'

'I didn't know. I still don't know. I made some excuse to go
home. Said I was all right. But I guess Michael was suspicious.

166

He came to check me out earlier this evening. By then I'd done some more thinking. He started to question me. I could see he was suspicious. I guess you'd say the scales had fallen from my eyes. So I accused him outright and said, "Why next door?" He asked me what I was talking about. I said he should have cleaned up properly. He started to get up, but I had prepared myself. I pointed Jim's gun at him. I said I'd give him ten seconds to tell me the truth. He tried to wheedle me out of it, but the more he tried the more I saw him for what he is. He then had some cock and bull story about I might be right, but it was Jim's boss's people from the other side of his house who had taken Jim. Something to do with an argument he'd had with Mr Aramgu. I pretended to be convinced and lowered the gun. Then I saw his thoughts in his eyes and I knew I was next. As he came for me I shot him. He kind of jumped backwards on to the sofa. His head . . . Oh God, his head . . . It was horrible!'

Gianna Iocacci let out a cry that strangled itself as she choked on the bile that surged into her throat. She swallowed hard and fell back into her chair, her throat burning. Stefano Iocacci felt physically dizzy. The implications of what they had just heard were so wide-reaching and dangerous that his mind processes seemed to be in a sort of free spin. Their guest, on the other hand, seemed now to be more composed, as if recounting the dreadful events had removed the cause of her strain. She took a sip of her drink and then another, but in a more controlled manner than the gulping of her earlier one.

Iocacci sought desperately for words, any words.

'Was there anyone . . . ? Servants . . . ? Is there anyone there now?'

Anne Dennison did not seem to be concerned regarding witnesses to her deed. She was still thinking through the circumstances of her husband's killing.

'So the only question is, who helped him? If everybody else is lying to me, why not you? Did you help him, Stefano?'

From the pocket of her golf jacket, the killer of Michael Silent produced a pistol and pointed it at her dumbfounded host.

'What are you doing? Put it down, woman! Of course I had nothing to do with it. Gianna will tell you, when we left Jim was alive.'

'Somebody must have helped him. He couldn't have buried Jim on his own.'

'You haven't convinced me that Michael did it. But if he did . . . '
Iocacci's mind was now working at full speed under the threat
of the barrel pointed at his midriff. 'If he did, those servants of
his would have helped him. Those Masai would do anything for
him.'

Whether his words had the desired effect Iocacci would never
know, because his wife had risen to her feet, crossed between
him and the threatening gun and now reached down and calmly
took hold of the hand holding it.

'Anne! You've killed one man tonight, you're not going to kill
another – my husband. Of course he – we had nothing to do with
it.'

Gianna Iocacci applied a little more pressure and to her husband's amazement and relief Anne Dennison released her grip
and allowed the gun to pass into the other woman's hand.

A very long time later, in the early hours of the next day, the
trio collapsed due to exhaustion, mental and physical, and, in
the case of Anne Dennison, alcohol. They had made very little
progress in deciding what to do next: Stefano believed the police
ought to be informed before they discovered the body or had the
shooting reported to them by one of the servants and came looking for Anne, but Gianna wanted to wait. Stefano, himself, realised that phoning the police in the middle of a coup was
unlikely to be fruitful. Anne Dennison, as the evening pro-
gressed, seemed to lose interest in the future as if she was dis-
associated from it rather than someone likely within hours to be
arrested for murder.

Because it was dawn before the Iocaccis collapsed into bed,
having laid their comatose guest on a bed in the guest room, they
were still behaving like zombies in their kitchen, putting
together the basis of a breakfast despite the approach of midday,
when the nightwatchman (who had stayed on the premises, regarding it as a safe haven) informed them of visitors at the gate.
Iocacci went out to check who his visitors might be, and was not
altogether surprised when he recognised the large black man
standing on the other side of the gate.

'Omb . . . Od . . . you're the policeman who was here before.'

'Correct. Odhiambo. Chief Inspector Odhiambo. Let us in,
please, sir. I need to see you.'

Iocacci gestured to his watchman and waited as the other man,
who he recognised as Odhiambo's companion from their pre-

vious encounter, drove the Land Rover through the opened entrance. He waved them ahead of him into the house and followed them through the door. Odhiambo swung to face him, coming straight to the point.

'Have you seen Mrs Anne Dennison since last evening? Is she here?'

Iocacci hesitated, but there was no way he was going to stick his neck out for Anne Dennison. He hadn't much liked her anyway, even before she had become the murderer of a friend of his.

'Yes. She came here last night. She was distressed. She's resting.'

'Did she tell you what she was distressed about?'

Before Iocacci could reply he heard his wife's voice from behind him.

'Why shouldn't she be distressed? There's enough for her to be distressed about. Her husband dead. Fighting in the streets. You think any of us should be cheerful, Inspector?'

'I must see her, if you please.'

'You want me, Mr Policeman?'

Odhiambo turned. There was his quarry standing half-way down the staircase, looking dishevelled as if she had slept in her clothes – which, he thought, was probably, the case. McGuiry, standing beside him, felt a great sense of relief. He didn't know what they would have done next if Odhiambo's hunch had proved to be mistaken.

'Mrs Dennison, could I ask you some questions, please?'

'Oh, cut the crap. You've found him, haven't you?'

'Him? Who are you refering to, madam?'

Anne Dennison had reached ground level now and glanced at her hosts before looking back at her questioner.

'Michael, of course. Michael Silent.'

'Yes. Mr Silent's body has been found in your house.'

'Well, I shot him. It was self-defence. He threatened me because I found out that he killed my husband. So there. That's what you want to know.'

Over the next fifteen minutes Odhiambo was given the same story that the Iocaccis had been given the previous night; the difference being that Anne Dennison was now composed and in control of her emotions. It was, Iocacci thought, as if she had been though a catharsis and emerged with all doubt and guilt expunged.

Odhiambo asked for the revolver and was given it by Iocacci. He probed further regarding the woman's actions.

'You say you went to the house next door believing it was there that this gentleman', pointing at McGuiry, 'lived?'

'Yes. Michael referred to him as a neighbour.'

'In your visits to Mr Silent's house, not just in the last few days, but as a member of his social group, did you ever see anyone living in that house?'

'I wouldn't have noticed. Why should I?'

'Did Mr Silent ever refer to the occupant of that house?'

'Not that I know of. I have no idea who lives there.'

'Why do you think your husband would have been taken there? Why would Mr Silent have the key to the place?'

Anne Dennison's composure began to crack.

'How the hell should I know? You should have asked Michael. Perhaps he was looking after the place for whoever owns it. What does that matter? Jim's pin was there and there's blood on the step. Why don't you go and test it if you don't believe me?'

'Oh, I do believe you, Mrs Dennison. I do. But I can't ask Mr Silent to explain his actions because he's dead. You shot him.'

Gianna Iocacci had joined the gathering during Anne Dennison's recapitulation of her story. She had sat herself down against the wall of the lounge they were in, looking strained, her fist once more pressed against her mouth. But now, seeing Odhiambo begin to turn the screw as he had done with her, she repeated her previous night's performance of suddenly commanding centre stage. She walked over to Anne Dennison and stood beside her.

'That's enough. Anne has been through too much. Her husband killed. Now this affair. She has told you what she knows.'

Odhiambo looked as if he'd been bitten by a previously friendly puppy.

'I'm sorry, Mrs Iocacci, Mrs Dennison has confessed to shooting someone. I must ask her to elaborate on her suspicions.'

'There's time for that. She's had enough for now. While you're in my house I still have some rights.'

Her husband's mouth opened as if to support his wife's stand, but then shut again. Gianna gave him a withering look of contempt. Odhiambo observed this little by-play with interest. He had a feeling that the male Iocacci didn't wish to be involved in defending Anne Dennison in case he got dragged deeper into the mess. What might be more fruitful was a chat with him.

'OK, Mrs Iocacci, I understand. Just a couple more questions then you can take her to rest. Mrs Dennison, you will need a solicitor. You understand that your story of self-defence cannot just be accepted? It will be investigated.' The woman nodded. 'Now, can you tell me why Michael Silent would want to murder your husband?'

'I don't know. But they had some sort of row. Stefano will tell you. I think he was afraid Jim knew something about him.'

'He knew quite a lot about him, didn't he? Drug supplier for a start. But you all know that. Was Mr Silent in love with you? Did he want your husband out of the way?'

Anne Dennison laughed, a genuine spontaneous laugh. It somehow seemed slightly shocking in the context of the strained atmosphere of the Iocacci household.

'Michael Silent didn't fancy me, he fancied my husband. Michael was queer. OK, maybe he could get it up occasionally with Gianna here, but it was the men in the group that got him going.'

Odhiambo allowed the women to depart, but asked Stefano Iocacci to remain.

'Mr Iocacci, you were a close member of this group. Do you believe Mr Silent killed Mr Dennison?'

Iocacci seemed to consider his position for a few moments, lips pursed in indecision. Then, a decision made, he spoke clearly and to the point.

'Yes. But not because of tensions within the group. Something happened that Monday night. Gianna remembers more clearly than me, but Jim seemed to threaten Michael. Not . . . what is the word . . . not explicitly, you understand. But he made it clear he knew something about Michael's association with somebody.'

McGuiry, who had been silent so long, made his first contribution.

'What? Sex, you mean? Blackmail because he knew he was linked with some prominent man.'

Iocacci shrugged, a very expressive Italian shrug.

'I suppose. But no, I don't think so. Recently they seemed not to trust each other. I had the impression it was some affair of business.'

Odhiambo grunted as if at last they were getting somewhere.

'Dennison worked for Mbayazi Estates which is owned by a prominent politician called Aramgu who was a leader of the coup last night. Did Dennison ever talk about his work?'

'Not much. He handled the exports of coffee, wheat, that sort of thing.'

'What about Silent? What did he do?'

'Nothing as far as I know. Wealthy man. May have had business connections. Shares, that sort of thing. But work he didn't do. He liked to say he moved to his house this year because it was beside his only place of work. He meant the golf course.'

'He hadn't lived there long, then?'

'No. Less than three months.'

'And what about Miss Florislow?'

'I've been thinking about her. If Michael killed Jim Dennison, then it's for certain he killed her. Gianna told you that when we went home that night Jim and Pauline were still there. Suppose Michael forgot she was still sleeping in one of the bedrooms. She had no car with her. She had come with us. We assumed Michael would take her home in the morning. Suppose she saw something which didn't worry her at the time, but later when she knew Jim was dead she realised it was significant. That it meant Michael had killed him. And Michael found out she had still been in the house when he got rid of Jim so realised she might have seen something and she was about to tell you.'

Odhiambo pounced.

'But how did he know? That she wanted to see me, I mean. Only you saw us talking and, perhaps, saw her give me her card.'

Iocacci raised his hands as if to ward off a blow.

'I didn't tell him. I swear, I didn't tell him. Only much later, but by that time she was dead. I've told you the truth. Perhaps Michael was planning to get rid of her. It was coincidence that she had just asked to see you.'

McGuiry nodded. 'Could be, James. These coincidences do happen.'

Odhiambo looked unconvinced and glowered at the uncomfortable Italian. Then out of the corner of his eye he caught sight of the attractive figure of Gianna Iocacci who had sidled back into the room. He turned towards her.

'Mrs Iocacci, your husband is being co-operative with us, which is wise. Now, you were the one who realised there was a problem between Silent and Dennison. Think hard. What exactly was said?'

The dark eyes locked with his own. She looked, thought Odhiambo, to be at the limit of what her nerves could stand. Nevertheless in her posture, in her gaze and in the vibes he could pick up he was in no doubt there stood some woman.

'I can't remember the words. I told you, Michael made fun of Jim's impotency. And Jim answered something about there was more to concentrate on than sex.'

'That's too general. Be more specific, please, Mrs Iocacci. It's important.'

All three men watched the woman intently as she struggled with her memories.

'I remember Michael saying Jim wasn't as up to it as his boss. Then Jim said something about being too busy for sex. Now I think about it, I think he was talking about this boss that Michael spoke of. And then Michael said he'd be better sticking to sex as that's where his only brains were.' She paused, straining her powers of recollection. 'Jim told him to be careful. He might have to change sides very soon. Then he said something about costs and then I remember he said, "He was lucky once but you shouldn't count on it again." '

'And that was all?'

'Yes, I think so. Michael went quiet. That's why I remember it. He seemed to be thinking. Shortly after he got up and left the room.'

Odhiambo looked at McGuiry and nodded. His hypothesis was standing up. Jim Dennison, carried away with drink or drugs or both, had signed his own death warrant. If only he could pin down the source of the Pauline Florislow information: that was the loose end. The Mbayazi Estates manager, Mantebe, was ruled out by Odhiambo's theory, unless he was playing a two-faced game himself. Too late now to find him once more: he would almost certainly have gone to ground if he had survived Aramgu's bungled coup.

Ten minutes later the two men left the Iocacci residence. McGuiry, hanging grimly on to the shaking steering wheel with both hands, could contain himself no longer.

'So where does that leave us, James? Did ye think the Eyeties gave us the confirmation we were looking for?'

'Think it out for yourself, Robert. Dennison was drunk and

angry at being insulted and blurted out too much. He didn't realise the extent to which the man he was used to having sex with,
or whatever, was in the political game too. I think Iocacci's right.
Pauline saw Dennison being taken out, but the significance
didn't hit her until after his body was found. But forget your
crap about coincidences. I don't buy it.'

'But she dinna give ye the final piece. She dinna have the
name.'

Odhiambo laughed. 'I'd have thought you might have been a
crossword puzzle solver, Robert. Obviously not.' He looked out
of the window of his door. They were passing some industrial
and office units. As he looked, the logo that caught his eye on the
side of the building was for one of the rapidly growing private
security firms. 'Stay Secure', it read in big letters and underneath
in smaller print, 'and Rest Easy.'

McGuiry, disgruntled at James' coyness in revealing his
thought processes, got his own back on returning to his friend's
personal problem.

'Cari was far from happy, mon. She went along 'cos of the
depth of your feelings. You shook me, shook me rigid. As if you
were possessed by your pagan Luo gods. Dinna break your
promise to her after this is over, mind. Not if you want to keep
my respect. Assuming you're still around. So now you reckon
you've got the evidence, over it goes to your boss to handle.
That's what I heard said to that fine gal of yours.'

'But there's the other matter, Robert. I told her to get hold of a
plane from her friend at Wilson Airfield at our expense. I said I
had to work out my destiny.'

The old Scot looked sideways at the profile of his passenger
and sadly shook his head.

'James, there's no changing ye. Now we're nearly at your station. Go in, hand it over, mon, and get back to Cari.'

'Watch where you're going.' The Land Rover had veered towards the pavement as McGuiry's eyes left the road. 'You drive
and I'll make the decisions. You nearly hit that sign-board.' Sign-
boards, signs. Suddenly he remembered the one he had seen two
minutes earlier and that in turn brought back another to his
memory. He grabbed McGuiry's arm, almost precipitating another lurch on to the pavement. 'Go on, through the centre. God,
Robert, I think I've got it. The missing piece. I knew I had the

174

answer somewhere. I need to check something. Down to Kenyatta Avenue and off to where that library is.'

The excitement in his voice brooked no refusal. The old man sighed, clutched the wheel even move firmly and headed in the direction instructed. To be fair, he admitted to himself, he hadn't had such fun in years.

23

Odhiambo climbed the stairs which he had climbed once before. The building in this mainly Asian business area had not escaped the attentions of the looters of the night before. When he reached the first landing, there were the two doors he had seen on his previous visit; now both were battered and ajar. The sign for the lawyer Singh hung down, attached to the door by only one remaining screw. The other sign was still intact. There was no indication of life from within either doorway. Odhiambo paused and then resumed his climb. The doors on the top floor were intact: the looters seemed not to have climbed the stairs. The Mustapha brothers would still have premises in which to conduct their valuations and Mbayazi Estates awaited their owners – should they be in a position to return. An inconsequential thought passed through Odhiambo's mind – he wondered what had happened to the ex-boxer, now sleepy doorman. Merely speculatively, he knocked on the door and then tried to turn the handle. It was no surprise when the door failed to open and no one came from inside to unlock it. Odhiambo retraced his steps to the floor below. A quick, instinctive look around, like a guilty schoolboy, and then he slipped into the gap left by the broken door guarding the holding company, Stasec. These were the offices directly under those of Mbayazi Estates. Apart from a couple of tables and chairs and an old metal filing cabinet, the open-plan office was bare. Opening a drawer in the filing cabinet at random revealed it to be empty. He pushed the top of the cabinet gently with his palm – the cabinet started to tilt. It was obviously nearly empty, although there was the sound of something sliding in the bottom drawer. Odhiambo looked around. The bareness did not give the impression of being caused by looting; there was no mess and nothing was overturned. It was as if the intruders, like himself, had cast an eye over it and found nothing of interest. If the lawyer's room was equally bare it was not surprising that the upper floor had survived untouched; the loot seekers would have given the building up as containing only run-down or abandoned offices.

Odhiambo bent down and opened the bottom drawer of the filing cabinet. He found himself looking at two large magnetic tapes – recording tapes. A frisson of excitement sent a shiver down his back. His pulse rate quickened in anticipation. He moved away from the cabinet and slowly searched with his eyes the upper walls and ceiling. He found what he was looking for almost immediately.

Cari Odhiambo, two hours after she had agreed with her husband's obsession, could scarcely believe she had given in so easily. Not only had she failed to veto this latest manifestation of his impulse to stay involved, to stick with whatever task he was engaged on, she was actually aiding and abetting it. She had managed to speak to her old friend, a private pilot, due to, first, the fortunate survival of the telephone line and, second, his restriction to his house because of the coup. Now she was driving towards Wilson Airport to meet him, having persuaded him to venture forth. As she drove she said aloud, 'You're mad, my girl, you're mad.' But she knew it was James who was more likely to be certifiable. She, like McGuiry, had been stunned by his insistence that fate had ordained his course of action.

'I'm willing to leave, Cari. I am. But you know I can sometimes see into my future with utter certainty and this is one of those occasions. If I try and leave without seeing Price-Allen we will be stopped or he will hunt us down. If I see him, I can promise him I'll keep what I know to myself if he will let us go.'

She had tried, for a time she had tried.

'But what you know, everyone knows. He's a killer, but a state-sanctioned killer. What can you say to frighten a man like Price-Allen?'

'There will be a lot of suspicions now. The people around the President will wonder who was loyal and who was ready to change sides if the coup looked like succeeding. There'll be secret trials. Everyone will be running scared. I know that Price-

176

Allen knew Aramgu was ready to strike, but he didn't stop him. This could do for him in the atmosphere there's going to be around this town.'

'But why didn't he stop him? Why play elaborate games?'

'Because that's the way he is. Or maybe there was some deeper reason he wanted Aramgu dead in a gun battle with the police. He certainly didn't want him taken alive, which means he feared what Aramgu might know.'

'Oh, anyway, who cares? You can't risk your life. I won't let you.'

'I have to, Cari. You know I have to. I've seen what I have to do. But it will be all right. When I get these flashes, it's to guide me. I will only come to harm if I try and defy what I've seen. Call it what you will, my Luo ancestors, or whatever, I can't help it.'

Cari had looked over, helplessly, towards the old Scotsman who had watched and listened to this exchange with a grave face.

'Tell him, Robert. Tell him he's a fool. It's all nonsense in his head. Caused by tiredness or strain or whatever.'

McGuiry had looked at her sympathetically, but then slowly had shaken his head.

'I'm thinking you know better, my dear. I've seen it with others born in James' part of the country. I've been here too long and seen too much to call your troubled lad a fool.'

And so it had gone on, but Cari had mentally given in after these words. Her last attempt had been based on the improbability of his plan working, but his answer to that was equally difficult to contest.

'It has to work, otherwise what I've seen as inevitably happening can't happen.'

So here she was now, at this airfield used by those with their own small planes and by small charter companies and tourist safari firms. Her friend Paddy Andrews was waiting outside the gate. Cari jumped out of her car and greeted him with a quick peck on the cheek.

'Paddy, it's lovely to see you. It's been a long time. Thanks for coming out.'

'Cari, you know I'd come much longer distances than this to see you. I've never got over you meeting that bloody policeman.' He smiled, a regretful smile. God, thought Cari, I'd forgotten how handsome he is. The lean figure, the tanned face, blue eyes and wispy fair hair. And, a rare asset in her view, the right size and shape of legs to be able to wear shorts and look good in them. The nearest she would ever likely come to having an affair with Robert Redford. But it had been when they were both young. 'You broke my heart and it's still broken, you Jezebel.'

'Pull the other one, Paddy. I heard you were chasing other girls the minute I'd left your life.' She gave him another sisterly kiss. 'But it's great to see you, it really is.'

'And to what do I owe the pleasure?'

'Have you ever heard of a man called Price-Allen?'

Her old flame's brow gathered in a frown.

'He's no fit company for you. Don't tell me you're mixed up with that bastard?'

'Yes, we're obviously talking about the same man. James, that's the bloody policeman you're still cross about, has to know where he's going this afternoon or evening. He'll be almost certainly flying out of here. Do you know whose plane he uses?'

'His security people have got their own. I know the guy who normally flies him. But we're not mates.'

'What about the control people? He has to file a route or something, doesn't he?'

'Not absolutely necessary, always. But there's a good chance. Yeah, I know those guys pretty good. I could see who's on and see what I can get. Can you let me in on the deal?'

'Not really. I'm not sure I know myself. James thinks he's going to the Masai Mara. But where exactly? And if you can find out, maybe there's a job for you.'

'Cari, I tell you that man is bad news. I'd sooner track a wounded buffalo. Are you sure you want me to do this?'

'Please, Paddy. For old times' sake?'

The pilot gave a short laugh.

'Memories are not enough. I'll take that great hunk of yours and secretly I'll be helping Price-Allen get him, then perhaps you'll realise I'm still available.' He saw the pain pass across the beautiful face he remembered so well. 'Aw, shit, I'm sorry. I shouldn't joke about such things. I'll look after him. But I'll insist on a dinner date.'

'OK. And it'll be a dinner on me. But don't stand here flirting, get to it, man. You were never a slow starter in the old days. I'll wait in the car. Then maybe we can have a beer down the road.'

178

*

McGuiry sat in a small room with the short-wave radio crackling in his ear. James was closeted with his Superintendent trying to convince him that his plan was not insane, whilst McGuiry had been shown into the radio room where an impassive policeman was helping him establish contact with an old acquaintance from his hunting days who was now in charge of the Masai Mara's anti-poacher squad.

The policeman nodded at him and McGuiry bent forward to the microphone, at the same time adjusting the earphones on his head.

'Is that you, Alex? It's McGuiry here, Robert McGuiry. Over.'

'Bob! What're you doing in Nairobi? Not the place to be, from what I hear. Good to hear you, anyway. What can I do for you? Over.'

McGuiry put his request, replied to the other man's astonished reaction, argued the case and finally relied on the bonds of loyalty between old white hunters.

'We'll be on the side of good, Alex, that's the point, mon. We never shirked a challenge in the old days. So if we land in hot water we've had a good run. But I'm telling ye, the police will back us up – I'm speaking from their central station now. Our final track together, Alex. Ye canna let me down, mon.'

First a grudging acceptance, then the voice lifted as Alex Hayling entered into the spirit of the enterprise.

'I knew you'd land me in it one day, Bob. You remember that time in the Taita Hills? Back in the fifties? When you wrecked that bar over the girl who was the daughter of that chief? You were a bad man to be with then and it looks like you haven't changed.'

Superintendent Masonga lit a fresh cigarette from the stub of the last, which he then ground into an already overflowing ash-tray causing a further spillage of ash across the papers on his desk.

'If Price-Allen goes after Aramgu, he has a right to do so. Aramgu is a fugitive from the State. If we interfere we're the ones breaking the law. You're asking me to sanction you and your friends interfering in State Security.'

179

Odhiambo pressed his fists on Masonga's desk and bent his head lower towards that of his superior.

'You know and I know that Price-Allen has no intention of bringing Aramgu back alive. Look at the lengths he went to in order to kill him and me yesterday. So an unofficial agent of the State is going to commit murder. No different to some of the others he's arranged, I agree. But in doing so he's prejudicing my enquiries into a double murder, so I have the right to intervene. Given the chaos here today, I don't expect a full police back-up so I'm exercising my option of seeking the co-operation of other government officials who also happen to have public safety responsibilities. It's a cast-iron case.'

Masonga looked at the man looming over him with mixed emotions of irritation and sympathy.

'Look, Odhiambo, I understand the thing between you and the *mzungu*. You think I'm happy to have him giving out orders to me? But he's got the ear of the Big Man, you know that. You get in his way and you know what will happen.'

'No, Mr Masonga. If ever there was a moment to stop him, this is it. Half the State Security people were disloyal to the government. Price-Allen kidnapped my wife, in order to stage a killing which included me – a Chief Inspector of Police. He's gone outside the law and his actions are suspect even within the outlaw mentality of State Security. Anyway, I'm going. All I'm asking you for is passive tolerance and then if things go wrong to make sure Cari gets out of the country. You owe me that much.'

'And what about your hunter friend? You're putting him at risk. What future is there for him if you cock it up?'

Odhiambo paused to relish his victory. If Masonga was querying peripheral matters, as far as concerned Masonga's duties, such as the future of Odhiambo's friends, it meant he was going to allow matters to proceed.

'McGuiry's an old bull. I couldn't keep him out of it now if I tried. Now, there's a couple of other matters I have to fill you in on. You've got Mrs Dennison, have you?'

'Yes. Ntende brought her in. And the Italians. Did she kill her husband as well as this other man?'

'No, of course she didn't. She's got evidence that Silent did it. That's the man she killed. Look, she may have a self-defence argument so look after her until I get back. As for the Italians, I don't think they're involved – not in the murders anyway. Drugs, yes. Ntende can have them for that. Deport them would be the easy answer. But coming back to Dennison and the Florislow woman – the one who fell, or was pushed, from her window – this is where I've got to and it means I know the story now and who did it.'

'Or think you do,' grumbled Masonga, lighting yet another cigarette. 'OK, let's have your latest theory.'

24

Felix Aramgu was a product of an urban environment, to the extent that if he felt any natural affinity to the rural areas of Kenya it was with the densely cultivated coffee farming areas around the foothills of Mount Kenya. The plains and wooded river valleys of the Masai Mara, which formed the Kenyan extension of the Serengeti plains – the great and ancient home of almost the entire spectrum of African animal life and the last location where it was possible to see grazing animals, like the wildebeest, in their scores of thousands – were alien country to Aramgu. Here now on a narrow, bumpy track, deep in the woodlands of the Mara, with the light of the moon giving an eerie aspect to the landscape, he felt distinctly nervous.

There was, of course, good reason why he should feel nervous, even very afraid: a failed coup leader in Africa could expect very short shrift if captured. Oddly, however, he felt his nerves to be drawn tight more by the strangeness of the environment he was in than by the life or death necessity to get to and cross the Tanzanian border. Aramgu was seated in the front of the four-wheel drive, rough terrain vehicle, alongside the driver. Three more were squeezed into the back: Sasaweni and Aramgu's two bodyguards. The noise of the engine drowned the night sounds of the park, for which Aramgu was grateful. When they had stopped half an hour or so ago for Sasaweni to relieve himself, Aramgu had found the cacophony of noises to be physically disturbing. The chattering, plaintive warning cries, coughing barks and spirit-like screams seemed to surround him and he had the feeling that his presence was known to a thousand eyes, while he stared into a motionless dark void.

They were all armed with hand-guns and the two bodyguards had automatic sub-machine guns, so Aramgu felt they stood a good chance of making the border and beyond. In the Serengeti there should be a more comfortable vehicle waiting to take them back to civilisation. The lions could have this place as far as Aramgu was concerned – he hoped never to be in it again. His bodyguard, who knew, or claimed to know, this track, had said the worst that could happen would be an encounter with a patrol of two rangers. If this happened they had the force to deal with it. The only risk of encountering a larger body would be if their presence was known and a proper search organised.

They were travelling with the benefit merely of sidelights, but the driver seemed to possess good night-vision and their progress was steady although not as fast as the fugitives would have liked. The track was little more than a pair of parallel impressions in the ground which had become bare and compressed due to the passage of vehicles, usually small buses full of tourists. Between the tracks the ground was raised, a mixture of grass and stone. The high clearance of Aramgu's vehicle meant that this caused no problem. Aramgu peered out of the windscreen, but could see nothing. Suddenly, however, the driver braked, not violently but sufficiently to cause Aramgu's head to jerk close to the windscreen.

'Careful, you heavy-footed idiot.'

The vehicle now was stationary; the driver, ignoring Aramgu's insults, was addressing someone behind them.

'The junction is here. The river is over there.' A slight gesture of the speaker's head to his right. 'One hundred yards.'

The bodyguard, who had set the escape up, spoke to the back of Aramgu's head.

'I'm getting out to make a small reconnaissance, *bwana*. We go left, but down other track they are staking meat to attract a leopard so that he stay in tree here for tourists to see. I better check that there no be rangers there. They may hear us and chase us.'

Aramgu could not see any great advantages in the excursion, but he bowed to superior knowledge of a hostile environment. As the bodyguard disappeared into the darkness the other men clambered out to stretch their muscles and their backsides, stiffened by the incessant bumping of the journey.

'If you're ready for another piss, Sasaweni,' Aramgu said, 'be careful the leopard does not leave you manless.' A laugh bubbled up from the great belly and split the night, seemingly bringing the denizens of the woods to a temporary silence.

'It is not a leopard that worries me.' Sasaweni's voice was suspicious. 'I'll take a dozen leopards rather than a trap set up by the *mzungu*.'

'I told you, Sasaweni, you son of a feeble woman, Price-Allen has enough to think about in Nairobi without coming game-hunting.'

'Why would that man disappear on his own? Are you sure you can trust him?'

'Of course. Unlike your men, mine are loyal. You heard him. He has gone to make sure our way is clear.'

The driver's voice brought the incipient argument to a close. 'There is someone near. I hear noise.'

Aramgu half turned. 'There is much noise. Too much noise. What do you mean, someone is near?'

'This noise is noise not of animals. I listen. I think we should mo . . .'

Further speculation was suddenly pre-empted by the shocking intervention of a powerful floodlight that blinded them all as it came to rest upon them. It was joined a moment later by a second that criss-crossed and finally merged with the further reaches of the first, displaying the four terrified men as if they were skewered meat.

The first to react was Sasaweni who dived to the ground and started to roll towards the vehicle, intending to grab one of the guns which they had left in it when they got out. A split second slower than Sasaweni, Aramgu's remaining bodyguard made for the darkness outside the rays of light. Neither achieved their objective. The noise of automatic weapons was muffled, yet pierced Aramgu's eardrums like a needle. Sasaweni's body arched in agony as the bullets hit him, then slumped face up beside the vehicle. The bodyguard was thrown backwards and temporarily disappeared out of the light beams, his cries taking the place of the rapid coughing-like noise of the guns. Aramgu's driver sank to his knees, his hands raised in helpless supplication. Aramgu himself, the largest target of them all, slowly realised he was unhurt – the firing seemed not to have been aimed at him. He stood his ground, partly because he was rooted to the spot by fear, but partly because, placed in this most terrible and helpless position, where nothing useful was for the time being achievable, his sense of pride made him face the unseen enemy with his head held erect. His eyes flicked downwards at the snivelling wretch on his knees and his great lips curled in contempt.

'So, Mr Ambassador, you have developed a taste for our game parks as well as for playing war games.'

The voice from beyond the light source was dreadfully familiar. Aramgu watched as a figure emerged into the light, closely followed by two men clutching their automatic weapons. Small, dapper, even out in this wilderness, dwarfed by two gunmen, but more deadly than the pair together.

'Price-Allen! May the hyenas lick your bones. You white-murdering . . .' He stopped as the three men approached closer and he recognised the man flanking Price-Allen on his left. 'You . . . Msumbe! What are you doing? You cannot go with this white devil.'

Price-Allen allowed himself a small chuckle.

'Ah, yes. Msumbe. I'm afraid he is not what you believed him to be. He is one of my most trusted men and indeed brought you to me tonight.'

There was the sound of a single shot. Aramgu's head turned involuntarily. He could see nothing, but the cries of the wounded man ceased. Only the muttered pleas for mercy from the kneeling man beside him punctuated his conversation.

'So. I have been betrayed.' He looked at his erstwhile bodyguard. 'How come I could not smell the stinking smell of a sewer rat?' He managed to restrain himself from further invective as the man grunted, as if he had been punched in the stomach, and brought the gun barrel up from its semi-inclined position. 'White man, take care. Your masters may wish to know things I know.'

'Msumbe!' The voice was quiet but brooked no denial, and the threatening gun sloped back towards Aramgu's feet rather than his stomach. 'Do not overrate your worth, Aramgu. You are charged with organising a coup for Kiwonka, a coup that has failed. We need nothing from you.'

Aramgu desperately tried to get his mind to work through his need for an excuse to stay alive. He was under no illusion that his survival beyond that of Sasaweni was no more than a delay of sentence.

'You are still a hired man, Price-Allen. Those above you may

184

yet have need of me. If they want Kiwonka, only I can persuade him into a trap.'

Price-Allen smiled, a thin smile and a brief one.

'True to your character to the last, eh, Aramgu? A shiftless, worthless mountain of lard with no loyalty. Remember you were once a close retainer of the President. You betrayed him, now you offer to betray your new master.'

'It was you, *mzungu*, who poisoned the ear of the President against me. But he had better trusted me than you.'

Price-Allen seemed to lose interest in his captive. He looked at the still-kneeling driver.

'Get up, you wretch.' He watched as the man rose to his feet, almost falling once more as trembling shook his legs. 'Help my men load the bodies. You are going to drive them back to where you started. And you will say what you are told to say. Or do you wish to die with your master here?'

The driver muttered his acceptance of his orders, his hands together in humble supplication.

'*Ndio, bwana. Ndio*. Yes, *bwana mkubwa*. As you wish.'

He was jerked away by a man who materialised from behind Aramgu. Price-Allen turned back to the giant figure in front of him. He was not satisfied. Aramgu was not yet totally humiliated.

'Now, Aramgu, we must consider what to do with you.'

Aramgu fought for control of his mind and his bowels.

'Do what you intend, I will not beg to white trash like you.'

Again, the fleeting smile. 'You hope to anger me so I will shoot you like a dog? No, Mr Aramgu, I have arranged something more special for a big man like you.'

A gesture from Price-Allen and the two men flanking him stepped forward and seized Aramgu by the arms. He tried to shake them off and succeeded in shoving one backwards in a stumbling stuttering of his feet. Msumbe was made of sterner stuff and as Aramgu struggled from his grip he quickly reversed his machine pistol and drove the butt into Aramgu's temple. The giant frame toppled and fell.

'Don't hit him too hard, you fool. We don't want him to miss the final scene.'

Aramgu came to sharply, driven back into consciousness by the terrible pain down one side of his head. The pain was worsened by the repeated jerking of his head up and down, causing

185

the centre of his agony to strike a hard surface. Gradually he realised he was in the back of a Land Rover bumping its way along what was obviously a rough track. He tried to look up, but only managed to keep his head tilted for a second or two such was the pain down the right side of his face and neck. In that one brief glance he saw the figure of his traitorous bodyguard sitting over him with the weapon that had damaged his face now reversed again so that the barrel was pointing at him. He tried to speak but could not; his mouth seemed not to belong to him and he was vaguely aware of his tongue stuck with sticky blood to his bleeding gums. More pain wracked him as his body was jerked forward when the vehicle sharply braked to a halt. The back doors were opened and he was dragged roughly from the floor, prevented from falling to the ground only by strong arms under his armpits. Distorted through the barrier of his pain he heard the voice of his arch-enemy.

'Remove that goat carcass and tie him to the tree instead.'

The pain, as he was dragged with legs trailing in response to this command, was such that he lapsed into unconsciousness once more. When again his mind returned he felt the extra discomfort of his arms having been extended and tied to branches of a tree; his body was held against the trunk of the tree by another rope. A torch was shining into his bloody face.

'Let me explain, Mr Ambassador. You are to participate in something of an experiment. The staff here secured the continued presence of a leopard by providing it with a goat every other night or so. As the leopard has not yet had its nocturnal treat we are going to vary its diet tonight, offering it a substantial feast of flesh of a different kind. It will be interesting to see whether it finds you equally to its taste. I understand cats of this type prefer to kill their own meat, so we are offering it that advantage.'

Even in his present state of mental confusion due to the pain of his broken jaw, the horror of his situation sent tremors through Aramgu's body. He was also able to grasp the uselessness of appealing to Price-Allen for mercy for he knew that sadism was the food on which his evil soul survived. He tried, therefore, to appeal to his fellow Africans, asking them not to sell their souls to this white devil, but at least to give him a dignified death. But, unknown to him, the words came out through his broken teeth and swollen mouth as indecipherable, guttural croaks.

Price-Allen surveyed his handiwork and was pleased. This most bombastic and domineering of men was now a wreck, mouthing strange sounds and slumped defeated against the ropes that secured him to the tree. Price-Allen remembered the taste of fear as he had struggled in the Nile, anticipating the crunch of the crocodile's jaws; now he could smell that fear from the body in front of him. Aramgu must reap what he had sown.

He turned to his two remaining assistants, the others having gone back in the vehicle with the dead men.

'Let us go.'

As they retreated the man called Msumbe voiced his doubt.

'Suppose the *chui* no come. And no lion. The tourists will find him in the morning early.'

'Ah, that is smart of you, Msumbe. Yes, with all this movement the big cats may stay away, although the smell of blood should attract the leopard or *chui* as you call it. But that is where you come in. Back a little way on the track there is a hide for watching that the rangers sometimes use. You will stay. If just before dawn our friend is still intact you finish the job. You understand?'

Msumbe had been looking forward to a bed after two hectic days, but he was too wise to admit so.

'*Ndio, bwana*. It will be as you say.'

'And you.' Price-Allen turned to the other man. 'You take me to the air-strip. Then you wait and you come back before dawn to pick up this man and join the others.'

A nod confirmed that this order too was understood. They were now back in their vehicle and the driver had turned in the space in front of the doomed man and headed down the track. He braked after only a few score yards.

'Here is the hide, *bwana*.'

'Good. Come, Msumbe, I will show you how these people keep watch. I have night-binoculars for you.'

Price-Allen and his aide got out of the Land Rover. Msumbe looked around with the aid of his torch. There was not much to see. The same mixture of scrub and trees showed up in the beam. He swung it round further to the left. Yes, there it was, horizontal logs covered with creeper just a couple of feet off the ground. Behind it, Msumbe assumed, would be a sunken trench of some sort to stand or sit in. He jumped, involuntarily, as his torch caught something moving. They were not alone.

25

Cari's old flame, Paddy Andrews, had flown Odhiambo and McGuiry to the Masai Mara, leaving Wilson Airport one hour after Price-Allen had departed on the same journey.

'Apparently he's going to land at the air-strip that serves the main lodge in the park,' Andrews had told them. 'And you say you want to land at the strip near the river? Near Buck Point.'

'That's correct, laddie.' McGuiry had his instructions from his friend Alex. 'You must know Alex Hayling. He and his men have their camp there.'

This had sparked a bout of further doubts from Cari, which had taken her husband some time to quell. Finally, she said her fearful farewells and they set off. McGuiry thought it was just as well there was room for only two passengers otherwise he believed James would not have been able to restrain his wife from joining the hunt.

Their faith in Andrews proved justified and he brought the plane to a halt without running off the edge of the grass strip into the river that ran through this part of the park. True to his word, also, Hayling was waiting with a driver and a four-wheel Japanese-made vehicle. McGuiry made the introductions.

'Alex, this is James. Chief Inspector Odhiambo, to be formal. He's after yon slippery fellow Price-Allen as I told you on the phone. James, this is the best tracker in East Africa, other than meself of course, Alex Hayling.'

Odhiambo liked the look of the old white hunter. Shorter than McGuiry and thicker-set, in his shorts and safari jacket with a pipe set firmly in his mouth he looked the part and the long appraising glance he gave the policeman was direct enough.

'Chief Inspector, glad to meet you. Bob and I go back a long way and he's probably as mad a bugger now as he always was. What he's asking me to do for you is frankly . . . well . . . bizarre. I know these are troubled times, specially after the *shauri* you've just had back in town, but I need to be sure that what you're up to is legal. And not just legal. Right. Correct. The proper thing to do.'

Odhiambo shook the proffered hand, which was firm and dry.

'I can promise you it is right. The Head of the Nairobi CID knows what I am doing. There's a coup leader in this park and he's being hunted by a government security officer – well, sort of – who is going beyond his orders. What we're going to do is unorthodox certainly, but it is dictated by the circumstances. Having just survived a coup, I've had no time for the paperwork. I'm on duty. As well as the coup, two murders have been committed. White people, one a woman. Price-Allen thinks Aramgu did these too. I need to speak to both of them, but I suspect only one will emerge from this park unless we intervene.'

'R.D. Price-Allen.' Hayling spoke the name with distaste. 'I've heard many whispers about him and none of them good. OK, Chief Inspector, I'll take your word we're on the side of the angels. Let's go.'

Once in the Suzuki, Hayling gave them the good news that his men had already picked up Price-Allen's trail. Odhiambo was concerned.

'I hope they won't reveal themselves. He's a careful man.'

Hayling gave a scornful snort.

'He may know his way around Nairobi, but I doubt his knowledge of the Mara. My men can track professional ivory poachers without giving themselves away. They'll be good enough for your man.'

They had landed just before the sun had set in a breath-taking blaze of colour which gave the African plain a reflected glow. But now darkness had fallen quickly after the great heavenly illuminations and Hayling needed his headlights as he pulled off the road into a track which led to a tented camp alongside the river.

'Welcome to our camp. Does this bring back memories, Bob? I hear you live in one of those tourist traps now. Drinking fancy cocktails. Do you good to visit a genuine camp again. I can offer you both a Scotch.'

Odhiambo declined, but after a shifty glance at the policeman, McGuiry accepted the offer. He needed a stiff snort to put him in the right mind for the evening's doings. He was not so much afraid for himself, but he had a premonition that there were ugly moments in store.

Pressed by his host, Odhiambo accepted a beer. It was in fact most welcome. In the blur of events in these last two days, it seemed like a long time since his last cold beer.

Once his guests were settled, Hayling raised his glass to McGuiry, but then got straight down to business.

'To old times, Bob. Now, Chief Inspector, I said I'll take your word. Backed by Robert here. But now it's your turn. I need to know what you intend to do and how you propose we go about it.'

'That's fair, Mr Hayling. I believe that Felix Aramgu, a leader of the failed attempt to overthrow the government, and at least one other prominent figure in that coup are going to slip through the park tonight and seek sanctuary in Tanzania. They'll have some protection around them, but probably not much. Mr Price-Allen, we believe, is aware of their intended route and intends to prevent their flight. So far so good. But we believe that Price-Allen does not intend to take them alive, for reasons that are not sanctioned by the government. We are going to stop Aramgu getting into Tanzania and we're also going to stop Price-Allen acting unlawfully.'

McGuiry looked at his friend admiringly.

'Hey, James. That's quite a speech. I never heard you say so much so fluently. Ye'd better give him another beer, Alex.'

Odhiambo addressed the other man. 'Don't listen to Robert. He likes to keep things on a light note. This is serious work, Hayling. Dangerous work. You have to know that. Aramgu and Price-Allen are both killers, and whoever they've got with them will be the same. You don't have to put your men into this, you know.'

Hayling looked from one to the other. McGuiry nodded in answer to some unspoken question.

'Call me Alex, Chief Inspector. And you're James, I gather. Nice to be on first-name terms with men you're going into action with. My men face men who will kill them with no more compunction than they kill an elephant. And as it happens some of these poachers are linked to your friend Aramgu, from what I've heard. And as for Price-Allen – he makes me ashamed of being a white Kenyan. We're game.'

McGuiry was watching Odhiambo closely. He knew he was holding back. But Hayling now had enough of the facts to make a considered decision. If James wanted to keep some cards close to his chest, why not?

190

Odhiambo, meanwhile, was watching Hayling. What he saw seemed to satisfy him.

'OK. Alex it is. Now we don't know precisely what route Aramgu intends to take or when. But Price-Allen does. So we keep in touch with Price-Allen and he'll hopefully lead us to Aramgu.'

Hayling went over to McGuiry's glass with the bottle of Black Label. The Scot looked at it longingly but shook his head.

'I canna trust you bastards. I'd better keep a clear head to look after meself.'

Hayling laughed. 'We'll finish the bottle later, Bob, and we'll keep a beer or two cold for James here. Right. I have a good idea what way they'll come. They will likely keep off the main tracks – too close to the lodges. There's a couple of ways over to the border that are quieter. Follow this river here. They might come quite close to us, as a matter of fact. So if there's no more drinking to be done let's join my boy with the radio and hear what's happening.'

Odhiambo had prepared himself for a long night. For no reason other than that the idea had entered his head, he thought Aramgu would make his run near dawn. In the event, they were in Hayling's short-wave radio tent for no more than fifteen minutes when a crackling message came through. Hayling explained.

'Price-Allen's vehicles are on the move. And one of my men says there is a vehicle coming towards them. It's on one of the tracks I'd have picked. Looks as though the balloon's going up.'

Odhiambo tried hard to keep the impatience out of his voice.

'Where are they? Price-Allen, I mean.'

'They're heading away from here but near the river. Six miles or so.'

'So what are we waiting for?'

'We can't just go blasting down the road, headlights full on. Don't worry, my men will keep in touch and once we can see where the action's going to be we'll get there.'

Half an hour later the waiting was over. Hayling's men reported that their quarry seemed to be settling in and waiting.

'It's near a place on the river called Leopard Rock. Aptly named, always leopard thereabouts. They put meat out sometimes to keep the cats from wandering. Then take the tourists out at dawn.'

'Then it's time to go?'
'Yep, reckon so. Looks like that's where the fun's going to be.'

26

Hayling's swearing revealed a range of obscenities which Odhiambo found impressive. The three men had left Hayling's camp and set off down a track which for the first mile or so ran through what seemed, as far as Odhiambo could tell from the limited vision provided by the Suzuki's headlights, open countryside – grassland and small bushes with only an occasional large tree showing up near the track. Then the number of trees and denser bush growth gradually increased until they seemed to be passing through woodland. It was after they had been travelling for about fifteen minutes that the radio in Hayling's vehicle crackled to life. Odhiambo could scarcely make out the sense of the report for the reception was poor and, in addition, the Swahili-speaking voice seemed to be out of breath. But Hayling understood and his language confirmed that the news was not good. McGuiry in the back seat had made nothing of the crackling voice amongst the static.

'What's up, Alex? What's the trouble?'

'My fellows lagged too far behind. Playing it ultra safe. They thought Price-Allen's people were waiting at Leopard Rock. There's a hide-out there. A viewing place. It seems the other vehicle stopped short of there and someone came to meet Price-Allen on foot. Then they vanished. My chaps stayed where they were expecting them to return. But they've just heard shots. Rapid firing. Automatics. I've told them to hang on and not to go rushing in.'

Odhiambo beat his fists on his knees in frustration.

'How far to go? Are we close?'

Hayling had accelerated whilst he was speaking, but now dimmed his lights, peering through the windscreen in an endeavour to stay on the track.

'Yeah. Less than a mile. We'll have to walk the last bit if our targets are still about.'

A minute later he braked the vehicle to a halt. Just as they were about to jump out the radio came to life once more. The reception was better now and all three men heard the Swahili words clearly enough.

'*Bwana*, they are coming back. One car only. I have one man in the place they make for watching the leopard. Make haste, *bwana*.'

The three men abandoned the vehicle and set off on foot, Hayling leading the way. McGuiry soon found himself panting for breath, and started to fall behind. Odhiambo caught his foot in a root that lay exposed across the track and took a heavy fall. Hayling stopped. 'Are you all right?' He was whispering. 'Are you hurt, Inspector?'

Odhiambo cursed nearly as fluently as Hayling's earlier effort.

'I think so. Turned my bloody ankle, but I think it's OK.'

McGuiry, given the chance to catch up, arrived panting.

'I'm too old for these games. You two go on. I'll follow in me own time.'

Hayling's whisper was urgent. 'It's not far. We need to keep silence now. Slowly does it.'

They proceeded more sedately, but had gone only another hundred yards when a figure emerged suddenly in front of them. Hayling and the new arrival whispered urgently to each other as Odhiambo and McGuiry waited impatiently. Hayling turned back to them.

'We're there. It's bizarre. My man says the *mzungu* – that's Price-Allen – has tied a big African to the tree instead of the goat-meat. What the hell is going on?'

Odhiambo felt a shiver run down his spine, partly, perhaps, because of the picture conjured up by Hayling's words, but mainly because his instincts told him the show-down was at hand. He didn't need two guesses as to the identity of the man Price-Allen would take the trouble to stake out for a ghastly death. But what about the others?

'How many?' he whispered to Hayling. 'How many men do we have to deal with?'

The new arrival understood and answered for himself.

'Only one man left of people they capture. He is the one they tie to tree. The *mzungu* has only two men with him.'

Just as the reasonable odds sank in to his listeners there was the sound of a burst of automatic fire, followed by two single shots. They dived for the cover of the bushes. As he lay with his face pressed to the earth, Robert McGuiry thought to himself, Never again, James Odhiambo, this is the last time I act as your Dr Watson.

Msumbe was a hard man: his involuntary jump and missed heartbeat as he caught sight of a head peering from the viewing hide scarcely delayed his reaction time. He brought the machine pistol up to the horizontal with the one hand which was holding it, rested the butt on his hip and fired at the hide. Price-Allen beside him gave a cry of surprise before turning to see what had happened.

'What are you . . .?'

Msumbe would never answer the unfinished question. A strong beam of light picked them out and as Msumbe swung towards its source, dropping his own torch and grabbing his weapon with both hands, two shots struck him, one scarcely nicking his ear, but the other catching him full in the stomach. He went down screaming.

Price-Allen was in a state of shock. The inexplicable developments of the last few seconds were too much for even his calculating mind to grasp immediately. But his self-preservation instincts were still functioning: he turned and ran towards his vehicle. He was within two strides of reaching it when the grinding of gears gave him the first indication that he was stranded. Before he could grab the door the terrified driver had found a gear and shot forward, leaving Price-Allen blinded in a burst of sandy dirt spewed up by the tyres.

A voice reached him from the darkness.

'Put your hands up, *bwana*, or we must shoot.'

Odhiambo did not confront Price-Allen immediately. It was almost as if he wanted to savour the moment. He watched from the darkness as Hayling dispatched two men to retrieve his vehicle and another used by his men. Price-Allen was forced to sit on the ground with his back to a thin tree and his hands handcuffed behind the tree. The screams from Msumbe continued, but apart from securing his gun nobody paid him any heed. Odhiambo felt rather than saw McGuiry move up beside him. He heard the short intake of breath as if the Scotsman was about

194

to speak, but no words came. Hayling, now with the strong torch that had pinpointed the unfortunate Msumbe, focused it briefly on Price-Allen and then moved to join Odhiambo.

'One's dying, the other's secure and I guess he's the one you want. The driver won't get far. The one we shot opened fire on one of my men who was waiting in the hide. So the others had no option.'

'You said earlier that they tied a man to a tree instead of bait. Where is the tree?'

'Hell's bells. In the excitement I'd forgotten the leopard bait. Mind you, I should think the cat will be miles away with all this disturbance going on. Come with me.'

The three men walked towards the track, Hayling lighting the way with his torch. As they passed close to where Price-Allen was tethered, he spoke for the first time since his capture.

'Is that you, Odhiambo? I know you're there. It has to be you. You've got some explaining to do.'

The two white men glanced at their companion, whose face they could just see in the reflected diffused light from the torch, but his features remained impassive and no answer came. They walked on down the track and then as Hayling levelled his torch they saw Price-Allen's handiwork.

'Christ Almighty!' Hayling's blasphemy was almost reverent. 'What have they done to the poor bastard?'

Aramgu's mind had gone. His head was raised towards the sky, the blood still running from his cheek and mouth, his arms outstretched in the crucified position, and from his throat came a continuous series of sounds as if he was giving a speech, but one without recognisable words. The whole effect, given the great size of the man, was dramatic and horrific. The three men gazed a moment longer, trying to take in the dreadful scene.

'Have you a knife on you?' Odhiambo's question was spoken while his head was still fixed facing the sight of Aramgu in his torment. Hayling handed him a knife from inside his knee-length sock. 'Thanks.'

Odhiambo walked forward; McGuiry hesitated only a moment before following. Odhiambo cut the ropes with a series of slashes and he and the Scotsman took the considerable weight and lowered it as gently as they could to the ground.

Thirty minutes later the scenes of the recent bloodshed had been, at least partially, cleared. The men Hayling sent to the location of the earliest fighting reported back signs of the shooting but no bodies. Aramgu and Msumbe were laid out in the back of a Land Rover for the journey back to Hayling's camp, and the man Msumbe had shot at in the hide sat in the front of the same vehicle with his arm in a makeshift sling.

Hayling watched the vehicle leave and turned back to Odhiambo.

'Right, the second vehicle can take the able-bodied and the prisoner. The driver of the first will get a radio signal out to bring in more help including a doctor. Although I doubt if the fellow with the stomach wound will live long enough. So, we can follow on in my jalopy.'

'You and your men have done very well.' Odhiambo took Hayling's hand in both of his and then released it, remembering that the British did not much like men gripping each other's hands. 'There's hope for our animals yet if your men are protecting them.'

Hayling grimaced.

'As long as there's no fall-out from this little *shauri*. What do you reckon will happen to him?' Hayling jerked his head towards the tree where Price-Allen was still tethered. 'I mean, if he has clout enough to walk away from this, I guess we're not going to be very popular.'

Odhiambo nodded. He had still not looked at or addressed the man in question. He could sense McGuiry watching him from behind.

'I understand. There's a lot of old blood on his hands, but now there's fresh. This time he's not going to walk away.'

Hayling looked at the stern face visible in the shadowy light provided by the four gas-pressured lamps now encircling the scene. There was a steely tone to the deep voice, but also, he thought, a note of reluctant resignation as if a difficult task had to be endured.

'Good. We rely on you. Pity we can't leave him out here for the leopard's dinner. Let's get him loaded up, then we can get going as well. I think we all deserve another drink.'

'I've got one more favour to ask, Alex. Get the rest of your men off. You and Robert get going too and leave me with our friend. I have to have a private interview with the man.'

There was an expostulation of protest from the Scotsman. Hayling concentrated on the practicalities.

'And how do you intend to get back? Walk? Leading your prisoner? The cats will get their dinner yet.'

'No. You get back and send one of your men to get me. By then I'll have finished.'

There was a pregnant pause, which McGuiry was the first to break.

'I'm staying with ye, James. Never know when you need a corroboration.'

'No. I'm sorry. This is my *shauri*. I have my investigations to conclude. I need to speak to him alone. It's the only way.'

Hayling looked quizzically at his old friend, who gave a small shake of the head.

'OK. You're the boss.' He turned and shouted to his senior ranger. 'Load the men up, we're pulling out.' He turned back to Odhiambo. 'What about the handcuffs? You want them taken off? At least to free him from the tree.'

'Take them off completely. He can't do anything with me here. Right, it's time.' The last remark seemed to be addressed to himself. He strode purposefully over to where Price-Allen sat, silent but with eyes that missed nothing. Hayling and McGuiry followed two steps behind. Hayling gave an order and the ranger assigned to watching over the prisoner reached down and, after a certain amount of fumbling, released the handcuffs. Price-Allen pulled his arms to his front and started to massage them to restore his circulation. Odhiambo spoke to the guard.

'Help him to his feet.'

He watched as his order was carried out. Price-Allen swayed a little – the restriction in his circulation had affected his legs also – but then pulled himself erect and looked up into the face of the policeman with something of the usual arrogance still in the pale eyes.

'And what now, Odhiambo? What further interference in an official operation are you going to stage?'

'Mr Price-Allen, I am arresting you for the murders of Mr Jim Dennison and Miss Pauline Florislow. Have you anything to say?'

27

'So, Odhiambo. After your absurd melodramatic gesture we are, it seems, alone. The ball would appear to be in your court.'

The two men faced each other, lit by the two remaining lights. Hayling and McGuiry had departed, reluctantly. Odhiambo was not entirely sure that they would, in fact, return to Hayling's camp. He suspected they would retire a decent distance, wait a while and then return. Odhiambo had hitched one hip on to the top row of horizontal logs that made up the wall of the viewing hide. Price-Allen stood, circulation restored, three feet away.

'It's not absurd, as well you know. I don't have to make up charges. Tonight alone would provide sufficient. What happened to Sasaweni and whatever guards they had with them?'

'I do not have to account to you for the execution of my duties. I and other official security men intercepted the leaders of the failed coup as they were trying to flee the country. There was some fighting and some died. But the only death of a security agent was caused by you and your unauthorised vigilantes.'

Odhiambo smiled, a grim smile without humour. He nodded slightly as if confirming to himself an assumption he had been holding.

'Yeah. As I would expect. And even torturing Aramgu, I dare say you'd boast about it in the right circles. But, you see, Denni-son and Florislow are my cases. You set me up to investigate them, so you must not complain if I am determined to find the solution.'

'I gave you Aramgu early on. You could have saved yourself and your resourceful wife a lot of trouble if you had listened to me.'

'Gave me Aramgu! You set me up to be killed arresting him, because you not only wanted him dead, you wanted him branded as the bad guy because he caused the death of a prom-inent policeman.'

'Politics is dangerous business, Odhiambo. This you have never recognised. I was trying to prevent a coup. If Aramgu had been removed from the scene the coup attempt could have been nipped in the bud.'

'I'm not interested in your complicated plots. Or I wouldn't be if you left me and Cari out of them. But Aramgu did not kill Jim Dennison.'

'How do you know? Dennison worked for him. Normally, it was just Aramgu's business dealings he was concerned with – some of them were shady enough – but he found out something about the coup preparations. Given his habits, including drug-taking with gossipy friends, Aramgu could not risk him talking. Dennison was at his friend's place next door to Aramgu's. What easier than to kidnap him as he left in the early hours, kill him and dispose of the body as quickly as possible.'

'And the woman? Florislow?'

'It is only you who insists she was murdered. But if, and I stress *if*, she was murdered, it was because Aramgu suspected Denni-son had already talked to her. She was at the same party. Denni-son was in a bedroom with her, high on drugs, and he talked. So the woman was a risk too.'

'You seem remarkably well informed about this party.'

'Simple deduction, Odhiambo. Which if you were to follow in your own work would result in less aggravation for everyone involved.'

'Simple deduction, or first-hand reporting?'

'I wasn't at the party, if that's what you mean. Whatever you think of me, I'm not into that sort of thing. No, Odhiambo, one source is Matavu. The Captain of the Ngong Golf Club. Denni-son was his Vice-Captain. Also he's the bank manager for Mbayazi Estates. Dennison was worried. Asked him on the golf course what was going on. You could have found this out for yourself. Dennison didn't like what he was getting into and so became a threat. Simple explanation, but you have to chase after complicated theories and end up in a big mess.'

Odhiambo looked at Price-Allen with something almost akin to appreciation. There had been a moment when he was hand-cuffed to the tree when the Price-Allen voice seemed to reveal a crack in that confident sense of superiority. Now, here he was bouncing back, trying to assert his usual dominance over his ad-versaries.

'So, that's your story. Well, now, let me give you the true ver-sion. Dennison worked for Mbayazi Estates sure enough, but he wasn't involved in Aramgu's political plans. Not normally anyway. Aramgu is not so stupid as to trust major secrets to a boozing, drug-taking man who likes to get into the kinky sex scene. But there was an exception. He knew about the plan to murder you during your visit to Uganda. He said so to Michael Silent.' In his mind Odhiambo could hear Gianna Iocacci repeating, 'He was lucky once but you shouldn't count on it,' and saying as she strained her memory that Dennison had mentioned 'costs'. Not 'costs' but 'Price', although she hadn't made the connection as she'd never heard of Price-Allen. 'Now, why should that worry Silent? Worry him enough to slip away just afterwards. To make a phone call?' Odhiambo paused but only rhetorically before proceeding to answer his own question. 'Because Silent is one of your unofficial stooges. He just moved into the house next to Aramgu. Was that to keep an eye on comings and goings? And on the other side a house owned by a man who was never there. We got hold of him today on the phone. He's in England, as you know. He admitted quite readily that he had an informal arrangement with you. You paid him for use of his property. It's one of your safe houses, isn't it? His brother-in-law, Hill-Templeton, knew something was going on, but he survives by seeing no evil and hearing no evil. Silent tells you what Dennison said. You decide you need to find out more. The dopey Dennison finds himself next door. You enjoy that sort of thing don't you? Did you mean to kill him or did you go a bit too far when torturing him? Perhaps the latter, because you had to get rid of him in a hurry – so you dumped him in the newly dug golf teeing ground. Gave you breathing space. How am I doing?'

Price -Allen smirked.

'All conjecture, Odhiambo. A figment of your imagination based on your antipathy to me. So I'm looking after someone's house while he's away. It's shut up. I keep an eye on it. That and probably the ramblings of a pair of Italians whose truthfulness is more than open to question.'

'When did you last do a good turn without getting something out of it? And it's not just the Italians, but we'll come back to that. It was the death of the other woman that puzzled me. Pauline Florislow. She wanted to tell me something, but before I got to her office she goes out of her window. I don't believe in that sort of coincidence, but I couldn't work out how you knew she was going to tell me something, unless it was the Italian or the Mbayazi manager. But I couldn't shake either of them. Then it came to me. Right under the Mbayazi Estates offices was a door with a tag saying "Stasec Holdings". I should have made the connection earlier. Stasec – State Security. I should have thought you could have come up with something more imaginative. You were bugging Mbayazi Estates. Trying to get as much as you could on Aramgu's movements and plans. Fair enough. But when you put me on to the Dennison case you knew I would interview the Mbayazi Estates people so you made sure the bug wasn't just recording on tape, but plugged through to you or one of your people. You knew I was going to see the woman so you got there first. Who did you send?'

Was there at last a change in Price-Allen's demeanour? The light was not good enough to see his eyes clearly, but Odhiambo's instincts told him that he had pierced Price-Allen's armour. He waited, but Price-Allen was silent, keeping his own counsel. Odhiambo continued.

'You made one more mistake. The morning after Dennison's body was found, Masonga allocated me to the case on your orders. Here you are, surviving a murder attempt, up to your eyes in trying to forestall Aramgu's coup plans, and yet overnight you hatch your plan for me to arrest Aramgu and for both of us to end up dead. Yet the plan was no good unless you knew who Dennison was. How he was involved with Aramgu. Just one Happy Valley *mzungu* found dead yet within hours you know all about it. The whole thing stank from the start.'

Price-Allen found his voice.

'I always knew you had talent, Odhiambo. I never underestimated you, unlike that oaf Aramgu. All you need is a steady hand to guide you and stop you drawing the wrong conclusions. You overcomplicate things. So you've saved Aramgu from a fate he well deserved. You may live to regret that. But I'm still prepared to look after you. Now, let's get out of this damn wilderness.'

'It's no good, Price-Allen.' Odhiambo drew a quiet breath. Now he had to put across the bluff. Surely Price-Allen had been too busy today to keep in touch with police news. 'Michael Silent has talked. At least about Dennison. He hasn't admitted knowing anything about the woman.'

He waited. He was sure that his story was true in its essentials, but he had to hear it confirmed from the man's own lips,

201

otherwise there would always be just the slightest doubt to exacerbate the inevitable feeling of guilt.

Price-Allen waved a hand petulantly and came a little closer to make eye contact with his interrogator.

'Who cares about people like Silent? A pervert, a parasite. Anything he did for me at least gave his life some purpose. Forget Silent, I can see to him when we get back. You are suited to higher things, Odhiambo. But you need me. Especially in these days to come. It will be important to have powerful friends in the atmosphere of suspicion which there will be.'

Odhiambo let out his breath with care. He knew he was almost there.

'What exactly did happen that night? Is Silent's version the truth?'

'It doesn't matter, I tell you. Dennison had Uganda connections. What he blurted out to Silent that night showed he knew of the plot to kill me in advance. He was the contact for passing the instruction through to one of his old acquaintances. We confirmed that when we questioned him. The man was nothing, just a messenger boy. But I had been in the damn water, Odhiambo, with a crocodile looking at me. And that bastard had helped to put me there. I've killed men for a lot less than that. Yes, I strangled him and I did it slowly.'

'Do you know, that's the first time I've heard you swear. Your dip in the Nile got to you, didn't it? You've given men worse deaths.'

'Perhaps. I don't mind pitting my life against others who are worthy of my attention. But Kenyan white trash? I think not. Kenya will be a better place without them.'

'And the woman?'

'Woman? Woman? What's the matter with you, Odhiambo? Is it not getting through to you? Stop concerning yourself with trivia. Plan with me how we can exercise control over this country. It's ripe for picking now. I am loyal to the government, but there will be spaces near the top after this Kiwonka affair.'

'I like to know. First tell me about the woman.'

'There is little to tell. According to Silent, he forgot she was still in his house. Asleep. She woke up and saw him taking Dennison through to the next compound where I had arranged to meet them. She put two and two together when she heard of the circumstances of his death. And if she had spoken to you, you

202

would have added it up to five. I sent one of my men around. There was not time to arrange anything neater. Now are you satisfied? Can we move on? You know you have no proof. In fact, I wonder if you told me the truth about Silent.'

'He's dead. Mrs Dennison shot him.'

'Well, there you are. All neatly disposed of. Where is your transport?'

'It will be here soon. So yes, the time for talk is over. I wanted you to tell me in your own words, you see. I wanted you to know why I have to kill you.'

Odhiambo was watching his man carefully and he noted that his words did not strike with as much impact as might have been expected. Price-Allen was no fool. He had a deep insight into how people thought and what their strengths and weaknesses were. During their conversation he had moved closer to Odhiambo and now he edged a little closer still. One hand had been in his trouser pocket throughout. Odhiambo could feel the tension within the man; he was like a coiled spring. Casually, Odhiambo eased his weight off the log on which he had hitched one buttock.

Price-Allen smiled.

'I know you too well, Odhiambo. You have one major weakness: you have scruples. You will not kill a helpless prisoner. Take me in if you must. I will not hold this conversation against you.'

Odhiambo slowly shook his head, his eyes remaining locked on those of the other man.

'No. You've always misread me. I'm a Luo, remember. You have blighted my wife's life by blackmailing her when she was young, kidnapping her parents, and now kidnapping and imprisoning her. And you arranged for me to be killed. I don't forgive those acts and they demand retribution.'

'But I looked after both of you. Who saved you from Aramgu when he had you in his hands before? Who got you promoted? I have been your patron whether you wish to recognise it or not.'

Odhiambo's voice resumed, even in tone but implacable.

'But as well as being a Luo, I am a Kenyan. You have hurt my country and now, if with your skill you get even more power, you will hurt it more. It must not be. For all the blood you have spilled your blood is now required.'

Price-Allen heard and recognised the finality in the voice. He had made an error in letting this man live on the grounds he could be useful. He was in check and one move from checkmate. The sharp stone he had managed to slip into his pocket when the handcuffs were removed was in his hand. Slowly his hand rose from the depth of his pocket and as it emerged accelerated with all his strength behind it to strike at the neck just a foot away. Odhiambo swayed away, his own hand taking the borrowed knife from his belt. As Price-Allen's lunge slipped past his shoulder his lower abdomen lay open to the counter-strike. In the microsecond of hesitation before plunging in his knife a sharp noise reached his ear and echoed through his head: Price-Allen's body jerked away from him and slumped face down, the arm that had struck at him catching on the logs of the hide, the stone spilling from the hand to Odhiambo's feet.

Odhiambo looked into the darkness beyond the area lit around him. Into the fringe of the light stepped the familiar figure of the old hunter, rifle in hand, looking as he must have looked a hundred times as he moved towards a fallen beast.

'I knew I shouldna let ye alone with him, James. Lucky, Alex had let me borrow his rifle to get the feel of its balance.'

Behind the old Scotsman, Odhiambo saw the emerging figure of Hayling, looking startled at the turn of events.

'Robert – you knew, didn't you?'

'Ach. You think you're a poker face, but I had a fair idea of your thinking. But I dinna underestimate him either. Decided to keep an eye out for ye.'

McGuiry had reached Price-Allen's body. He prodded it with the barrel of his rifle, jerking it over to see the face. He bent and pressed his fingers to the neck before straightening again, satisfied with the single-shot, clean kill.

'It was my *shauri*, Robert. You should have left me to deal with my own problem.'

'Dinna talk daft, mon. I heard yon Price-Allen. He was right. You're a man with a conscience. While me now, I've got blood on my hands of beasts that were better, far better than this snake. For young Cari's sake I couldna think of you moping about like my fellow Scot, Macbeth. Now, let's have that knife so I can return it to its owner.'

Hayling added his contribution.

204

'I saw him strike out. Thought he had a knife. Lucky this old reprobate can still shoot straight. Saving a police officer in the execution of his duty, that's how I see it.'

Odhiambo looked from one to the other.

'You *mzungus* always stick together, don't you.' He paused, then placed a hand on McGuiry's shoulder. 'I'd have done it – you know that, don't you? But thanks anyway.'

McGuiry smiled. He felt almost young again.